THE APOLLO

THE CONSTELLATION THIEF BOOK ONE

GRACE WARD

COCKATRICE PUBLISHING

THE GREAT IC
POLISLAV
BÖRJ
THE GREY SEA
THE BIANCO TRADE EMPIRE
ALVANII
SHAHEEN
IRAJMI
AURORA'S SANDS

TO THE TUNDRA
WILDLANDS
FOREST OF
SILVA
AGRIPPAN
MOUNTAINS
MYNOS
VERONII
SEA OF SALICIA
TO THE EAST

For Corban —

A dear friend who always dreamed of having his name in a book. I hope you write one yourself someday. I'll buy the first copy.

And For My Students —

Because today is going to be AMAZING.

Chapter One

Avira had resigned herself to being in disguise all the time, even during her sleep.

"My name is Cesario," she said, practicing her introduction as she stared at herself in the tiny mirror fastened to the wall of her cabin. She'd been gazing at herself all morning, getting used to the grubby-looking boy who blinked back at her.

Her ebony hair was cropped short against her head and, although it was a rather unstylish look; she thought it complimented her fair skin and petite features to have less hair. Her hair used to look like it was eating her alive. The updos the servants had to do to get it out of the way were heavy and bothersome, like carrying a stack of books on her head. When she had her way, she'd worn it in a single braid that stretched down her back like a slippery black snake.

Despite her hair, Avira's face was unmistakably feminine. She opted for a small straw hat with a round brim to obscure her button nose and high cheekbones. Her baggy sailor's uniform did well to cover up any feminine curves.

"My name is Cesario," she said again, this time making her voice as low as she could.

"And I'm Nicolo!" a voice from behind her said. Avira couldn't help but jump.

She turned and found herself face to face with a frail boy with auburn hair and a hopelessly sunburnt nose. From his generally ginger complexion to his thin lips and flowing light blue tunic, he looked like a true Veronan.

The boy's hand was stretched out to shake, but Avira blinked at it for a long moment before taking it. She was used to men taking her hand and planting a kiss upon her heavy gold rings. Shaking hands was not instinctual for her. She'd have to get used to that.

"Cesario, was it?" Nicolo said. Hearing more of his accent, Avira was sure the boy was from Veronii.

"Yes," she responded bluntly.

"Well, it's nice to meet you, Cesario. Which bunk is mine?"

Nicolo threw his satchel down on the floor. He began rummaging through it, eventually pulling out a pillow.

"My pap used to work on the sky ships too. He told me captains never remember pillows for the crew, so you've gotta bring yer own."

"Oh," Avira said softly. That made sense. Working on the skyships was generational, and fathers frequently passed down tips and tricks to their sons when they picked up the family trade. She probably looked like a flaming idiot.

"Forgot one, eh?" Nicolo said.

He produced a second pillow from his bag and tossed it at her. Avira barely had time to understand what was happening before catching it.

"How did you afford two of these?" Avira asked when she realized the pillow in her hands was made of silk, fine silk, probably something her father had imported from far away. It wouldn't have been cheap.

"My pap says good sleep is worth its weight in gold," Nicolo said and shrugged. He spoke so casually. It was strange for her. People had never spoken to her so casually back home. They'd barely spoken *to* her at all.

"Think of it as a token of my friendship." Nicolo smiled at her and tossed his pillow on the top bunk. "If you don't mind, I'll take the upper bunk. Reminds me of home."

Avira took her pillow and placed it gently on the lower bunk. It was settled then.

"Thank you."

"Good to have friends. Especially considering how much time we're about to spend together. By the time we make port in Shaheen, I'll know every one of yer secrets."

I doubt that, Avira thought to herself.

Sure, Nicolo being friendly was convenient, but Avira didn't have time to make friends, at least not until after the ship left port. She'd been hired four days ago, and since then, she'd successfully laid low in her cabin except for her scheduled shifts as a kitchen boy.

The kitchen was awful. It was a tiny room filled with steaming pots of spices and leafy greens that boiled down so far they were almost porridge. Despite the smell, she only had to share a shift with one other sailor. The privacy made it all worth it.

"You're from Veronii?" she asked quietly.

"Nah. I'm from the North, though. There are little villages in the hills with goat farms and such. I grew up on one of them! And how about you? You've got one of those uppity Alvanian accents."

Every muscle in Avira's body froze. An *uppity* Alvanian accent?

What does that even mean?

"Oi... Cesario... you okay?"

Avira snapped back to reality, her eyes still wide.

"Sorry. I shouldn't have made fun of yer accent. I assumed you was some kind of kitchen boy for the folks up on the hill in Alvanii, eh?"

Of course. Avira relaxed.

"Oh no, it's okay, really," she said coolly. "I was surprised you could read me so well based on my accent alone. I mean, I've only said a few sentences. That's all."

"So, you were an upscale kitchen boy! I knew it. My pap says I can read a person like a book. That isn't much of a compliment because I hardly read books. But I know people, yah know? I'm a people-person."

Avira smiled but tried not to use her teeth for fear Nicolo might notice how white hers were compared to his.

"Do you have your assignment yet?" Avira probed, trying hard to change the subject.

"Ropes." Nicolo shrugged. "Prob'ly cuz I'm so small I can climb up and fix bad knots if I need to. I'll be like a monkey or somethin'. Have you ever seen a monkey?"

Avira had. Her father had monkeys brought to her tenth birthday celebration. The monkeys were dressed in gold and silk robes like tiny kings.

"I haven't," she said blankly. "Maybe there will be one in the Shaheeni port!"

Nicolo smiled at this idea.

"I'd better get a nap before we shove off, eh?" Nicolo said, climbing up to his bed. "Ropes men work the night shift; moon up to sun up."

Avira went to the door.

"Nice to meet you, Cesario," Nicolo said as he rolled onto his side to face the wall, and in an instant, he fell asleep. Avira shut the door behind her.

At least her bunkmate worked nights. That would help. She worked one kitchen shift in the early morning and one in the evening, so their rest time would rarely overlap. Nicolo seemed nice. Maybe in a different life, they could have been friends.

As Avira climbed the ladder from the bunks to the ship's deck, she contemplated Cesario, her false identity, and the backstory she'd tell.

A kitchen boy from Alvanii who dreamed of adventure aboard the famed Apollo? They'd probably heard that story hundreds of times. It was the Age of the Airship — everyone wanted a slice of the adventure. Nobody would have any reason to assume she was lying.

She couldn't help imagining what would have happened if she'd told Nicolo the truth. He'd probably heard about her disappearance or seen the missing posters. The port was plastered with her likeness.

When Avira reached the deck, the sunlight glared against her face, heating her skin. She'd never spent so much time in the glaring sun, and she suddenly felt thankful for her straw hat.

Avira remembered the streak of freckles across her nose and cheeks that her mother had always warned would grow should she spend too much time in the sun. Maybe the freckles would take over her face, and she'd become completely unrecognizable. She turned her face up to the sun and smiled in the heat.

From her left, a commotion rang out. Avira opened her eyes. The ship wasn't set to take off for another five hours. What could all the noise be about?

She found the source quickly. It was across the deck, where the rope ladder from down in the port connected with the ship. Malvolio, a tall, tattooed man who looked like he'd spent the last 30 years of his life in the sky, was holding a well-dressed Shaheeni boy over the edge of the ship. Avira watched, trying to stay hidden behind a crate of spices. Perhaps the boy was a stowaway. She'd initially planned to hide on deck until the ship took off from the port, but now she was glad she didn't.

For the last three days, Avira had hidden in her room, terrified that one of her father's men would board the ship and drag her kicking and screaming back home. Or worse, her father could have sent her fiance, Gavriel Castillo, to find her.

Avira had known Gavriel since she was a child and he, slightly older, was a new recruit to her father's armed forces. As a boy, he was almost kind. But he'd grown into a violent man. He would slaughter whomever it took to "save his bride."

Little did he know she didn't need saving at all.

Avira slipped into the kitchen. The head cook, a leathery, gray-haired man named Diego, was dropping whole onions and cabbages into a pot to boil. The smell was rank and getting worse by the second, and the balmy kitchen air was nearly impossible to breathe.

Just a few hours to go, and the ship would be moving. Once there was a growing distance between her and her father, she'd let herself breathe easier. Maybe she'd even have a chance to take in the view of the clouds. But until then, she wiped the sweat off her palms and began cutting the tops off radishes.

"Cesario, you're late for your shift!" Diego shouted to her over the boiling pots.

"Well, I'm here now," she fired back.

Four more hours. Then she could relax.

Chapter Two

Avira Bianco had been missing for seven days.

Matteo De Luca arrived in the port city of Alvanii just after dawn. Matteo was barely twenty years old, but he'd already negotiated the safe return of at least twenty missing noble children.

After a falling out with his adoptive older brother, who controlled the family estate, Matteo had set out on his own at the ripe age of fifteen. He'd soon learned that his lack of family, lack of culture, and lack of history made him powerful as a private detective. People never expected much from him, so he could always take them by surprise. The past five years had been filled with adventures large and small, dangerous and docile, but this was the first case of his to bring him to Alvanii. Somewhere deep inside, he knew he'd always been avoiding it.

He'd been up for hours, reading a book of Shaheeni myths by lantern light. Alvanii was famous for its sunrises. The oranges and golds of the sky above the Sea of Salacia had been lauded by poets and painters alike. But Matteo barely noticed the light. He had work to do.

Matteo knew about the Bianco family; it was hard not to. They were the most powerful trading entity in Veronii and Alvanii, perhaps the most powerful trading entity *anywhere*. Their fleet of sky ships traveled at dizzying clips, hauling spices, fruits, perfumes, and precious jewels from the rich soil of the Southern Continent. The patriarch of the Bianco family was a man by the name of Grigori Bianco. He was notorious for his temper and unmatched wit. Matteo was a bit frightened of him.

Alvanii was known for its ports, where wealthy merchants like the Biancos boasted more power than anyone else in the city. There was a monarchy in place, sure, but they had gone broke years ago commissioning merchants like Grigori Bianco to bring them back all the riches of the world. Now not even the clergymen could boast the power of the trade barons.

Veronii, where Matteo had grown up, was Alvanii's. Every oldest son in a Veronan household was encouraged to join the priesthood, while women were taught to be modest and soft-spoken. Ceremonies to honor the Sky Goddess Aurora were held nearly every week in Veronii. Many Veronans whispered over dinner about how far from The Goddess Aurora their Alvanian neighbors had strayed.

Matteo had never particularly loved Veronii. He never felt like he truly fit in there. He didn't look like his peers, nor act like his peers, nor aspire to the same positions high in the priesthood as his schoolmates or brothers. Veronan women were of little interest to him either. But he'd never strayed far from the city of his birth because he reckoned he wouldn't fit in much better in Alvanii, the sister city to the south of his home.

Every woman who passed Matteo on the street was adorned with gold and draped in deep orange silk and red velvet skirts. Their bodices were cut low and tight to reveal every curve and collarbone. Matteo remembered his adoptive mother and the way she'd alway worn a simple house dress cut all the way up to her chin. The fashions of Veronii were certainly less attractive than these gaudy frocks but, for some reason, he was beginning to miss them. Alvanian women looked like pastries. He wondered how they could possibly stay cool in the hot sun under all that fabric.

On every corner Matteo passed, there was a vendor selling some spice he'd never heard of. One salesman boasted seventy-two unique strains of rice. Another sold sapphire rings, insisting that the fashion was to wear one on each finger. Matteo tried to imagine getting anything done with a ring on each finger. It would be rather hard to cook, or write, or read a book with heavy jewelry dangling around everywhere. *That must be the point*, he thought to himself.

The carriage driver had been appalled when Matteo asked to be dropped off at the public carriage station rather than at the gates of Bianco Manor. Matteo calmly explained that he liked walking the streets of new places. Mostly, he was tired of sitting. Sitting never did him any good. Matteo liked keeping his hands and his mind moving at all times. If he stopped, he would get stuck.

Rows of red-bricked townhouses lined the streets. Matteo noticed that almost every house boasted a lush garden terrace. Clematis and trumpet vine climbed up the walls of some of the houses and occasionally an orange or a lemon tree peaked out from the cracks in between the streets.

Orange trees were in full bloom everywhere he looked. Their scent hung heavy in the air. Matteo had always thought orange flowers smelled like an old woman's perfume, but it was nice to smell something other than horse droppings and his own sweat. The carriage ride had not been glamorous.

Once as a child, Matteo and his adopted family had made the

journey from Veronii to Alvanii. He didn't remember much about their trip except for his deep fear of the sea that crashed up against the city. He couldn't imagine how anyone felt safe living so close to Salicia's terrible waves.

It was not unique to fear the sea. Alvanians had taken to the sky for exactly that reason. Sailing on the waves was dangerous. At any moment Salacia could strike your boat down or swallow you in a storm. Airships could hover above the clouds, riding the ever-persistent wind in any direction they chose. To fly through the sky was to be truly in control.

The modest terraces eventually dissolved into massive gardens, showcasing the wealth of the villas to come. The Biancos were the wealthiest of the Alvanian merchants, but plenty of other families lived on the top of the hill looking out on the city and the sea. Their villas were protected by shade trees and exotic flowers imported from Shaheen and other nations even more southward.

Finally, Matteo reached his destination, a massive gate. At the center of the gate was a golden falcon emblem. Matteo reached his hand and grazed it across the cool metal. He could tell it was made of pure, soft gold by running his fingers along it. Two shimmering gems had been used as the falcon emblem's eyes. Matteo couldn't be quite sure, but they looked like star garnets. Where on earth did Grigori Bianco find star garnets?

Matteo hadn't waited for long before a scullery maid, clad in a uniform of cream and gold with a little gold falcon pin at her shoulder, came out to retrieve him. Strange that a scullery maid would come to rescue him rather than a footman. Quickly, it became clear why.

"I had to box the footman's ears to be the one to come get you," the maid said in a hushed tone as they walked towards the hulking villa. "But I had to be the one to see you first."

The maid had skin the color of cinnamon and curly dark hair pulled back behind her ears. From her head to her toes, she was Shaheeni, save her uniform, which had all the gaudiness of typical Alvanian dress.

Matteo couldn't help himself. He was so curious. There were not many Shaheeni people in Veronii. "You're from Shaheen," he said. His voice came across as more confrontational than he'd intended.

"Which is why I trust you," she said quietly. Matteo then remembered that, to the girl, he probably looked just as Shaheeni as anyone else. His dark hair fell in little ringlets all around his head, and his skin was, like hers, the color of ground cinnamon. When he was younger, he'd had his nose pierced with a gold ring. It had been impulsive, a futile attempt at connecting to his roots. He kept the nose ring but never quite got used to the way it looked on his face. Though Matteo looked Shaheeni, he didn't know who he was or where he came from. Veronii was the only place he'd ever called home.

"My name is Yasmina."

"I'm Matteo."

"I know who *you* are."

Yasmina was more fierce than any maid or servant Matteo had met before. He practically winced at the bite in her voice. Then he kicked himself. He was there on Grigori Bianco's special request. Of course, she knew who he was.

"I was Avira's lady's maid. We spent day and night together from the time she could walk. I even heated her bed on the cold winter nights. There is nobody in this villa who knows her better than I do." Yasmina was talking fast, as though at any moment someone might round a corner and force her to stop.

Matteo stopped in the path. "Do you know who took her?"

Yasmina shook her head slowly.

"All I know is that Lady Avira asked me to pack a few sentimental items into a small silk satchel and hide it under one of the lemon trees on the outskirts of the property. I did as I was told. That was seven days ago. Nobody has seen her since."

Matteo nodded.

"I also know," Yasmina continued, "that Grigori Bianco always lies."

"I find it's not good to speak in such absolutes," Matteo scoffed.

"I don't care what you've found or what you believe. I know Grigori Bianco. He always lies."

Matteo bit back the urge to ask a hundred questions. "Thank you, Yasmina."

They had reached the great doors of the manor. Yasmina opened the door and pointed down the great hall past a series of massive portraits.

"They're waiting for you in the garden, Master De Luca," Yasmina said, barely a whisper now. And then she disappeared into the bustle of the house.

Matteo walked towards the outdoor terrace, stopping to look at a portrait of a young woman whom he could only assume was Lady Avira Bianco. In the picture, she was about fourteen or fifteen, still small and rosey in her cheeks like a child. Her hair and eyes were the color of ebony, but her skin was a smooth porcelain color. Every feature on her face was petite, as was her frame. She couldn't have stood taller than

Matteo's shoulder. As Matteo looked closer, he swore he could make out a smattering of freckles along her nose, though it was faint. In her dark eyes was a sparkle, something Matteo rarely saw in portraiture.

He reached towards the oil painting, letting his fingertips rest on the wooden frame. Although he didn't want to admit it to himself at the time, he found the girl quite beautiful. The kind of young lady he might pine over had they met under different circumstances.

"That's her," a soft voice croaked back at him from the other side of the room. Matteo looked up, startled to see a small woman, even fairer than the girl in the painting, staring back at him through tear-stained eyes. "That's my daughter."

She looked run down, like a skeleton garnished with just the most delicate layer of skin.

"Lady Bianco." Matteo gave a deep bow, realizing he didn't know what was customary when greeting a woman of such wealth but no nobility. "Your daughter is beautiful."

"She looks so young in that picture. I miss the light that was in her eyes then."

Matteo nodded sadly. It was true, the girl in the portrait in front of him did have joy about her. She looked like she was planning something absolutely brilliant. Her painted eyes practically glowed with inspiration.

"My husband is waiting for you." Cristina Bianco hung her head. She clearly did not want to look at the portrait any longer. It was too painful for her. Matteo had seen this in almost every mother he'd worked for who had lost a child, right down to the somber, slow way Cristina breathed. It was like her body barely wanted to take in the air any longer.

The terrace was even grander than the inside of the villa. Wisteria vines twisted along a golden pergola, soft strings of purple blossoms hanging like ornaments everywhere. The ground was paved with red bricks and, unlike the paving of the streets, not a single weed dared poke its head through.

Cristina took her seat at a little yellow table with a glass pitcher of iced tea and chairs for three. A man with dark hair streaked with slight traces of silver sat with his back to Matteo.

"Master De Luca is here to see us."

The man slid around in his chair ever so slightly to get a good look at Matteo.

"So, the rumors are true. You are Shaheeni."

Matteo shook his head. "I was adopted as a child. Veronii is all I've ever known."

"What a unique situation. And your brother is the high priest, Julio De Luca?"

"Adopted brother," Matteo corrected. He didn't want to waste any time talking about Julio. He wasn't worth the time.

Grigori frowned. "Please sit down, Master De Luca. We have much to discuss."

A chill ran through Matteo's body, but he did as he was told. Yasmina emerged from what felt like nowhere and poured tea into a cup of ice. Matteo didn't dare ask how the Biancos obtained ice this time of year. He'd heard stories of mines in the Far North that farmed ice and shipped it to wealthy merchants in the South.

Yasmina garnished the tea with a handful of tiny blue borage flowers from her pocket and presented it to Matteo as though the two had never met. She bowed deeply.

"So, Master De Luca. I hear you are the best at what you do."

Matteo nodded. "I've negotiated many children's safe return, sir. Kidnapping is all too common in Veronii."

"You should know that my daughter, Avira, is not just any child. She's exceptional... and important."

"You and your wife must be devastated."

Cristina let out what Matteo could only assume was a soft sob, stifling herself with her iced tea. Grigori just shook his head, chuckling.

Matteo went on. "Certainly, you and your wife have considered the possibility that Avira is being held for ransom?"

Grigori rolled his eyes. "We'll be considering no such thing."

"I'm sorry?" Matteo could feel confusion on his face. Out of the corner of his eye, he could see Cristina hang her head. They were only two minutes into this conversation and already, Grigori was making this job harder than it had to be.

"Why would I pay ransom for a child who so clearly left out of her volition?" Grigori said.

"You believe she's run away then?"

"I know she has."

Matteo's head was, once again, filled with questions but the reality set in quickly that Grigori would not be the man to answer them. After all, Yasmina had warned him Grigori was a liar. How much of this could really be true? Certainly not all of it.

"You're just saying this because you hate her." Cristina didn't shout. She sat stiffly as a lady, a single tear running down her cheeks. She stared daggers into her husband. "You've always hated her, and you're glad she ran away."

Matteo drew back is head. It would appear that Yasmina was right, and Matteo wouldn't even have to pry to find the truth.

"She's a spoiled, selfish brat with big ideas about the world and no follow through. Why would I miss her. I never wanted a daughter anyway."

Grigori looked to Matteo as he spoke, probing for sympathy in the boy's eyes. He found none. Matteo was growing impatient. He was about to spend weeks, maybe even months of his life searching for this girl.

"You see, Master De Luca, my daughter and I have a *complicated* relationship. She is my only child and heir, so of course, I need her. But she is also a girl, meaning she can't inherit my fortune. The only hope for my fortune is marrying her off to a worthy man. She and I are not close. I've never had a fondness for her"

Cristina, it seemed, could no longer maintain her composure. "Excuse me," she said, more of a commandment than a request. And she bustled away, trailing her velvet skirts behind her. Yasmina gave a quick curtsy to the men and followed Cristina away. Grigori watched, sipping his iced tea as though he thought this meeting was going well.

"Forgive my wife. She's more and more distraught these days. As I was saying, a little over a week ago I announced her engagement to an esteemed captain from my fleet. She was less than pleased and, selfish as she is, she ran away. I need her back. And I will pay you handsomely to deliver her."

Matteo was growing less and less excited for this case by the minute. He wanted to be through with Grigori as soon as possible. "Do you know where your daughter may have run to?"

"Of course, I do. She's aboard The Apollo, rolling in the hay with that abhorrent Captain Artemis Cascella and his crew of thieves and beggars and witches."

Clearly, Grigori Bianco and Artemis Cascella had a history. It didn't take much deduction on Matteo's part to notice that. Artemis Cascella was a legendary sky captain, a fairytale hero in the flesh. It had always been a marvel to Matteo that Artemis worked for Grigori Bianco.

"Let me be clear about your assignment, Master De Luca. You are to board The Apollo, find my daughter, and return here alive before her marriage in September. I will pay you thrice your weight in gold if you can do this." Grigori thought more. "Here, take this as an advance." Grigori removed one of his massive rings. As Grigori placed the ring in Matteo's palm, Matteo could feel the icy cold of the man's skin.

"And you're sure she's on board The Apollo?"

"I announced her engagement nine days ago. The Apollo docked here eight days ago. She went missing seven days ago and is now nowhere to be found. I am not one to give merit to coincidence, Matteo. Are you?" Grigori's use of his first name made Matteo shudder. He didn't trust the man, but he'd come all this way, and a new desire began to burn within the boy's chest.

Wherever this girl was, she was a liability to the Bianco family, which made her a gold mine to any enemy of Alvanii that found her. She had to have known this. Matteo couldn't help but smirk. *What a witty young woman,* he mused to himself.

"I'll find her, sir," Matteo said.

"Then you best get to it. The Apollo takes off towards Shaheen tomorrow at sunset."

Matteo stood without saying another word, slipping the ring onto his finger, bowing his head, and leaving Grigori alone on the terrace.

As he walked back through the hall of the manor, he could feel a spring in his step. A new adventure was on the horizon, *one that would take him to Shaheen.*

But before Matteo could finish his daydream about finding his family in Shaheen, a set of hands flew out from behind a curtain, grabbing him and pulling him into a room he hadn't seen before.

Once Matteo gathered his senses, he faced Yasmina's clear brown eyes again.

"Come with me."

She took his hand, holding on tight, and guided him down the dark hall towards a staircase. They scampered up the stairs and through a set of golden doors. In the room at the top of the stairs, light spilled in, illuminating little specks of dust.

"This was my lady's room."

The room was massive, with smooth marble floors and a bed the size of a carriage right at the center.

"Look here." Yasmina guided Matteo to the bed and, before grasping what was happening, pushed the whole bed away from the center of the room and towards the wall. Matteo had to look at it for a long time before he knew what he was looking at. A giant map was painted onto the floor where the bed had stood.

Matteo had never seen anything like it. Maps of the world weren't easy to find. Merchants made their own as they developed their trade routes. Everyday people like Matteo tended to live out their lives without ever knowing exactly how the world around them was shaped. Sure, he knew Veronii was North of Alvanii, and there was a sea between Alvanii and Shaheen, but he'd never seen it in such detail.

And even when he'd caught glimpses or seen sketches of maps before, they'd never had this kind of evident care. Every city-state was labeled in what he could only assume was Avira

Bianco's curvy handwriting. Most of the map was the Sea of Salacia. In one of the bottom corners, Shaheen jutted out. Matteo had never realized it was a peninsula. Past Shaheen was a sizable octagonal shape labeled *Southern Continent.* Above Veronii, mountains had been drawn, and a little dot was labeled *Polislav.* While he knew they were people In The Far North, he'd never known they had an entire city-state.

"I've never seen a map like this," Matteo heard himself say. His mouth was hanging open.

In smaller handwriting were dozens of little labels, most on Shaheen and Southwards. *Nutmeg, Allspice, Pink Salt, Rice, Tea, Long Grain Rice, Cinnamon, Sapphires.* Up North, near Polislav, there were labels like *Wool, Lard, Diamonds, Burlap,* and *Wheat.*

"Her father's trading ports," Yasmina explained. "See how many?"

Matteo studied the map. All the details made one thing clear: Grigori Bianco had the entire world at his fingertips.

"She wanted to inherit the company," a voice whispered from behind them. Matteo and Yasmina swung around to reveal Cristina. Yasmina dropped into a low curtsy.

"When my husband told her that because of her sex, she'd never inherit his fortune, she swore she'd start her own business, captain a ship to Shaheen, and even further than that. She said she'd never marry and someday become even richer than her father. He hated her for it."

Cristina shook as she spoke. *The poor woman*, Matteo thought.

"When she ran, she took something precious to my husband. He doesn't really care if she comes back. He wants his map."

"His map?"

"A trade map *far* more detailed than this. She stole it. There are other maps, but this one was particularly vital to my husband's efforts in Shaheen. If you don't find her, I fear someone far more dangerous will."

Cristina took another quavering breath.

"Perhaps, she'll come home. Perhaps you can talk some sense into her, and she'll be home and married by September. But if she refuses, please promise me you'll keep her safe."

Of course, if Matteo didn't bring her home, he'd never get paid, but he nodded and took the woman's hand. The least he could do was bring this woman some peace.

Cristina placed a small chain in his hand. A necklace, not gaudy like the ring, but simple and dainty. A tiny gold falcon pendant hung from the chain. Matteo lifted it to the light before placing it around his neck and tucking it into his shirt for safety. It sparkled.

"Give this to her, from me, when you find her?" Cristina said softly.

"I will."

"And be sure she knows she's loved."

Matteo tightened his grip on the woman's hand.

"Thank you. Thank you both," was all he could think of to say. "I'll find her. I will."

Chapter Three

Nine days before Avira ran away from home, she and her father shared their first and only kindred moment. He hated her. She knew that. She'd never pressed him or asked him to feel differently about her. She'd learned that the best way to never get your heart broken was to never expect anyone to be anything other than exactly who they were. She knew who her father was. She never expected more.

They were in his study, well past the time of night when her mother usually went to bed. The house was silent save for the sound of Avira flipping through an ancient book of maps and the tinkle of ice in Grigori's glass of brandy. Avira knew what lengths her father went to have ice in the kitchen. It had to be mined by workers far up north in Polislav and then carried by carriage through the highest mountain passes so it remained cold enough. It cost him a fortune. He had fortunes to spare.

"Can I have a glass of brandy?" Avira had asked. She didn't

quite know what compelled her to do so. She knew all too well what her father's answer would be. Besides, she didn't like brandy much anyway.

"Brandy is a men's drink." Grigori had huffed, not looking up from the map he was studying. It was splayed out across his polished walnut desk. Avira desperately wanted to look at it but every time she got close, he shifted so he stood between her and the map.

"I don't see why women can't drink brandy." Avira had made up her mind to be as absolutely petulant as possible.

"Fine." Grigori caved. He pulled a crystal glass from the shelf behind his desk and decanted a small amount of the deep purple liquor, it was barely more than a swallow. Avira took the glass and toasted it gently towards him, lifting it to her lips dramatically. The dark liquid flowed across her tongue and Avira fought back a wince. She didn't like brandy. She pressed her lips together as tightly as she could but, despite her effort, a cough escaped her lips.

"I told you it was too strong," said Grigori, returning to the map he was studying.

"You told me it wasn't for women. You didn't say a word about how strong it is." Even as she spoke, Avira coughed again. Grigori chuckled. Avira threw back another large gulp of the brandy, determined to make it through the whole glass. She wanted to prove her father wrong.

"You study that book so diligently." Grigori gestured to the book Avira had been reading just a few moments before. "I've always wondered why. It's not like knowledge of geography will do you much good as a wife, save for understanding where your husband is off too at any given time."

"I think maps are interesting." Avira tried to hide how deflated her father's words made her feel. He'd been bringing up the concept of her having a husband more frequently these days. There was only one thing that could mean. Marriage was on the horizon.

"Girls don't need to find things interesting," Grigori retorted.

"Well, I do!" Avira placed her hands on her hips and straightened her back. She barely stood tall enough to reach father's shoulder. She felt so petite in his shadow.

"Fine, if you love maps so much, tell me where the mistake is on this trade map of mine." Grigori stepped away from the map on his desk, finally allowing Avira to look at the whole thing. Her eyes found the mistake instantly. The map was a relatively simple one. It had Alvanii and Veronii marked clearly on it as well as Shaheen to the south and Polislav to the north.

Dotted lines indicated mountain passes that were safe for carriage travel and golden lines marked popular skyship routes. She'd studied hundreds of maps just like this one, some from her father's library and some stolen from his desk in the night.

"There," Avira said as she slammed her index finger down on the map. She pointed at an island that was floating a few inches above the Shaheeni coastline. "That island is marked as Alvanian territory, but it falls well below the 36th parallel so it would technically be Shaheeni territory. Calling it Alvanian soil would be a violation of the Lalla-Mereyem Treaty."

Grigori raised an eyebrow. "It would appear you are correct. How do you know about that treaty?"

Avira's heart swelled. She'd found the mistake in her father's map. She'd outsmarted his best cartographers. She forced down the urge to jump for joy. "I read about it in one of your books."

Grigori snorted. For the first time ever, Avira saw a glimmer of pride in his eyes. It was almost addictive. She desperately wanted to ask him to show her another map. Instead, he said, "You are certainly going to give Gavriel Castillo a run for his money."

Gavriel Castillo? Avira didn't know what her father was talking about. Gavriel was one of Grigori's most trusted pilots and confidants. He was known by one and all to be a favorite to take over as captain of The Apollo when Artemis Cascella retired. He was a fool, a drunk and violent young man. Avira had known him since early childhood, and she'd never much liked him.

"What does Gavriel have to do with any of this?" Avira asked her father. He shook his head and their moment of fondness was over. The next morning Gigori made an official announcement of his intention to have Avira and Gavriel married. Gavriel had dropped to one knee and presented her with a ring that held a gigantic sapphire. Avira had been too stunned to protest. She'd spent the rest of the day hiding in her bedroom, staring at the map she'd drawn on her floor. *I can draw all the maps I want,* she thought, *but I may never see the world.* The idea alone was devastating.

Avira dumped another chopped cabbage into the stewpot. Warm oil splattered up into her face as she did. She pulled away, her hands flying up to her face. She'd never had an oil burn before. She'd hardly cooked at all.

"Get it together Cesario," the kitchen master, Diego said, growling at her, not even looking up from the bread he was kneading with his bare fists. Avira had seen the undersides of the man's fingernails. She didn't like thinking about how much filth was transferring from his hands into the bread dough with every knead. "First you're late and now you're making a mess of the stew. Trust me, you don't want fifteen angry ropesmen asking why their stew's burnt."

"Sorry, Diego," Avira muttered. She wasn't used to this, any of this. She felt like one of the tropical flowers her mother had imported from Shaheen. The flowers were beautiful in their natural habitat, but the soil in Alvanii was different. None of them were ever able to thrive. Avira didn't want to be fired from her position on The Apollo before the ship even left port.

Diego set the bread on a shelf to rise and started working on a brine to go with the stewed cabbage. He pulled a wooden bowl out from one of the cupboards. It was the most beautiful bowl she'd ever seen, it practically sparkled.

"What kind of wood is that?" Avira asked. She knew it wasn't typical of a kitchen boy to ask questions like this but she couldn't help herself.

"Wouldn't you like to know?" Avira could have sworn Diego winked at her as he said this. He pulled a few jars off of a shelf and removed the tops. Then he took a fistfull of a red powder and tossed it into the bowl. To Avira's shock, the red powder began to twist and turn as though it had been possessed by a summer breeze. It was like magic. Diego tossed in a pinch of pink salt crystals, and they also whirred to life.

"You're a sorcerer?" Avira had heard stories about wizards like this. They had magical powers and could bring inanimate objects to life. Diego laughed in Avira's face.

"I'm not magic, the bowl is." He threw some yellow spices in with the salt and the red powder and they all continued to mix until they were a brilliant orange color like marigolds in August. "It's made of the same kind of wood as The Apollo. It's magic wood, you know. How else do you think ships can fly?" "Science?" Avira said, feeling stupid as soon as the words escaped her mouth. Deigo chuckled kindly. Avira had to remind herself that he was drunk. His eyes were so cool and calm.

"I think you'll find that there are not so many differences between magic and science once you're in the sky." Diego picked up the bowl and dumped the spices on top of the cabbages Avira was boiling. He scoffed as he looked into the stew pot. "You're gonna need to chop at least fifteen more cabbages. I suggest you quit staring at me like I just pulled a snake out of my butt and get back to work."

Avira did as she was told. She slammed another cabbage onto the cutting board and began working twice as hard.

There was a strange energy on board The Apollo. She didn't care if it was the people on board the ship or their cooking utensils that held the magic, she felt happy to be in their company. Anything was better than where she'd come from.

CHAPTER FOUR

That girl better be here, Matteo thought to himself, looking around at the vastness of the ship and the brilliant cerulean sky that hung like silk curtains all around it. But his gut said she was. And Matteo trusted his gut.

The Apollo, the greatest skyship in all of Alvanii, was many things. It was colorful. The massive balloon that kept it aloft had been painted with gigantic golden suns. It was state-of-the-art. The rumor went that it took at least 100 men to man the ship across the Sea of Salacia and back. It was also old enough to garner a swath of legends, one claiming that the ship's captain, a southern man by the name of Artemis Cascella, hadn't set foot on land for fifteen years, so committed to life in the sky that spending time down on earth was impossible for him.

One thing the Apollo was *not*, however, was easy to board. Matteo arrived at the docks early in the morning, hoping a plank would take him from the land to the sky. Instead, he found a giant rope ladder, 200 meters long at least, stretching high up to the clouds. Matteo realized that all the cargo loaded and unloaded from The Apollo's mahogany deck was loaded via a complex pulley system. This meant the crew never had to step off the ship when picking up or dropping delicate cargo. It also suggested, Matteo speculated, that it would be relatively easy for a dainty young woman such as Avira Bianco to stow away in between a barrel of spices. He swallowed his nerves and began climbing the rope ladder into the sky.

The physics of Alvanian sky ships were lost on Matteo. The way they hung aloft in the clouds felt nearly impossible and looked as much to the human eye. The balloon that floated above the ship's wooden body looked about the size of a city block. The rigid body was fastened with two massive aluminum wings for steering. As Matteo climbed the ladder, the ship growing closer and closer with each step, he felt lucky not to have packed more in his satchel. Even his one change of clothes and leather-bound notebook felt heavier with each ladder rung.

After fifteen minutes of climbing, Matteo found himself on the glossy deck of The Apollo, the docks below looking like a sprawling ants nest from so high above. A tall man, covered from head to toe in deep green tattoos, approached Matteo.

"Who do you think you are?" the man grumbled, "crew or otherwise?"

"Otherwise," squeaked Matteo, "I'm here on behalf of Grigori Bianco-" Before he could gasp out another word, the tattooed man had him lifted by his shirt collar and his feet dangling in the open air below.

"We don't take well to *that* name up here." The smell of onions on his breath made Matteo's eyes water.

Before Matteo could formulate a half-decent argument for why the tattooed man shouldn't hurl him through the sky and to his death, another voice called out from out of his line of vision.

"Malvolio, send the boy with me." The voice was calm and confident, with the spice of an accent Matteo had never heard around the edges. The tattooed man, Malvolio, did as the voice said.

That is how Matteo found himself face-to-face with the infamous Captain Artemis Cascella. "What's your name, boy?" Artemis said, never raising his voice in the slightest. He didn't have to.

"Matteo. Matteo De Luca." It was clear that Matteo needed to get the upper hand here and fast if he was going to get assistance from the Captain. "And I'm not a boy," he said. "I'm a man, and I'd like the respect of one."

Artemis laughed. "You're what? Twenty years old? Take a turn in the sky, and then I'll call you man." Matteo bit his lip. He'd already humiliated himself only two minutes into the conversation.

"I hear you fancy yourself the finest detective in Veronii," Artemis said.

"I do, sir." With every passing moment, it became more apparent that Artemis could sense how nervous he made Matteo. Perhaps Artemis made everyone he met just a bit nervous. Maybe he'd come to expect it.

"Funny, I had expected you to look a little more Veronan. If I didn't know better, I'd have assumed you were born in Shaheen."

"I'm not here to speculate on the logistics of my birth, Captain." Mattco straightened his spine to look the captain right in the eye.

"Of course. You're here to find the girl."

Matteo felt his eyes brighten. How could Artemis know so much about the Bianco family if he never even left his ship?

As if he'd read his mind, Artemis smiled through his teeth and said, "News travels fast, Master De Luca. Even faster when it's airborne."

A chill ran down Matteo's spine. Like a hundred eyes were watching him and Captain Artemis square off.

"Perhaps we might discuss this in private," Matteo suggested. Artemis, smirking, extended an arm toward the center of the ship.

"Be my guest, Master De Luca."

Captain Artemis was not a tall man, though he exuded the spirit of someone far more significant than himself. He was not from Veronii or Alvanii, but Matteo couldn't imagine him being from Shaheen either. His skin, eyes, and hair were all as dark as night. His smile was cocky, and his teeth glittered white like seashells in the tide. His hair had been braided close to his head, and in the braids, Matteo noticed half a dozen precious gemstones secured tightly with the hair. The stones caught the sunlight in a hundred different ways, sending patterns across walls as Artemis passed. Artemis wore a fitted crimson coat like nothing Matteo had seen before. His pants were tight to his body, and his boots were clean, black, and stretched to his knee. Artemis was fashionable but not in the haughty way of the women Matteo had seen in Alvanii. No, Artemis dressed like a man who was genuinely sure of himself.

When Matteo and Artemis reached the captain's cabin,

Artemis pulled off his coat and hung it on a hook behind his massive mahogany desk. Matteo could now see a golden amulet around Artemis' neck, hanging down against his collarbones. At the center of the amulet was a golden sun, each ray laced with tiny diamonds. Captain Artemis Cascella was a man of immeasurable wealth. But, unlike Grigori Bianco, his wealth did not make him any less human. Matteo's gut said to respect the man, and Matteo trusted his gut.

Artemis hadn't stopped smirking since he sat down. He fumbled around in the cabinet behind his desk until he found a set of crystal wine glasses. "Do you drink, Master De Luca?"

Matteo struggled for words.

"This is good wine. Of course, you do." It was settled. Artemis pulled a bottle of pink wine from another drawer and poured it with his heart. He was handing the first glass to Matteo and pouring an even larger glass for himself.

"I got this bottle from the south side of Shaheen. It's sweeter than anything I've found in Alvanii and more full in flavor than anything from Veronii." Artemis snickered as though he had an inside joke with himself. "Mind you. I'd consider Veronan wine more mead than anything else."

Matteo lifted the glass to his lips and took a small sip. He wasn't one for wine, but he also wasn't one to turn down hospitality, especially from an ally he needed as severely as Artemis Cascella. It was indeed sweet. It tasted more like juice than anything.

"I've been told that real men don't dabble in sweet wines," Artemis rambled. "But I'd rather be castrated than give up Moscato."

Trying to play along, Matteo lifted his glass. "I'll toast to that."

Without skipping a beat, Artemis got down to business. "So, you're looking for the Bianco girl. I hear she's been missing for a week now."

"And *I* hear The Apollo's been docked at this port for that same time," Matteo remarked, trying hard to match Artemis' energy. "Some coincidence, don't you think?"

"I assure you, she's not on board my ship. I handpick every man on my crew myself."

"All one hundred of them?"

"All one hundred *and eleven* of them."

Matteo's confidence broke for just a second. Artemis was smart. Even if he had kidnapped the girl, he would hide it well. Best to be direct.

"I hear rumors that you took the girl for ransom."

"And I hear rumors that you're the bastard son of Shaheeni

nobility. As you can see, we've both done our research."

Artemis took a hearty drink of his wine, letting it swish in his mouth for a moment before swallowing.

Matteo's gut twisted. An idea. Perhaps a different approach was best. He and Artemis were at an intellectual stalemate.

"A battle of wits is pointless then," Matteo started, "perhaps an alliance would serve the both of us better."

Artemis scoffed. "You work for Grigori Bianco."

"And?"

"Of the one hundred and eleven men aboard my ship, not one trusts Grigori Bianco. Your alliance would do me no good."

Matteo pursed his lips. "Make it one hundred and twelve, then. Let me work for you. I will do whatever service you need while I search for the Bianco girl. I trust my gut, Captain Cascella. And my gut says she's aboard The Apollo."

Artemis thought about this. "You would make a mediocre kitchen boy at best."

"Then let me sweeten the deal."

"I'm listening."

"My deal with Grigori Bianco is that I bring his daughter back alive. What happens to her between here and there is none of my worries. If I find her, you may hold her for whatever ransom you like in Shaheen, punish her for stowing away, use her however you please as long as I may return her to her father alive next time The Apollo docks in Alvanii." Matteo dropped the massive Bianco ring onto Cascella's desk for good measure.

Artemis' face fell. Before Matteo had a moment to consider what he may have said wrong, the Captain spoke. "Careful, boy. We don't treat women as objects aboard my ship."

"But you don't hire them either." Matteo stood his ground.

Artemis was not the type to kidnap a woman. If Avira was here, and Matteo felt deeply that she was, she was here of her own volition, and she'd somehow made it past even Artemis Cascella. Matteo maintained a straight face but inside, he was grinning. Such a witty girl. His desire to meet her was growing every minute.

"And thus, our alliance is sealed," Artemis said dryly, taking the ring. "You find the girl, wherever she's hiding on this ship, and report her identity to me when you find her. We'll go from there."

Artemis extended his hand to shake. Matteo took it and shook it firmly.

"We launch at sunset. Report to the kitchen by 10 PM sharp."

"Yes, sir." Matteo turned on his heels.

"And Master De Luca," said Artemis, stopping Matteo with his words.

"Yes, sir?"

"You are just one of one hundred and twelve. Don't expect any special treatment."

"Of course not, sir."

"That's *Captain* to you."

Artemis gave his signature smirk as Matteo exited the captain's chambers. Midday was breaking.

Chapter Five

Before this week, Avira had never been on a skyship. At least not a skyship like this one.

She'd ridden with her father along the coastline, his brightly colored luxury vessels designed for the wealthy of Alvanii to take in the view of the countryside with minimal effort. This ship was at least five times that size. The Apollo was like a floating city. Avira knew there were decades of science behind the flying ships, but after her encounter with Diego and his magic bowl, magic was beginning to feel more likely. After all, what gave humans the right to fly a mile above the earth like this?

Perhaps a mile is an exaggeration, Avira thought, as she peered over the edge of the ship. But the height alone was enough to make the bottoms of her feet tingle a bit. Watching the Sea of Salicia crash so far below, she wondered if she could jump down to the water from this high up. Probably not.

She'd heard stories of sailors falling overboard. Their bodies had shattered like glass upon impact.

Above her head, the ropesmen worked. Each crewman was tied to an intricate pulley system that lifted them above deck and kept them safely harnessed as they checked for any sign of wear and tear. The Apollo had been sky bound for years. Avira couldn't remember a day when it wasn't in the air. When she was a child, Captain Cascella's sun-painted vessel was the diamond of her father's fleet. Grigori Bianco chartered many feisty sailors like Artemis. He could offer them safety, consistent trading, and fortune in exchange for their loyalty to the Bianco Trade Empire.

The Bianco Trade Empire.

Avira rolled her eyes at the thought of it all. Her father's exorbitant wealth was enough to swallow even the best of men whole and her father was *not* the best of men.

Once Avira's father had caught her picking lemons from his private grove. He'd slammed her fingers with a branch from a lemon tree until they bled. Lemon trees have thorns across their boughs, so every blow was met with a dozen tiny stab wounds. Avira was only ten years old. She'd wanted to make lemonade to share with her mother, who was pregnant and having lemon cravings.

Her mother hadn't carried that baby to term. Avira was an only child, which left her lonely most days of the week. Yasmina had told Avira never to mention her lack of siblings. The miscarriages that came before and after Avira had left Cristina heartbroken. But Grigori wasn't just heartbroken at the loss of so many babies. He was furious with his wife, who, in his eyes, had failed to give him a son. Each miscarriage seemed to carry more and more of her mother's soul off with it.

A softness filled Avira's chest as she thought of her mother, who was bearing the brunt of her daughter's absence. She thought she was about to cry. It felt so foreign to her. The gentle tingle morphed into a twist in her stomach, and she realized the ship had begun to move! The relief was twofold. She wasn't crying, and The Apollo had finally started its voyage.

Avira had been taking a break from the pungent odors of the kitchen. She was trying to catch her breath and distinguish what onion stench was dinner and what was her own body odor. The instant she noticed the motion, Avira caught a glimpse of Captain Cascella. He stood at the ship's wheel, eyes fixed on the Southern horizon.

"Prepare for open-air," he shouted.

Avira wondered if she was supposed to know what to do. It appeared that the men with jobs to do knew what they were supposed to be doing. The rest of the crew members made themselves scarce.

Avira attempted a casual stride across the deck back towards the kitchen but found it was much harder to walk while the ship was moving in the opposite direction. Elation bubbled inside her with every wobbling step. She'd made it. Now she could breathe!

She was aboard The Apollo and moving farther from her father every second.

She'd been gone for eight days. Eight days was no short amount of time. She was certain few other girls running from arranged marriages had made it as far as she had. Much less successfully disguised themselves and obtained employment in the most famous skyship in the world. As she opened the door to the kitchen, she didn't even notice the smell. She let the stench wash over her and said a silent thank you prayer to the sky goddess, Aurora, for getting her this far.

This is precisely when she ran face-first into a wall of sticky, hot flesh.

"What are you thinking?" she said before even having the chance to take in her surroundings. She surprised herself with how low her voice sounded, especially spontaneously.

Her quips were met with an outstretched hand as though

this bothersome stranger was taking pains to make a friendly introduction. Finally looking up, Avira's eyes met with a set of massive, unblinking brown eyes.

No, not quite brown. Darker than brown, like the sky on a moonless night.

The man's pupils were barely distinguishable from the dark color of his irises. Avira had never seen eyes like this. She was absolutely lost in them.

"My apologies," said the owner of the eyes, hand still outstretched. "I was looking for whoever left this pot on." The man gestured to a massive stock pot Avira had left unattended when she stepped out for her breath of fresh air. The pot didn't look anything like how Avira had left it. The broth had bubbled over, streams of greenish foam dribbling down the sides every which way. It looked like human refuse had been bottled up, shaken, and exploded like champagne.

"It's boiled over," the stranger said rather unhelpfully.

"Well, aren't you a perceptive one," Avira said instinctively. She ran to the stove and doused the flame with a cloth, careful to snuff it out. Avira gagged on the steam and its putrid smell. She tried to swallow down her disgust, hoping that the strange boy hadn't noticed.

Avira swung around on her heels, ready to direct all her

anger toward this nuisance of a boy. Screw his enrapturing eyes. He hadn't even had the sense to douse the flame when the soup boiled over, and now a pot of soup that could have fed at least fifty men was ruined.

But before Avira could begin scolding him, she recognized him. He was the Shaheeni boy she'd seen the Malvolio holding over the ship's edge. That was only a few hours ago. What on earth was he doing in the kitchen now?

"I'm Matteo," the boy said earnestly, his hand still extended. His dark eyes made more sense now, given his Shaheeni appearance. He had those same dark curls her lady's maid, Yasmina, had had. His ringlets were far less well-kempt than Yasmina's though, she noticed. It looked like he'd never bothered to style them at all. Perhaps he didn't know how.

"Cesario," Avira said, shaking the boy's hand. He'd had it outstretched for at least a minute now. It felt like the polite thing to do.

"I'm sorry about your... er... what is that exactly?"

Avira turned to look at the soup. "It was supposed to be dinner for the night crew."

The boy looked puzzled.

"The night crew?" Avira pressed. "The ropesmen and furnace crew and-"

"Cesario is a nice name," the boy said, interrupting her. He'd located an apron on the far side of the kitchen and was tying it on over his suspiciously well-pressed pants. Avira noticed something when he spoke this time. He didn't have the pang in his voice that Nicolo did so that he couldn't be lower class. But his words didn't italicize in the same brisk way she knew those of Alvanii did.

He must be Veronan, Avira thought, *a wealthy Veronan at that.*

Veronans were far less inclined to take to the skies, and high-born young men generally didn't need to. Besides that, Avira's father hated Veronans and rarely hired them.

Even more strange, the boy looked more Shaheeni than he did Veronan. He didn't have the pasty complexion or ginger hair that set most people from Vernonii apart from their Alvanian counterparts.

Avira realized she'd spent more time contemplating the boy than conversing with him. She formed a response, "It was my brother's name." She immediately kicked herself. Now she'd have to elaborate more.

"You were named after your brother?" Matteo asked.

"He died before I was born." Avira felt like a fish pulled from the water, slapping around on the docks and gasping for air.

"I'm the youngest of twelve, you see."

"I like the name," the boy said. She noticed him give her a look with only his eyes so quickly she could have missed it. His eyes said, *I don't believe you.*

He already had her on her back foot, and she'd only met him a moment ago.

What if he saw right through her disguise? He could report her to Captain Cascella, and she would be tried on Sailor's Law. Even her fortune couldn't save her then. She'd be thrown overboard.

"How can I help?" the boy asked. He had a pressure in his voice that made Avira worry he'd already asked her this while she'd been busy inside her head.

Best not to get friendly, she decided.

"Throw that pot overboard."

"The whole pot?"

"Not the whole pot, you idiot, just the soup. Then get back in here, clean the stove, mop the floors, and start on the bread. I'm assuming you can make a half-decent bread."

Nothing about this boy told Avira that he could make bread. She couldn't even do it herself. But if he was to be her shift mate for the next few hours, maybe she could at least use him.

"Hop to it. We've got mouths to feed!" She put on her

best 'hardened sailor' voice and hoped it might work. To her surprise, it did. Matteo gathered the entire charred pot in his arms and took it out of the kitchen, dumping the burnt stew overboard. "Look out below" He shouted. Then he came back and, without saying a word, plunged the pot into the wash basin and began to scrub vigorously. He didn't even complain. Maybe she was getting better at this whole Cesario act.

Avira went back to cutting vegetables, the same thing she had done earlier. Dropping them into a fresh pot of water and waiting for them to boil. She thought she would have been more annoyed to have to start over completely, but she found the chopping cathartic, relaxing even. After her shift, maybe she'd track down the Kitchen Lead, a gruff man named Diego. She could ask who on earth assigned her the new guy. Even though she'd only been there a few days, she felt she deserved better than this. Feeding the night ropesman was an important job. They kept the ship aloft while everyone else slept.

As he mopped, Avira let herself glance up at the strange boy. Something about him felt familiar. That couldn't be good. Her mind wandered to all the ways this could be a trap of her father's or Gavriel's. He could be a spy. Anyone on board the ship could be a spy. Her father did own the ship, after all. But Avira remembered the boy in her cabin, Nicolo, who had been kind to her even when she was cold and suspicious with him. If she was going to make it through this journey, she'd need friends. And she couldn't make friends if she walked around suspicious of everyone all the time. Besides, this boy appeared to be far too daft to succeed in the world of espionage. He couldn't even keep a pot from boiling over. As she cut, she relaxed into the mundane chopping motion. She let her mind wander away from the boy, away from her worries for only a moment.

She imagined the map she'd drawn on her bedroom floor, so many miles away now. And She let her mind drift to all the trade routes she'd imagined but never dared put on the map in case her father found it and stole her idea. If she was to be his most significant competitor, she had to beat him at his own game. Her mind had always wrapped well around facts and figures. She was better with numbers than any other girl in her classes. Her friends had taken to copying her answers on math tests. Avira felt she could change the whole world using only numbers, a pen, and a blank sheet of parchment. She could map the entire future of Alvanii, if only they'd let her. If only she'd been born a boy.

She remembered the small bag she kept locked safely in the chest of her cabin. Inside it was a handful of things, but she only truly cared about a roll of weathered parchment. It was a complete map of the Bianco Trade Network, every port from Shaheen to Veronii, across the Southern Coast to places Avira hadn't even heard of, every route from Polislav to Irajmi. It was the most comprehensive map she could get her hands on, it even included her father's secret military forts.

Avira smiled. Someday she'd make a map of her own and share it with the world. After all, few people had access to maps in Alvanii, and she assumed it was the same in Veronii. Trade barons like Grigori had kept their secrets so close to their chest that the everyday man didn't even know what the world looked like.

Someday, Avira would change all that. But first, she had to get through this kitchen shift.

Chapter Six

Matteo knew who she was the minute he saw her. Well, the minute he ran headfirst into her.

The sun was setting, and it had only taken him a minute to settle into the small room that would be his home for the next month and a half. He'd locked up his journal, change of clothes, and book of Shaheeni myths in the chest provided to him and changed his shirt to look a little more casual. Then, he decided to make his way to the kitchen and check in for his shift early. In Veronii, the kitchen was strictly a place for wives and mothers. He'd spend barely any time cooking in his life. He'd never even learned how his adoptive mother made the thin, doughy bread they ate with almost every meal. He suspected it was just walnut flour and water but he had no way to be sure.

When he'd made it to the kitchen, Diego, a plump man with gigantic hoop earrings, was in a drunken stupor, complaining about how lazy his crew was. Matteo had introduced himself politely, and Diego had made a sweeping gesture to a rack of aprons in one corner and a pile of onions before stumbling out the door. Matteo was alone in the kitchen with at least five gigantic pots boiling on every open flame. The room was scalding hot and so muggy he could barely breathe.

One pot had only onions and cabbage in it, set to a simmer. The aroma of salt and spices filled the air but it was hard to pinpoint exactly where it was coming from. None of the food looked to have much in terms of flavoring. It looked like a gray sludge. Matteo wasn't one to complain, but he had always assumed The Apollo offered slightly better dining options, considering its fame. *The least they could do is serve some kind of meat,* he thought.

Another pot was at a rolling boil so intense Matteo feared it would spill over and ruin whatever bile was cooking. Matteo decided it would be wise to find the kitchen lead, Diego, and ask for advice on what to do next. He'd turned on his heels and dashed out the door. That's when he'd run into the girl.

She was dressed as a boy, sure. One could even say the costume was passable, but having seen her portrait on the wall at the Bianco Villa, Matteo recognized her immediately. From the daintiness of her features to the smattering of freckles across her nose — notably more intense in person than in the painting — to her pale, glass-like skin. Matteo had tried to quickly cover up his recognition by holding his hand out in a shake, but the girl had locked eyes with him so intently he worried she knew he knew. Matteo could feel himself blushing. Her gaze was so intense. It overwhelmed him.

It was probably a good thing she wasn't particularly friendly. Distracting her with the pot boiling over had seemed to work well and pretty soon, she was ordering him around like some old haggard sailor who hadn't touched earth for a decade.

Matteo had felt confident he'd find the girl. He'd once negotiated the safe return of a Veronan senator's infant child who couldn't even speak, much less leave a trail of clues as to where she had gone, as Avira had done. But it was always much harder to find people who didn't want to be found. He'd expected Avira to at least evade him for more than a single day.

As he watched her work in the kitchen, cutting onions masterfully though he could only assume she'd never stepped in a kitchen a day in her life, he noticed how graceful she was. Even with the ship rushing underneath their feet and pitching back and forth from time to time when it caught a gust of wind, Avira danced between the counters and the flaming stoves. It was like she'd been born to be in the sky.

Avira asked Matteo to make a loaf of bread, and he'd failed miserably, garnering many under-the-breath insults from her. However, he couldn't help but notice that she didn't appear to know what to do with the yeast or flour either. They were one motley pair, two people pretending to know how to work in a kitchen. The night ropesman would have to go without bread tonight.

Matteo figured the best way to secure the girl's safe return was to gain her trust without revealing his intentions. If she'd recognized him instantly as Matteo De Luca, the Veronan detective, Matteo doubted she'd have been so calm around him. In hindsight, he could have given her a fake name, but he'd told all the other crew members his name was Matteo. *Way to go, Matteo.* He cursed himself for being so clumsy with his true identity. The girl had distracted him.

The kitchen shift went slowly. From 10 PM, when the sun set to 4 AM, when the night ropesman had a shift change and came to the kitchen for food, they worked away in the steam and the dim light of the kitchen. A single lantern swayed with the rocking of the ship and lit their way. They were nearly wordless for most of the night.

At one point, Matteo asked the girl, Cesario, as she had introduced herself, what time her shift had started. She shrugged and said she didn't mind working a double since her bunkmate was far too spritely for her to get any sleep in her bed anyway.

"He wants to become friends. I didn't come here to make friends."

By the time their shift ended, the stars were out. Matteo had never seen anything quite so brilliant as the stars. They were closer than he'd ever seen before. Instead of tiny fireflies or candle flames, they looked like torches lighting the night. He wanted to reach out and touch them. Matteo had stopped and called out, "Cesario, look at the stars." But she'd already disappeared below the deck of the ship.

So Matteo returned to his bunk, where his cabin mate was already out on a shift. He couldn't remember, but he thought he remembered his cabin mate's position was something he'd never imagined could be a job on a skyship – like sail stitcher or mast painter.

Matteo drifted into a deep sleep, promising himself that one of these nights, he'd stay awake long enough to watch the sunrise from the deck. He couldn't exactly picture it in his head, but it had to be brilliant -- probably even more intelligent than the ones that made Alvanii so famous.

He fell into a dreamless sleep and awoke to an unearthly sound. Some kind of copper bell rang from every corner. Or maybe it was ringing from *inside* his skull.

Matteo sat up so fast he nearly whacked his head on the ceiling. He wasn't accustomed to sleeping on a top bunk. When he'd learned of the bunking system, he'd been quite appalled. What would happen if the ship took a hard pitch to one side in the middle of the night? Would he fall right out of bed? Some night of sleep that would be.

Matteo slid on his pants and shoes, throwing on a muslin tunic he'd forgotten he packed. His bunkmate, it seemed, had already made it out of the room. The copper bell droned on. Matteo poked his head out of his room and found every man on the ship moving down the hallway in the same direction. He figured he'd better follow and join the crowd as they climbed up to the ship's deck. Artemis stood waiting for them. From what Matteo could tell, the men lined up in order of what position they worked and how long they'd been on the ship. Newbies like him were pushed, rather aggressively, to the front.

It only took a moment for Matteo to find the girl in the crowd. She was the only one who looked half as confused as he was.

"Good morning, my little sunshine!" Artemis called. He wasn't standing regally like a military general. Instead, he was hanging from a rope ladder a few dozen feet above his men. One leg was hooked into the ladder so he could gesture wildly with his arms as he spoke.

"For those new here, welcome to your first morning aboard the greatest sky ship in all of Alvanii, Veronii, and the world."

There was a great cheer, primarily instigated by the more seasoned crewmen. Matteo wondered if this speech happened after every launch.

"I wanted to gather you all here," Artemis continued, "so I can look at every one of your faces at least once before we are miles from land, and I'm stuck relying on you to keep me afloat. Each of you was hand chosen by me, no easy task, so know that there can be no secrets between us. If you think you are hiding something from me, think again." Matteo fought the urge to look at Avira. He wondered if she was nervous at all. He couldn't imagine anyone was keeping a bigger secret than her, especially with how men on this ship appeared to feel about the Bianco family.

"Now I know what this ship's charter says. It says that all of you technically work for Grigori Bianco. It *says* that he owns everything you do. But you know what I say?"

The men gave a cheer, egging Artemis on. "If Grigori Bianco wants to control my ship, he can come up to the sky and try to take it from me."

Matteo was impressed at Artemis' ability to work the crowd. These men respected, even idolized him. How could they not? This man had singlehandedly outsmarted the wealthiest man in Alvanii and beat him at his own game. Sure, the initial money for The Apollo had come from Grigori, but it was clear that Artemis ruled the skies. Matteo wondered what it must feel like to be so unafraid of the world.

"I am your captain. I am your friend." Artemis had a sick smile as if he was about to do something completely unexpected. "But I am also the law." He motioned with his hand to a blonde man with three nose rings who stood smack dab in the middle of the crowd. It was clear that the man didn't know why.

"Do not lie to me," Artemis said, taking pains to put on a show.

The tattooed man and another tall muscly fellow began making their way through the crowd, grabbing the blonde man by the shoulders and lifting him above the crowd.

"Are you a spy for the Grigori Bianco?"

The blonde man stammered, "N-n-no sir."

"Call me captain," Artemis pressed, "and tell me the truth. Do you work for Grigori Bianco?"

Matteo watched in horror. If this is how Artemis felt about Bianco's spies, was he next? Maybe Artemis had just lured him up here to toss him into the ocean like a ragdoll.

"I'm not a spy, Captain," the blonde man begged.

Artemis pursed his lips. "Malvolio. Throw him overboard."

"I'm a spy! I'm a spy," the man pleaded. Artemis nodded, and Malvolio set the man back on the deck, where he collapsed to his knees and wailed. Malvolio grabbed the collar of his shirt and began dragging him towards Artemis' cabin.

Matteo felt sick that the man's punishment was far from over.

"That's what happens when you lie to your Captain. Fifty-two days and fifty-three nights we will spend in the sky together. Do not break my trust." Artemis climbed down from the ladder and strode across the deck to his cabin. With a slam of the door, he called, "Dismissed."

The deck erupted into chaos. Some men were laughing, others quaking in fear. Matteo looked around for 'Cesario,' but the girl was gone. By the sun, he had a few hours until his next shift started, so he spent some time exploring the ship. The deck was massive, easily the size of the Bianco Villa, and shone in the sunlight in a bright walnut color. It was shiny like it had been polished and waxed that morning. Matteo reckoned he could run his hand along even the roughest patch of the deck without getting a splinter at all.

The ship was shaped like a gigantic almond with glittering silver wings and a giant balloon. In the center of the vessel was a large furnace that burned day and night, pumping hot air into the balloon to keep the whole thing aloft. It was a marvel of technology, that much was certain. But, as Matteo explored a little more, he realized it was also a complete work of art. The guard rails along the deck were intricately carved with what Matteo recognized as images of the goddesses Aurora and Salicia. There were entire stories sketched out along every inch of the ship. The balloon, from a distance, looked to have twenty or so massive suns painted on it, but as he looked closer, Matteo could see that the suns were mosaics of smaller, more intricate images. The mast of the ship had a massive carving of a woman in a golden slip that hugged her body so tightly. Matteo wondered how a wood carver could make walnut look like natural silk.

The ship was as helpful as it was beautiful. Three cargo bunkers were beneath the deck, each accessible from the top only by a slick wooden ladder. One cargo gave off the pungent smell of spices, some were easily identifiable as pepper or cinnamon, but others were new to Matteo. Growing up in

Veronii, the food was famously mild.

Even a few feet away, the smell of the spice bunker burnt Matteo's nose. Another cargo bunker was locked with a complicated latch, and the other looked to be filled with clothing and other luxury items. The back end of the ship was a raised quarter deck with a steering center. Standing at the wheel were two men studying a map. Matteo guessed these were the men who controlled the wings.

Matteo made his way below deck and to his room. He fiddled with the latch on the door, which seemed sticky and unruly. He hoped he'd get a little nap before his kitchen shift, which was set to last most of the evening into the night.

As soon as he stepped into the room, it was clear that a nap was not in the cards.

His bunkmate was nowhere to be found, and on the upper bunk, Matteo's bed sat Artemis Cascella. He was eating an apple whole which Matteo thought made him look particularly malicious. Artemis's eyes didn't sparkle in the room's darkness as they did in the sun. Instead, they reflected Matteo's face.

"What did you think of my little show up there? Did it help you find the girl?"

Matteo winced. "Don't you give that speech before every voyage?"

Artemis chucked. "I added some special effects to this one just for you. You didn't like it?"

Matteo didn't know what to think. What was Artemis trying to say? That the whole thing had been staged? Or that he knew he'd found the girl.

His mind flashed the image of the man screaming as they dragged him into Artemis' quarters. He'd promised Cristina he'd protect Avira, but Matteo didn't trust the captain enough. What if he tried to hurt her too?

"It's been twelve hours," Matteo said coolly. "How could I have found the girl already? The ship has what? One hundred and twelve men?"

"I didn't ask if you'd found the girl," Artemis hissed. "I asked if you liked my show."

"Am I next? I work for the Biancos, too, you know."

Artemis considered this for a long moment, taking another bite of his apple and letting a drop of the juice run down his chin and drip onto his neck like a bead of sweat. Matteo watched the trail it made along his dark skin.

"I knew that boy was a spy long before today, Matteo. I found out shortly after hiring him before my last voyage. But I liked him. He did good work in the furnace and didn't seem to cause any trouble. As you should plan on doing, he stayed on my good side." Artemis could be wicked.

"It's often hard to realize how tight a cage is if it is dripping with gold," Artemis continued. "It was unsafe to let the boy free any longer. Not with the war brewing."

"War?" Matteo had heard rumors of conflict in the Southern Skies but nothing of too much note. He'd never heard it referred to so plainly as a war.

"I received word from one Gavriel Castillo that Grigori Bianco is gathering his charter ships near Shaheen, hoping to destroy a blockade the Shaheeni queen has built. The Apollo has been requested. I need my bargaining chip."

"*You need the girl*," Matteo said, not asking but confirming what he already knew. Artemis gave a curt nod. "I do not want to fight in Bianco's war. But to defy him, I must provide something he wants."

"And what happens to me if I bring you the girl?"

Artemis gave a smile. "Smart boy. Good businessman. I will give credit where credit is due when the time comes. We'll turn her in. You will get your money. I will be free of my charter, and Grigori is free to wage his stupid war on Shaheen should he so please."

Matteo was speechless. It felt so much more complicated than he'd initially understood. He'd dealt with politics before.

Once Matteo had rescued a young bastard child whose family had been so deeply connected with a violent gang that the chances of returning him alive felt slim to none. But this felt different. This was a war.

"So, I ask you again, Matteo De Luca," Artemis said, now so close to Matteo's face that he could smell the apple on his breath, "Have you found the girl?"

Matteo shook his head.

"No," he lied, "But I will."

"Good." Artemis jumped down from the bed and sauntered out the door. "I look forward to our partnership."

And the door slammed behind him.

Chapter Seven

Avira quickly noticed that days in the sky had passed differently than at home. Her first full day of rest was one of the most relaxing days of her life. Crew members' rest days were on a rotating basis, and, as one of the most junior members of the crew, she had to wait nearly ten days for hers. But it was well worth it. The maids at home got one day off a month, which Avira realized was entirely too few, especially for the added stress that came with serving her father.

Without shade trees to block the sun, mornings came earlier and felt longer in the sky. It felt like high noon by 7 AM. All the same, dusk fell slowly. The sun would set for hours, starting at one end of the sky and gently melting together until darkness enveloped them all. While most of the crew members appeared pretty well adjusted to the brutal schedule of the ship, Avira still found the adjustment dizzying.

Generally, Avira worked through the sunset and into the

night, but she always tried to catch a moment out on the deck to watch the sky.

Diego, the kitchen lead, didn't appear ever to be sober. This made it challenging to prepare food besides his regular staples of boiled cabbage, boiled potatoes, boiled onions, hot broth, and soda bread. It only took a week for Avira to get pretty sufficient at baking a loaf of bread, though she hadn't yet figured out how to make them keep their shape in the oven.

Her night shift soon became her favorite; she got to work with the Shaheeni boy, Matteo. Matteo had a dry sense of humor that complimented hers well. She felt a bit more at ease around him than anyone else. He never gave any sign that he might suspect she wasn't Cesario, the kitchen boy from Alvanii. Either she had him fooled, or his poker face was unmatched.

Avira worried Nicolo had begun to grow suspicious, but she tried to ignore the matter, and it appeared he had taken the same approach.

Just over two weeks after their launch, Avira awoke from her afternoon nap to a terrible dream. The Shaheeni boy, Matteo, was in it. He was facing off with her fiancé, Gavriel, whose steely gray eyes didn't show even an ounce of mercy. Even as a child, when Avira was ten and Gavriel was a rising captain in her father's fleet, Avira had thought his eyes made him look almost like a shark. Gavriel, in her nightmare, had stabbed Matteo in the stomach and looked her directly in the eyes as he did. Only after Matteo took his last breath did Avira realize the real problem at hand, the ship had begun to freefall through the sky, dragging her and everyone else down to the sea below.

At the moment the ship collided with the water, Avira woke up.

She was breathing quickly and had to fight to slow her breaths so as not to faint. From the light through the boards of the ceiling, Avira guessed it was reaching evening hours and decided she might as well start her shift early. Diego seemed to like it when she showed up and relieved him of his duties, so he could find an old pal to play a game of cards with. Avira always wondered where the old man kept his liquor, there didn't appear to be any stocked in the kitchen, and Avira had looked for it!

Anything to bring a little flavor to the hot slop they prepared each day. The new ropesman hadn't quite gotten used to the "stews" yet, so most meals were met with hearty groans. But the older men seemed accustomed to the smell and the green color and ate quickly without complaining.

When Avira got to the kitchen, she saw she wasn't the only

one who decided to start their shift early. Matteo stood at the kitchen island, slicing onions into long strips.

"I thought we were supposed to cube the onions," she called from behind him, dropping her voice down an octave.

"We are," Matteo said without turning around, "because it makes them easier to mash into the stew. But I don't want to mash them tonight, so I'm not going to cut them that way."

"You're already tired of the stew? Diego will be so upset!" Avira mused as she took the bread dough she'd been letting rise off the corner shelf.

"Maybe he would be," Matteo shot back, "if he were sober long enough to notice."

Avira laughed. She hadn't quite managed to laugh without sounding like a young lady yet, but she figured everyone was embarrassed by their laugh anyway, so perhaps nobody would notice hers.

"I'm going to pan-fry them tonight as a topping for the bread. Like toast." Matteo was excited, which made Avira excited.

"I bet the night ropesmen will love that."

So, they set to work together, cutting the onions into their strips and baking loaf after loaf of bread. Twenty-seven ropesmen worked the night shift, and nine furnace workers. It would take at least a dozen loaves of bread to feed them all, and Avira found the math as to how many onions that entailed dizzying.

"Should we make a stew, too, just in case?"

"You think they'll turn down solid food?" Matteo said. One eyebrow was raised ever so slightly in defiance. It drove Avira crazy.

Avira stubbornly began tossing cabbages and onions into a pot of water. The stew wouldn't be the focus for tonight, but perhaps if they had at least tried, they'd be in less trouble with Diego.

Avira didn't know how long they'd been cooking, but at one point, she looked up from the loaf of bread she was braiding together and watched Matteo for a moment. He poured oil into the bottom of a wide pan and slowly added onions. He was looking at those onions intently like they were the cure for some horrible disease or something. Avira couldn't help but notice his long eyelashes batting away the steam. She didn't realize how long she'd been staring until she was slammed out of her head by an ear-splitting sound she'd only heard once before.

A copper bell.

Her head snapped to the door and then to Matteo. She had

no idea what the bell could mean. It was late in the night, certainly not a crew meeting. But then she heard the voices from outside the kitchen.

"Lockdown! Lockdown! Get to your bunks!" Men were shouting from every direction. Avira looked at Matteo; she knew from the fire in his eye that he'd heard the men too.

"Cesario get down," he shouted just as the glass from the kitchen door shattered inward just behind her head. Outside the door, she heard laughing and loud footsteps, like those of steel-toed boots.

Matteo had snapped into action. Forgetting entirely about the onions, he motioned for Avira to crawl towards him slowly to avoid the broken glass. Then, he ushered her into the cleaning closet where the two sat, each with their back to the wall. The cabinet was so small that their knees had to be wrapped together, and their faces nearly touched. It should have been pitch black with the door shut, but it wasn't.

Above them was a dim flickering light, like lanterns drifting through the floor. Footsteps slammed above them, and then they heard a calm, familiar voice with an accent she couldn't pinpoint. From the sound of it, they were directly below Artemis' cabin.

Matteo held a finger to his lips, reminding Avira to stay

quiet. But that wasn't hard because the next thing she heard made every muscle in her body freeze.

"Gavriel Castillo," said Artemis, "To what do I owe the pleasure?"

Avira could barely see the glint of Matteo's eyes reflecting the light from above them; they were opened wide, his focus trained on the floor. She wondered for a moment what he was thinking about before realizing he was listening to the conversation happening over their heads. She didn't want to do that. The idea of Gavriel walking just above her head was enough to make her blood run like ice. As long as she'd known him, he'd reminded her of a snake, the kind that could sense the warm blood of its prey even from far away. She wondered if he could feel her there, all it would take was him firing his pistol through the floor a few times to open up a hole big enough to find her.

"Don't play dumb, Artemis," Gavriel hissed.

"That's Captain Cascella to you," Artemis shot back, garnering an ever-so-small bit of silence.

"You know why I'm here, though, don't you?" Gavriel continued, unfazed.

"The girl."

There was a slamming above, a hand smacking a wooden

table. "I just figured I'd drop off a missing poster in case you run into her on your voyage."

There was the sound of paper crinkling in someone's hand and bouncing across the floor.

"Missing posters? Grigori must be getting desperate, then. Is his little detective agency not working out?" Artemis didn't show much emotion in his voice aside from maybe a sense of humor.

"The girl is proving hard to catch."

Avira relaxed ever so slightly. Maybe her father hadn't traced her to The Apollo at all.

"And Grigori is certain it's not a kidnapping?"

Gavriel laughed right in Artemis' face. "Girls don't just go missing two days after their betrothals are announced. She ran."

"I didn't know the Bianco girl was engaged. Was she unhappy then? How awful could her fiancé be?"

"You're speaking with him," Gavriel snapped. Something told Avira that Artemis had known this fact. It wasn't precisely private knowledge that Gavriel was her father's favored match for her. Their betrothal had been nearly inevitable.

"I'd run too." Avira could barely believe Artemis' gall, speaking to Gavriel like that. She barely heard the words before a sickening, gut-twisting sound rang out above them. Not a gunshot but a smack and a moan. Avira couldn't exactly tell what she was hearing, but she assumed Gavriel had kicked Artemis in the stomach or punched his jaw.

"You know how much hiding her would cost you, Artemis, darling, don't you?"

Gavriel's voice unsettled Avira. Its sweetness was just earnest enough to be believable, but his words were terrifying. He'd always been this way. "Your life and, even worse, your ship."

"I don't fear you, Gavriel. No man on my crew fears you. And if we do not fear you, you cannot control us. You are a little puppet. What happens when daddy lets go of your strings?"

Another smack. Another moan, this time from Gavriel. And then footsteps, a slamming door, and silence. Gavriel had gone. Neither Avira nor Matteo moved a muscle. She couldn't bring herself to. What if it was a trap? What if they opened the door and Gavriel was standing with ten swordsmen all pointed at her? And if they found her, they'd probably kill Matteo too, not for any reason besides his proximity to her.

"Cesario," Matteo whispered to her after an eternity of silence, "you're shaking."

"I'm afraid of the dark," she lied. "When will we know if it's safe to come out?"

Matteo shook his head, "I can go out and check, if you'd like. Will you be okay all alone in the dark?"

Avira nodded, and Matteo slowly pushed open the door with one hand, the other raised in a fist. He slid out of the closet, closing the door swiftly behind him. Avira could hear his footsteps outside the door. She listened to every step, expecting them to cease and the closet door to be smashed open by one of Gavriel's men at any moment.

"Cesario?" Matteo called, startling her. "You can come out. The coast is clear."

Matteo opened the door, letting light pour in onto her. He gave her his hand to help her up. Her head rushed with blood when she stood, making her feel faint. And then everything went black.

She awoke to the smell of burning onions with Matteo and Diego kneeling over her. In her mind, she thought she could hear Matteo calling, "Avira! Avira!" But as she gained her senses more, she realized Diego was slurring, "More water! More water!"

That's when she realized her face and body were soaking wet. They must have had to douse her with water to wake her up.

"Are you okay?" Matteo said urgently.

"Just a… a headrush," she said, nearly forgetting to drop her voice down when she spoke.

"Take an hour, Cesario. Wash up," Diego said. "I'll help the boy with this monstrosity he calls dinner."

"I let the onions burn while we were locked down," Matteo said with a wink.

He didn't seem too upset about it. Avira couldn't say anything more. She stood from the floor, not even attempting to go slowly should she faint again, and practically ran from the kitchen. She descended the ladder to the bunks faster than she ever had and collapsed onto her bed in a heap, sobbing.

Nicolo was sitting on his bed but didn't say a word. Instead, he set down the sketchpad he'd been working on and escaped. Avira didn't care that boys her age didn't cry like this. She was scared, worried, and angry. The feelings melted and mixed until her emotions felt like one of Diego's horrible vegetable slime soups.

She didn't know how long she'd been crying before her body ran out of tears, and she just lay there, staring at the wall of her bunk, letting the movement of the ship rock her back and forth. Eventually, her breathing slowed enough to step off her bed and open her trunk. The trunk barely had a thing in it save for the small bag Yasmina had packed for her before she'd left.

Avira grabbed the bag and dumped it out on her bed. She pushed her father's map out of the way and ran her hands over everything she'd kept of her old life. There was a tiny notebook her mother had pressed orange blossoms in every year to compare the fragrances. Avira held the book to her nose and inhaled. With her eyes closed, she could almost pretend she was at home in the garden on a spring day. There was a men's sapphire ring her mother had bought for her at the market one day because Avira didn't like any of the ones designed for women. The ring only ever fit on Avira's thumb, but she enjoyed holding it and watching it sparkle. There was a rolled-up sketch Avira had done of Yasmina, who, for most of her life, had been Avira's closest friend. In the sketch, Yasmina's shoulders looked entirely too large, and her nose was the wrong shape, but they'd pretended it was fantastic because they were children.

Last of all, folded so tiny she'd completely forgotten it was packed, was a lacey evening slip of her mother's. It was a light gray color with strands of sparkling silk woven into it in certain places to make it look like the wearer's body was glowing in all the right places. Avira wasn't much for the fluffy dresses most women in Alvanii wore, but she'd been obsessed with this nightgown since she was a child. On the night of her betrothal to Gavriel, just a few weeks ago, her mother gave it to her, not as a congratulatory gift but as consolation. Avira had begged her mother not to make her marry Gavriel, but neither of them was given a choice.

Avira didn't know she had tears left to cry, but she did. As she stripped herself of her wet tunic and pants and slid into the nightgown she sobbed like she'd never sobbed before. She touched her hand to her dark hair, which was more fluffy than anything. Looking at herself in the mirror, she saw the lady she was supposed to be falling away into little pieces. The nightgown, while beautiful, made her feel even worse. Like she didn't fit in her body at all anymore.

She was not the perfect fragile feminine toy her father had designed her to be. Instead, she was feminine rage, feminine power. All the bits of her that should have been dainty wanted to go to war and battle for her own life. *Her own life.*

Avira's face fell as she thought those words to herself.

She stripped off the gown and shoved it back into the bag without a single fold. Sliding back into her pants and the baggy tunic that ever so slightly obscured the curves of her body, she crawled back to her bed and curled in a ball.

Maybe if I stay here, she thought, *I'll become part of the ship and never have to touch the earth again.*

84

Chapter Eight

Matteo had been so worried about Avira that he'd barely processed his surroundings. She'd shaken violently the entire time they hid in the closet. He was forced to keep his hands resting on her knees to keep her from making a sound. She hadn't even noticed.

The truth was, he felt guilty. When the glass broke behind her, he'd been late calling out to warn her. He'd almost called out 'Avira' instead of 'Cesario' and had to stop himself.

He'd tried his best to listen to Gavriel and Artemis as they talked, but his focus had been so intense that he could now barely retain a word they'd said. A wanted poster. A punch. A threat. Matteo tried to jog his memory as he re-sliced the onions. Diego had been peeved at Avira's need to rest, so Matteo volunteered to finish the shift alone. He was learning quickly that the fastest way to Diego's heart was making the workday a little shorter for the old drunk. Matteo didn't mind the long shifts, especially since he spent most of them with Avira gaining her trust.

But he was worried sick. Every sound of footsteps outside the kitchen caused him to turn around, hoping she'd come through the door looking fresh as a daisy. As much as he wanted it to happen, he knew it was unrealistic. The girl was terrified of Gavriel Castillo, *her fiance,* Matteo remembered. She was 17, old enough for most girls in Alvanii to be married. But Gavriel Castillo had to be at least 30 and, from the sounds of it, quite the snake. Even Artemis had commented on how unhappy the girl must have been in the match.

But being unhappy in a match is one thing, and being terrified of your suitor is quite the other. Matteo couldn't remember hearing much of Gavriel Castillo when asking about the Biancos, but he'd seemed important. At least he sounded quite self-important when he spoke.

Matteo had just placed the new set of onions in the pan when the door to the kitchen flung open, so violently the glass might have broken had there been any left. Artemis stood in the doorway, knife in hand. He swayed as he stood, obviously drunk. Matteo couldn't help but notice the purplish bruise around the captain's left eye.

"What's the word on the girl, De Luca?" Artemis said, holding himself steady in the doorframe to keep from falling over.

Matteo shook his head, trying his best to indicate that he knew nothing without saying a word. He had a sick feeling that no comments could console Artemis.

"Where is she?" Artemis pressed further, spit flying from his mouth as he shouted.

"I don't know, Captain. I haven't found her." Matteo could hear the fear in his voice and hoped it translated as fear *of* Artemis rather than fear *for* Avira. He couldn't let on that he'd found her– not with Artemis in this state.

Artemis slammed his knife into the kitchen island so hard it stuck into the wood, standing in place like a scarecrow. "That's not good enough!"

Silently, Matteo thanked the Goddesses that Avira wasn't in the kitchen for this. Her Cesario act was strong, but something told him that she wouldn't be able to keep her composure through this.

"Two days," Artemis slurred, "or I'm telling my men whom you work for."

And then he was gone. Matteo tried to steady his breath before returning to cutting vegetables, but his hands wouldn't stop shaking. He had a soft spot for the girl. He wanted to protect her from everything, from her father, Artemis, the impending war, and especially Gavriel. But what could he do? He worked for Grigori Bianco, after all. He was just as treacherous as the blonde man from the first day of the voyage, and for all he knew, that man had been tossed overboard.

Matteo wiped his hands on his apron. He didn't know what tomorrow would bring, but he'd chosen for tonight. He had to find the girl.

He set the pots to boiling, careful to make sure nothing would burn or boil over in his absence, and slid a couple of loaves of bread into the fire to bake while he was away. Then, he took off his apron and slinked out onto the darkness of the deck. Above him, he could see the lanterns of the night ropesman as they worked. The furnace illuminated the ships by night but only in a dim amber glow.

Matteo wondered what it was like to spend the darkest hours of every night so high above the ship with only a lantern to light your way. The moon was nowhere to be seen. Tomorrow it would be back, a single silver sliver growing nightly until it was whole again. By the time the moon was full once more, The Apollo would be ported in Shaheen.

Matteo climbed down the ladder to the long thin hallway with doors coming off it in each direction. Most ships didn't offer private sleeping bunks as The Apollo did, and it was easy to see why. It took much space, giving everyone a private bedroom, but it did well to keep morale high.

Matteo passed his room, counting every door to the left after that. He'd observed Avira a couple of times as she returned to her room, and if his counting were correct, it would be twelve doors down to his left.

When he reached the twelfth door, he knocked gently. It was met with silence.

"Cesario? It's Matteo from the kitchens."

"Go away," a voice called softly. "I'll be back upstairs soon; I just need a little longer."

"I was coming to check on you. I was worried."

"You'll burn the bread."

"So little faith in me?" There was silence, then the sound of feet on wood and a latch click. Avira opened the door and stared deep into Matteo's eyes. She looked sallow. A skeleton wrapped carelessly in silk. Her eyes, which usually sparked, were sunken and dark.

"Are you all right?" Matteo blurted, somewhat without thinking. Even he could hear the care in his voice, like he was tending to a child or, worse, a lover. That wouldn't do if he were to convince Avira he didn't know her secret, so he added, "You look terrible."

"Thank you," was all Avira could scoff back at him.

Avira sagged against the doorframe as though she could barely stand.

"I was just worried."

"You keep saying that."

"I was also wondering," said Matteo, leaning in entirely too close to Avira's face and hushing his voice to a whisper, "If you'd like to help me steal some lemons from the cargo bunker."

Avira stumbled backward in shock, "Why would you want to do that?"

Matteo shrugged. "I'm craving lemonade, and I figured the night crew might be too?"

"We'd need sugar," she said defiantly.

"There's gotta be sugar somewhere around here. Listen to the ship. It's dead silent up there. Everyone's spooked from being boarded, and I figure tonight's the night."

"Tonight's the night? The night for what?"

"To cause some trouble."

The "Cesario" that Matteo had grown to know was a reserved boy who liked to be right and didn't talk much except to correct him. But Matteo knew there was more under that facade, a daring young lady who loved a challenge. He wanted to meet that girl; he wanted to know her. This was all he could think of to bring that side of her out or at least send a message that she was safe with him.

"I'm in," she croaked. "Just let me get my boots back on. And if we get caught, this was your idea. Deal?"

"Deal."

The two decided it was best to go back to the kitchen first to ensure the bread wasn't burning and make a plan.

Matteo had noticed a massive bin of ripening lemons in the cargo hold, but sugar was a little more challenging to pin down. They were confident Diego had some on hand for special occasions but finding it was another story. They'd torn the kitchen to shreds before they found, tucked in the very back of a cupboard, a tightly packed sack of white sugar.

The little victory made them confident. Now, all they needed were the lemons.

"Is it safer if one of us goes and the other stays, or should we both go?" Avira asked him.

"I'll go, you stay," He told her, though he didn't particularly want to let her out of his sight, "You've had enough excitement for one night."

"How long should I wait before I go looking for you?"

"If the bread is finished and I'm not back, you can worry."

Avira gave a nod of approval. Not wanting to waste time, Matteo slinked out the now windowless door and towards the cargo hold. The deck was quieter than usual. Most nights, you could find men drinking or playing cards up there, but he figured that wasn't likely with how on edge everyone seemed to be. It didn't appear that Gavriel's crew had done any harm to crew members, but he couldn't help but notice long scratches along the deck of the ship and a collection of broken barrels that had been swept out of the way.

"Bastards," he muttered.

Matteo reached the trapdoors that led down to the cargo bunker. He frequently checked over each shoulder to ensure he wasn't being watched. He also studied above his head, nervous that a ropesman could see him from a bird's-eye-view and turn him over to Artemis.

Once he was confident the coast was clear, Matteo lowered himself down the ladder of the first cargo hold. The room was massive, like a large stomach at the ship's center. Matteo could hardly believe that The Apollo had space for *three* bunkers like this. He slid between barrels of wine and liquor until he found a row of crates holding different citrus fruits that grew bigger in Alvanii than anywhere else in the world, lemons included. Next to the lemons, he noticed at least fifteen barrels of popping pepper.

Popping pepper only grew in the very high mountains near Veronii, and it was known for being so spicy that it combusted upon impact with heat. People in Shaheen considered it a delicacy, but Matteo had always thought of it as more of a liability.

He'd just pried off the lid of the lemon crate when a low voice about fifty feet away caught his attention. Matteo ducked low and let his body hug the box as closely as possible.

"And you're sure they were Grigori Bianco's men?" the voice said. Matteo could see candlelight flickering.

"I was on the lookout when they arrived. Their ship bore the falcon crest," another voice responded. This voice spoke in a jilting fashion. Matteo could make out some accent though he was pretty sure it wasn't Shaheen.

"Why would Bianco board us? There's no need."

"You've heard the rumors. About his daughter, being stowed away on The Apollo somewhere."

"Among us? She'd have to be dressed as a boy."

Matteo noticed he was holding his breath in some subconscious effort to remain completely silent.

"It's ridiculous," the first voice scoffed. "Just a rumor. Next, you'll tell me you believe in mermaids."

"Still," the second voice pressed, "you've heard what the

ones close to Artemis say about our charter. It could be pulled at any moment, and then what? All of us would be enemies of the Bianco family. They'd sink us."

"Grigori Bianco would never sink The Apollo. He needs it. It's his most powerful ship."

"I'm not so sure."

Matteo's foot slipped, making the quietest shuffling noise. As he readjusted, he tried to take a silent breath, but it didn't work. The voices of the men stopped suddenly.

"Did you hear that?"

The men were silent, listening. Matteo held his breath as tight as he could.

"The walls have ears."

The light began to grow fainter and fainter as the men walked away, as though they had a silent understanding that it was not safe to discuss such affairs here. Matteo waited a little longer before returning to the lid of the lemon crate, straining his eyes in the dark. He fumbled through, trying to find the ripest fruits. Of course, the fruit was green when loaded onto the ship, so it would be grown when it reached Shaheen. But judging by the aroma of the lemons, some were already ripe enough to juice.

Matteo put seven lemons into the deep pockets of his pants,

tightening his belt, so they didn't fall, and climbed the ladder back to the deck. It was just as quiet as it had been before, and he made it back to the kitchen just in time to run face-first into Avira.

"Don't you ever look where you're going?" she snapped. But Matteo could almost detect something else in her voice, worry perhaps.

"I got the lemons." Matteo gestured unhelpfully at his pockets which, in the light of the kitchen, he now realized looked ridiculous.

"The bread finished, and you weren't back. I was scared."

"Cesario," Matteo grabbed her shoulders gently, trying hard to pretend she was a schoolboy friend and not a woman of high birth, "I'm okay."

And without another word, he began unloading the lemons from his pockets onto the counter. "How much will this make?"

Chapter Nine

As Avira cut the lemons into thin, circular slices, all she could think about was her mother. Of course, she couldn't tell Matteo this. She'd even considered all the ways she could talk to him about making lemonade with her mother without revealing that she wasn't, in fact, a kitchen boy from Alvanii. She'd mostly been silent as they prepared the lemons, placing each slice into a bowl with as much sugar as they could take from Diego's stash without noticing its absence.

Matteo had been quiet too. It was a joyous silence, filled with excitement from their rebellion. Avira didn't want to make waves aboard The Apollo; at first, she'd worried that making the lemonade would draw too much attention to her. But Matteo's proposition was so sweet, thoughtful, gentle and kind. She couldn't have passed it up.

Maybe somewhere deep within her, she was beginning to realize her feelings for the boy with the dark curls, golden nose ring, and cavernous dark eyes. But she would never admit that to herself.

It wasn't as if he could reciprocate the feelings. He thought she was a rebellious kitchen boy, not an heiress. As she cut the last lemon, she wondered what Matteo would say if he knew who she was. Would he like what he saw if shown a portrait of Avira Bianco in all her glory?

Avira didn't miss the dresses, and, in all truth, she didn't miss her long hair much either. The preening part, where her ladies' maids were instructed to scrub and polish every inch of her until even her elbows glittered and dripped in femininity, was awful. But she did miss the way she could turn heads when entering a room. She was beautiful, just like her mother. She knew that because it was all anyone had ever talked to her about. It didn't matter in the slightest now.

For a short moment, Avira let herself wonder if Matteo would find her beautiful, had they met under different circumstances. She pushed the thought down quickly.

"So, we smash the lemons together with the sugar," Avira heard herself saying mindlessly, "And the sharp edges of the sugar grains help the juice of the lemon extract better."

Matteo began jabbing at the lemons and the sugar with the wrong end of a wooden spoon.

"You don't need to be so aggressive," she spat out through an ear-to-ear grin, "The sugar does most of the work for you."

"I'm finding it cathartic," Matteo said, defensive. Avira let him keep smashing as she found a large pitcher and filled it with water from the clean side of the kitchen basin. She knew the water on board the ship couldn't be ideal but she'd tried not to think about that. The other option was beer or mead, which most of the more senior crew members seemed to drink by the gallon. Avira thought beer tasted like pee, so she just took the risk with the water. If the other crew members were half as tired of gruel and stale water as she was, the lemonade would surely be a smashing success.

Once Matteo had tired himself out from the mashing, he poured the sugar and lemon mixture into the pitcher with the water, and Avira stirred. She watched as the lemon juice blended in with the water just as it had when she would make it as a child, ever so slightly tinting the drink a sunshiny yellow. The crushed lemons, having been drained of their juice, rose to the top of the pitcher. Avira always loved that part. It made the drink look lavish despite only being three ingredients.

"Is that all?" Matteo asked. "Rather anticlimactic."

Avira just smiled and pulled an empty jar out of one of the cupboards. She filled it halfway with lemonade and handed it to Matteo.

"First glass? I couldn't."

She gave a curt shake of her head in response.

"You're the one who risked your life stealing the lemons from the cargo bunker."

"But you knew the recipe so well. We'd have lemony water if not for —"

Avira cut him off by pressing the jar to his lips and forcing him to have a drink. He sipped greedily, and a smile crossed his face.

"You—" His grin grew as he spoke. "—are a master."

"Well, of course, I am. I'm a kitchen boy, after all." The lie was feeling more and more real every time she said it.

"Not anymore. You're a crew member of The Apollo now. An explorer of the skies."

Now Avira was smiling too. Matteo was special. He could make everyday life feel like an adventure, or at least his life always came across like one. Avira realized just how little she knew about him.

Matteo glanced at the clock on the wall that usually ran either thirty minutes fast or one hundred minutes slow, and it was impossible to tell which.

"I think we'll be expecting company soon. The night shift is almost halfway through, and they'll want their dinner."

Matteo put his hands on his hips, looking out with pride over the sauteed onions and soda bread, the stew bubbling in the pot on the stove, and the massive pitcher of lemonade.

"It's a shame the lemonade isn't cold," Avira mumbled to herself more than anyone.

"I don't think anyone will mind."

And he was right. They didn't. The night crew showed up in droves, having heard a rumor that dinner would be extra special tonight. Nicolo was one of the first to come by and get his rationed amount of food. When Matteo offered him an onion sandwich, his eyes looked like they were about to pop from his head. Solid food had been so rare that something with even a little texture was beyond welcome.

The furnace crew got off their shift next and were thrilled to have lemonade with their meal. They'd been told by their friends on the ropes crew that dinner would be extra special, so they'd arrived ready to eat. Matteo was afraid they'd run out of bread. But by the end of the meal break, after the ropesman, furnace crew, lookouts, and even a few straggling cargo men had eaten, there was just enough food for Avira to have a sandwich and Matteo a second glass of lemonade.

Their shift was over after the meal break, the early morning crew arriving ever so slightly late to begin the preparations for breakfast. It was still hours from daylight, but most of the morning shifts started at dawn, so breakfast had to be ready by then.

Matteo apologized in advance to Cory, a greasy bald cook who was preparing the usual cabbage stew. He figured the word would get out about the lemonade, and there would be a disappointment on the part of the morning crew. Only then did Matteo consider the wrath of Diego that he and Avira would likely face when the old drunk found out about their lemonade escapade. Matteo chose not to worry about this. His night felt special, the kind of night you remember when you're old and sitting senile in a rocking chair.

Avira took off her apron and wiped her hands on her trousers as boyishly as she could. Matteo was almost out the door, but something compelled her to call his name.

"Matteo, stop."

He did, turning around and focusing his brilliant eyes right on her.

"I'm going to look at the stars, maybe watch the sunrise. I'm afraid I'll have nightmares about the lockdown if I sleep. Would you like to come?"

Matteo gave a grin that could only mean yes, and the

two of them made their way to the front of the ship. Avira perched herself facing the sky with her legs shoved between the guardrail and the side of the vessel, toes dangling in the open air. Matteo watched as she did this and then tried to copy. His long legs were much harder to slide between the guard rail, but after a few tries, he made it work.

"It's such a clear night," Avira said to nobody in particular. "So quiet."

"It's hard to believe that the lockdown was only six hours ago, isn't it?"

Avira just nodded. The memory of that glass window shattering behind her plagued her. She hadn't seen who had done it. What if it had been Gavriel? He would have recognized her if she'd been facing the other direction.

"You're shivering." Matteo broke her from her thoughts as he spoke, "Is it from fear or from the cold?"

She responded softly, "I think it's just my body catching up with my brain."

Matteo sat quietly with this for a long time. Avira didn't mind the silence. She looked out over the clouds, watching them dance and shift in the wind. As a child, her mother had told her stories about Aurora, the goddess of the sky. Her mother always said that the clouds made shapes so Aurora could tell humans secrets or share premonitions. Once, as a little girl, Avira wandered out in the garden and found her mother lying on her back in the grass. At first, she'd been afraid her mother had fainted or hurt herself, but as she'd walked closer, she'd realized her mother was just watching the clouds. Avira hadn't been able to tell at the time but thought she'd seen her mother crying and whispering a prayer. It had scared her, and she'd run away before she could hear what her mother was saying.

"Do you believe in the old gods?" Avira said. She spoke in a whisper and wasn't sure if Matteo heard her or if the words had disappeared on the wind.

"Well, growing up in Veronii I had to," Matteo said just as softly. "But I don't know anymore. I don't think they're quite as powerful as we make them out to be. But I don't think they're all imaginary either, if that makes sense."

"You grew up in Veronii?" Avira blurted out. "But you're Shaheeni!"

"I was three years old when they found me and my mother in a garden in Veronii. We were tucked away beneath a tree in the orchard beneath a coating of fresh spring snow. My mother had been killed, but I was safe. The owners of the orchard didn't know what had happened. There hadn't been a commotion or anything. They felt so guilty that my mother had died in their orchard that they took me in and raised me themselves. For all I know I'm just some Veronan Nobleman's bastard."

"You look Shaheeni, though."

"Really? I hadn't noticed." Sarcasm dripped like honey from Matteo's voice. Avira felt like a fool.

Her family had hired many Shaheeni staff members, and her father had frequently entertained noblemen from the Southern Continent. From his curls to his golden nose ring, Matteo looked as Shaheeni as could be. "I think I was born there." He shrugged. "But I don't know for sure. I was hoping I'd find answers if I went south."

"That's why you're on the Apollo?"

Matteo was quiet for a long time. "I think it is," he said finally. "I should sleep, though."

He yawned a yawn that Avira thought looked somewhat forced, slid his legs out from between the guard rail and the deck, rather ungracefully, and bid Avira goodnight.

Once he was all the way out of sight, Avira sunk down into her shoulders. She was tired too, but she wanted to let Matteo get to his room before following him. He had clearly wanted to be done talking.

Eventually, she headed to her cabin, where she found Nicolo already fast asleep. She noticed a letter of some sort in his hand. He must have been working on it before bed, she thought. It was signed with a heart. Smiling to herself, Avira curled up into her bed, warm under the scratchy wool blanket.

Just before falling asleep, she realized she hadn't said thank you to Matteo for helping her forget how frightening the night had been. Gavriel had boarded the ship only a few hours ago. If it hadn't of been for Matteo, she might still be curled up sobbing in that closet. Instead of thanking him for his kindness, she'd pushed for his life story, which clearly upset him.

Guilt filled her stomach. Matteo's dark, lonely eyes were the last thing she thought about before drifting into a fitful sleep.

Chapter Ten

Matteo had never seen a daytime sky so dark. It was as if the ship had plunged into the heart of the night. Black clouds wrapped it up, tendrils of wet sky tracing their way like fingers along the deck. The air was so wet it had gotten hard to breathe. It was impossible to determine which was less pleasant, the dank kitchen or the wet skies.

Diego had told Matteo that storm heads like this were perfectly normal, and The Apollo had navigated hundreds without issue. But it was still deeply unsettling to step out of his room and find darkness, even during midday.

When he'd gone to bed after making lemonade with Avira, the sky had been clear and still, like it was sleeping blissfully all around them. But by the time he woke, the clouds were so thick he could barely make out the ends of the ship's wings even when he squinted. Day felt like night, and the night felt even darker.

After the excitement of the ship being boarded by Gavriel Castillo's crew, the crew was somber and quiet. There was far less drunken laughter echoing through the bellows of The Apollo, mostly just eerie silence.

Artemis had given Matteo two days to find the girl. But since Matteo knew exactly who and where she was, the 48 hours after the lockdown was spent toiling over his decision. He'd laid out every possible outcome in his head. In the worst-case scenario, Artemis surprised him with his cruelty; throwing Matteo overboard as soon as he found the girl and killing Avira immediately – mailing her head back to Grigori Bianco. In the best-case scenario, Artemis let them both free, maybe loaning out a glider or sending them home by boat once they'd reached Shaheen. Then maybe Matteo could help Avira start a new life, and in thanks, she would stay his friend. Matteo considered a life where he never told Avira of his dealings with her father but it felt unlikely. Things like that tended to come up. Secrets were dangerous and had the potential to hurt people. Matteo would have rather died than hurt Avira.

The storm made his decisions feel all the more dramatic.

Recently, all his deepest thinking happened while chopping vegetables, usually cabbage or onions. He'd even developed some sort of immunity to the onions, they had always used to make him cry.

Artemis' ultimatum weighed heavy on Matteo through his night shifts, especially the ones with Avira. He'd clearly gained more of her trust, and she'd begun to speak more, even cracking jokes here and there.

It was just after dawn on the day he was supposed to tell Artemis he'd found the girl when the sky broke open. It was like someone had taken a saber and sliced through the clouds. Matteo wasn't sure if it was the fact that The Apollo was much closer to clouds than the ground was, but he'd never experienced such violent rain. The raindrops were the size of coins and fell so hard that they left tiny bruises on some of the men. It sounded like the deck of the ship were being assaulted by a million pebbles. Even from his bed in the stomach of the ship, it felt like the rain was falling from every direction. He couldn't sleep.

As he walked to the kitchen, figuring he could spend a few extra hours chopping vegetables and thinking before Artemis came looking for him, he noticed a small circle of men praying in an old dialect. He recognized the ground walnuts that they tossed into a candle, mimicking a ritual he'd seen many times at home in Veronii.

They were praying to the Goddess Aurora, no doubt asking

her to spare them in the storm and ensure a safe landing. Matteo had never been a religious type, but he did envy the men's ability to place their trust in something they couldn't see. His adoptive mother, Mona, had been extremely devout. She'd always hoped Matteo would join the priesthood like her six biological sons had. Nevertheless, he'd seen how much comfort she'd found in devotion to the Goddess, and he wished he could find the same. His soul was rarely at peace the way hers was.

On deck, long, thick ropes had been spread out like a spider's web for men to hang onto as they walked through the storm. Diego had told him that there was more than one instance of a crewman losing his way in the rain and walking right off the side of the ship, falling to his inevitable death. Just the thought of falling through a storm into the crashing waves of the sea made Matteo's blood run cold.

The ropesmen didn't go up in the storm; the winds made it far too dangerous. Instead, they tended to the ropes that crossed the deck and helped the furnace crew. It took twice as much man power to keep the flame alive during a storm as wet as this one. Matteo noticed some of the men had packed thick wool jackets with hoods to keep their faces dry. He hadn't been so wise and so by the time he reached the kitchen, he was soaked through to the bone.

"What's with you? You should be sleeping," Diego shouted as soon as he saw Matteo through the kitchen window which now was just a hole in the door since the glass had been broken. Rain was blowing in through the gap, leaving a slick puddle on the floor just inside the kitchen. Unsurprisingly, it had not been mopped up yet.

There was something different about Diego's voice… was he sober?

"Couldn't sleep." Matteo wiped the water off his face and tried to wring water out of his curls. "Need extra hands?"

"The Captain came looking for you 'bout an hour ago. I'd go straight there if I were you."

Diego didn't ask questions, something Matteo appreciated. If the roles were reversed, Matteo knew he would have been insufferable, interrogating Diego until he knew every last detail.

"Could I just help in here for an hour or so? I want to dry off," Matteo lied. He didn't know yet what he was going to say to the captain.

"I can't stop ya. Plus, the ropesmen are all obsessed with your cooking. Don't know what for." Diego gestured to a cutting board of onions and Matteo grabbed an apron. "But if Captain Cascella comes by looking for ya again, you've gotta go with him. I 'ain't gonna save ya then."

Matteo gave a small nod of understanding and started chopping the onions. The kitchen smelled almost pleasant when mixed with the scent of rain. Plus, the water had given every crew member an involuntary shower which, after almost 20 days in the sky, was desperately needed. One of the crew members had told Matteo that the crew took turns going to the bathhouses when they reached Shaheen. It would be a fine day on board The Apollo when all one hundred and eleven men finally got the grime, sweat, and stench off their skin.

Matteo was happy to learn that Diego was quite chipper when he was sober. He had a curt, dry sense of humor and was always first to a punchline. Matteo hadn't enjoyed a shift without Avira this much before. Diego had happily explained why he only ever made stews anymore. Turns out the diets between Veronii, Alvanii and Shaheen varied so much that it was hard to prepare any meal without making someone sick to their stomach for one reason or another. The cleaning crew had politely requested that Diego prepare things that were easy to clean up should someone puke. He'd learned pretty quickly that it was far easier boiling everything into a slop anyway and the habit stuck.

Cooking had sufficiently distracted them both from the

ear-shattering sound of the rain pelting the deck of The Apollo. At one point Diego looked up from the potatoes he was mashing down into the stew and said, "Eighteen years in the sky, and I've never seen a storm like this."

"That's comforting," Matteo shot back in jest.

"Don't you worry. Aurora herself would never sink us."

"And why's that?"

"Because, unlike the other ships that have been swallowed by the sea, this one is piloted by a truly good man."

"Artemis?" Matteo couldn't hide the suspicion in his voice. Wise, sure, but "truly good" felt like a bit of a stretch for the captain.

"He can be a bear at times," Diego's tone was matter-of-fact. "He's a terrible drunk, a bit of a show off, and he leaves a trail of broken-hearted ropesmen wherever he goes. But his soul is good. He sees the world through a clear lens, unlike so many of his colleagues."

Diego's gaze was set on the empty hole where the kitchen window used to be and Matteo knew he must be referencing the rest of the Bianco fleet. Funny, Matteo had never considered that Gavriel and Artemis were co-workers. Didn't they both have the same goal at the end of the day? To make their fortunes in the sky.

It was almost like Diego had read his mind. "Artemis craves adventure more than gold or riches or fame. He wants to see the world as it is. And so, he does. And so, the Goddesses will keep us afloat."

As if on cue, the ship lurched so violently it hurled an onion off the kitchen island. Diego seemed unfazed, his knife unflinching. As the ship adjusted itself, Matteo's stomach lurched violently. He hadn't had any issues with motion sickness for the entire journey, but as a child it had plagued him. He ran to the waste bin and emptied his guts.

Diego gave a disgusted grunt. "Hungover, are ya boy?" Matteo's only response was another round of puking.

"Get out of here and rest. I need ya for the night shift." Diego used his free hand to usher Matteo out towards the storm. As Matteo turned to go, he felt something thwack the back of his head. He turned around to find a loaf of bread, slightly burnt but fresh from the oven.

"Don't tell the other boys," Diego said with a toothy grin. "I'm not supposed to pick favorites."

Matteo took a deep breath and stepped out into the rain, which stung his face as it hit him. He buried the loaf of bread in his shirt and clung for dear life to the ropes that held him onto the deck. He'd made it about halfway to the stairway to the bunks when the ship lurched sideways again. Matteo could see his knuckles go pale from clinging so tightly to the rope. He felt his stomach twist again and vomited right where he stood. It didn't matter though. The rain rinsed it away almost instantly. Once he was sure his stomach was empty, he pressed forward.

He'd only barely dried off when he was in the kitchen but now he was, once again, chilled to the bone and soaking wet. His bread was turning to mush even though it was tucked away.

He focused on each step and each breath, listening to the rain and trying to remember times when he was a boy when the rain was relaxing for him. He'd struggled terribly with sleeping, and his adoptive mother had opened the window and let the sound and smell of the rain in to help him drift off. It had been the only thing that worked. This, unfortunately, was not quite as relaxing a rainstorm as those of his childhood.

Through the rain, he could almost make out something else. A low, stilted sound. A laugh. He snapped his head around to see a figure draped in a silky poncho with a hood that covered his face. Under the hood Matteo could make out the glint of gems braided into the man's dark hair. Artemis.

"I believe," the voice said, hollering over the rain, "you owe me a conversation."

And with that, Artemis grabbed Matteo's hand and swept him out of the rain.

Chapter Eleven

Avira hated thunder. When she was a little girl she was so afraid of it that she'd bolt up out of her bed on stormy nights and climb in with her mother. Her mother and father hadn't shared beds since Avira could remember, and her mother never protested the company.

Avira lay awake in her bed, twisted on her side in the only position she found comfortable. She listened to the thunder roar and the rain hammer the deck of the ship as she stared at the wood grain of the walls. She could make out little shapes, similar to how one looks for shapes in clouds. It wasn't yet morning, she knew that much, because Nicolo hadn't returned from his shift yet. Usually, she finished her night shift in the kitchen and had about four hours before he came back from his shift. Sometimes they saw one another on his meal break but usually, they didn't talk. At first, Avira had worried Nicolo was suspicious of her but now she assumed he was just tired most of the time and thus not especially chatty.

She'd changed out of her sweaty clothes and spent a few moments lying under her blankets, wearing absolutely nothing before throwing on a large tunic that hid her curves. This had been the hardest part of having a roommate. When she was awake she could easily hide her femininity or play it off casually. But in her sleep, she was vulnerable. What if her tunic rode up in her sleep and Nicolo caught a glimpse of her girlish figure? What if she had a dream and somehow revealed her identity without

The storm had come from out of nowhere. The nights had been clear for the entire voyage so far, barely even a gust of wind. But this storm was loud, like the sky was angry. Maybe the Goddess Aurora was trying to sink them.

It wasn't the storm that kept Avira awake, though. It was a familiar feeling, a twisting pain in her stomach, and not the kind of twisting Matteo's eyes caused. This was physical, familiar, deep within her body. The pain had started at the beginning of her shift, and she'd been able to ignore it until about halfway through when it began to throb so terribly that she'd buckled over. Matteo had been worried. He'd run to her and rested his hands on her shoulders in a way not entirely appropriate. She'd tried to push that down though, it was just her imagination getting the better of her. She assured him it was just a twist in her gut, too much bread. Bread irritates anyone's stomach if it's their only food group. She could tell from his eyes that he didn't quite believe her. He'd have to live with that.

She'd used a chamber pot on her way back to her room and checked her pants for a blood stain, nothing yet. But she knew what was coming, and she was kicking herself for not thinking of it sooner. Of course, masquerading as a boy wouldn't give her a man's body. Bleeding every month was inevitable but she'd been so caught up in the intricacies of her escape that she hadn't thought to bring any sort of rag to catch the blood.

Men are so lucky. Avira thought to herself. *Their bodies don't attack them internally every thirty days. Of course they run the world.*

Avira decided it was probably best to wait until the bleeding started before leaving the cabin again. Heaven forbid it to start while she was on a shift with Diego or another kitchen boy. Matteo would help her, she assumed, he seemed like a kind boy and would probably not even ask questions about her deceit before getting her the help she needed.

As the cramps grew stronger and morning grew nearer, a new fear rose in Avira's mind. What if the bleeding started while Nicolo was in the room? He usually slept during the day, and she couldn't imagine cleaning herself and making a makeshift pad with him sound asleep on the bunk just above her.

Her stomach churned from anxiety and from pain.

When her bleeding had first started, years ago now, her mother had requested the finest of teas and silk bedsheets be brought to Avira's room. She would be pampered for four days of the month until she was well enough to leave the house again. She'd take long baths in herbs and floral salts while her mother talked her through every intricacy of what was happening inside her body. Avira missed her mother so much she wanted to cry. But she didn't let herself.

Finally, after minutes that felt like hours, she felt a familiar feeling she'd always dreaded. A trickle of blood ran its way from between her legs, along her thigh and down. It was warm and brought with it a painful, tingling sensation. She'd been ever so slightly in denial until now, hoping she wouldn't have to deal with it.

Avira let herself melt even further into her bed, pulling the itchy wool blanket around her and breathing through each set of cramps the way her mother had taught her to. She counted how long they lasted and felt the blood grew from a trickle to a gush. She let herself cry, not hard, not sobbing, but the silent and slow cry she'd gotten so used to at her father's house. It was the kind of cry where tears fly down your cheeks and drop off your chin before you realize you're crying all.

And then the door opened, slowly and silently, she heard it but didn't turn to look. She knew it was Nicolo. He always tried to be silent when he got back to their room so as not to wake her up. She heard him slide off his boots and tuck them away into his chest and scale the ladder to his bed, which sat directly above hers. She slowed her breathing, trying to pretend she was asleep. But she sniffed at exactly the wrong moment, a snotty, teary-eyed sniffle. It was pathetic.

She could tell Nicolo had heard because he froze in his place and fell completely silent. Avira needed to make a decision now. She could tell Nicolo what was going on and maybe get some help from him, which meant blowing her cover and risking her escape. Or she could wait until he fell asleep and try to deal with the mess herself from there. She had two pairs of pants. She could tear this one apart to make some sort of rag and then put the other one. But the bleeding was heavy and she desperately wanted a sponge bath of sorts, and that would be hard to do with Nicolo asleep right above her.

"Nicolo," she heard herself say, "I need your help with

something." There was no going back now. She heard Nicolo sit up, and then his head popped down from his bunk, hanging comically upside down, his big eyes blinking at her.

"Oi mate! I thought you was sleepin'." He had a gentleness to him that Avira appreciated. "What d'ya need?"

Avira sat up slowly and wrapped herself in the blanket to conceal her pants which she could now feel were soaked with blood.

"I've been lying to you about something." Her voice was almost a whisper. "I'm not a kitchen boy from Alvanii."

"I knew it!" Before Avira could process anything more, Nicolo was sitting beside her on her bed. He didn't look angry at all. "Yer accent is all wrong! Where are ya from then?"

"I *am* from Alvanii," she corrected. "I'm just not a kitchen boy. I'm not a boy at all. I'm a lady."

Nicolo was silent. Immediately. all of Avira's worries that he'd been suspicious of her dissolved.

"Yer a lady?"

Avira nodded.

"But yer hair!"

"I cut it."

"Why? Are you runnin' from someone? A marriage?" He said, his words tumbling out of his mouth all at once.

Avira chewed her lip as she spoke, "Yes and no."

Nicolo ran his hands through his shaggy ginger hair over and over, obviously still processing. "Well, ya sure fooled me."

Avira couldn't help but smile.

"Well, what's your real name? *Cesaria*?" Nicolo was clearly joking. Avira appreciated this.

"It's I-" but she realized that maybe it was safer for both of them if she didn't share her full name, "It's Avi."

"Nice to meet you, Avi." Nicolo stuck out his hand, which was calloused and grubby from working on the ropes. Avira shook it. "And since we're sharing secrets, I'll tell ya one of mine, eh?"

"You have secrets?" Avira felt like an idiot. Of course, Nicolo had secrets too.

"I've actually got a boy back home. His name is Benjamin and I love him more than anything. I'm workin' this job to save money so we can go to Shaheen together and have a big wedding! Maybe you can come."

Nicolo was a marvel to Avira. His heart was so full of love and kindness. He seemed utterly unphased. He just wanted a friend.

"Oi, you told me you needed help! What's yer being' a girl got anything to do with that?"

Avira had, for just a moment, forgotten her own issues.

"Well, I'm a lady. And I'm... bleeding. Do you understand?"

Nicolo's face went from confusion to understanding to concern in a matter of seconds. "I've got sisters! Eight of 'em."

"So, can you help me?"

"Of course, I can! I've got extra pants you can wear and—" He snapped his fingers as though an idea had hit him at a million miles an hour. "Do you think the kitchen has warm water?"

And Nicolo jumped out of bed, seemingly not tired though he'd just spent 10 hours working in the pouring rain. He slid his boots back on and started out the door.

"Nicolo?" Avira called after him.

"You stay right there!" he said with a tender smile.

"No, I just, I wanted to say thank you and..." Avira floundered for words. "I hope I can meet Benjamin someday. He sounds wonderful."

CHAPTER TWELVE

Matteo had abandoned the fantasy of his bunk staying dry as soon as he'd heard the rain set in. And he was right to do this, of course, because his bed was soggy within the hour. A wooden ship the size of The Apollo had ways of letting water seep into its very core.

But it was impossible to ignore just how dry Artemis' cabin stayed. Even in the dim candlelight, Matteo could tell that not a drop of water had soaked into the books, maps, curtains, rugs, fine wines or silk sheets of Artemis' bed.

"You look like you've just crawled out of a duck pond," Artemis said, looking Matteo up and down. "Prosecco?"

Artemis poured a tall glass of wine for himself and an equally massive one for Matteo and promptly took a seat on a velveteen sofa that was nestled in the corner of the room near a giant map of the sea. Matteo couldn't help but notice that this map paled in comparison to the one Avira had made on the floor of her bedroom back in Alvanii. As Artemis splayed himself out across the sofa like a cat, he gestured to an armchair. "Sit."

Artemis had downed nearly half his glass of wine before either of them spoke again. "You're not drinking your wine? Why not?"

"My stomach," Matteo responded softly. "I've been sick all morning and I'm not sure it would be wise to pour wine on top of it."

"Very well then. I'll finish yours when I'm done with mine. It's excellent, you know. Made in Shaheen from the most delicate, tiny little grapes you've ever seen. They practically blush when they see you."

Matteo was losing his patience. He didn't want to talk about grapes anymore, not with Avira's safety on the line.

"I know you didn't call me in here to talk about wine." His sentence came out as more of a snarl than he was intending, but it seemed to have the desired effect on Artemis who, for once, stopped drinking.

"Ah, yes. I wanted to revisit our little visit from the kitchen a few days ago. You remember, yes?" Artemis swirled his wine in the glass in a way that drove Matteo absolutely up a wall. How could he act like this was all completely novel?

"I find it hard to forget. But before you ask about the girl -"

Artemis stopped Matteo with a wave of his hand. "Do not speak. You have nothing to say for you are ill-informed, ill-equipped, ignorant, and also a liar."

Matteo opened his mouth to protest but before he could Artemis continued, "But so am I."

"What do you mean?" Matteo asked, trying to mask his absolute confusion as much as possible.

"It would appear that neither of us has been completely honest with the other. This might make other captains angry, but I consider it a sign that you and I are a true intellectual match and, more importantly, I can trust you."

And then it all clicked. Artemis had been testing Matteo. From the moment he set foot on The Apollo, Artemis had been one step ahead of him, playing a game. It was brilliant.

"You've known who the girl was this whole time?" Matteo tried not to look as stupid as he felt.

"From the moment I interviewed her."

"How?"

"Her disguise is decent, but not exceptional. Her frame is so petite. And, more than anything, she looks a great deal like her mother, who I know quite intimately. When I learned that the Bianco girl was missing, I assumed she'd make her way aboard my ship at some point. Her fiancé is quite a beast, and I vowed to protect her as much as I could without losing my ship's charter. Really, Matteo, you should consider yourself lucky to have never met Gavriel Castillo." The memory of the sound of Gavriel's fist colliding with Artemis' jaw snapped through Matteo's mind and he cringed.

"But then you came along, sent from Grigori himself. I had no way of knowing your true intentions so can you blame me for lying a few times?"

"Not at all," Matteo said, smiling through his annoyance. "But I am upset I didn't realize sooner. I am a detective, after all."

"You were a detective. But I think you may have found that your heart desires more than just the pleasure of returning Miss Bianco to her father."

Artemis dug through his pocket and tossed back the ring Matteo had tried to use as a bargaining chip; it was so well polished that it glistened even in the dim light of the cabin.

"You desire more than just your weight in gold, Matteo. You want to do what is truly good. And perhaps that was easy in Veronii where all the noblemen are pious and true to their Goddess. But in Alvanii, and in the sky, the good and the lawful do not always see eye to eye."

"And what are you, good or lawful?"

Artemis didn't answer, but Matteo didn't need him to. Instead, the captain just kept talking. He could talk himself into oblivion if someone let him.

"I placed you with the Bianco girl in the kitchens knowing you'd realize eventually that she was your target. I put pressure on you to tell me, but you didn't, quite valiant of you. But what I hadn't accounted for was Gavriel Castillo's visit. Grigori does not just feel angry that his daughter is missing, he feels powerless. That's dangerous."

Artemis had finished his glass of wine and reached for Matteo's, adjusting himself on the sofa again.

"If he cannot get his daughter back, then he will use her disappearance as a means to wage a war."

"War?"

"There is a queen in Shaheen. Her name is Adipe, a dear friend of mine. The Biancos have run her country dry of most natural resources. She's put her foot down and built a blockade keeping all Alvanian ships from making port on Shaheen until Grigori signs a treaty to leave her people alone. I've received word today that Grigori does not plan to let her win."

"What do you mean?"

"My trading charter comes at a price. If needed, I am to volunteer my crew to fight on behalf of the Biancos. I've received word today from Gavriel that The Apollo is needed to destroy Adipe's blockade. But, as you know, I do not have much in common with my employer."

Matteo was growing agitated. None of this made any sense, and, while it was unfortunate that the crew of The Apollo had to be a sort of volunteer army, it had nothing to do with Avira.

"Let Avira and I go then. We are not soldiers." Matteo heard the words come out of his mouth and immediately regretted them.

"No. You are not. But Grigori plans on accusing Adipe of kidnapping his child and murdering her. He has already sent a ransom note to her. If Avira can be returned it could save many lives -"

"I won't let you return her. She is in danger there. Women deserve—"

"Nobody knows more about what women deserve than Adipe, the Queen of the Shaheeni people. Her people deserve peace. And if that costs one girl's freedom, it is worth it."

Matteo stood, rising into his full height in a way that he wasn't usually comfortable with.

"She is a human being, not a bargaining chip in some sick game."

"It is not a sick game." Artemis stood too, and though shorter than Matteo he was made of muscle and glimmered with confidence. "It is the way of the world, which is by and large much bigger than you or one girl. We all make sacrifices. A week ago, I could have sent the girl back to Grigori myself, but I didn't. I am not the villain here, Matteo. I am just one man trying to do what is good."

"So, what happens next?" Matteo could feel himself shaking. He had so many questions, but his heart was beating too loudly for any of them to form into words.

"We will reach the blockade in a week. My highest-ranking men know of the change of plans, but I won't tell the rest of the crew until there is no escape. We will give the girl over to Adipe, who will give her over to Gavriel and grant my crew protection. The war will be postponed, and lives will be saved. It is the best we can do."

"Send me with her."

"What?"

"When you give Avira over to Adipe, send me with her. I don't want to leave her sight."

"You love her."

Matteo barely registered Artemis' words enough to argue. Instead, he fired back, "I promised I'd protect her."

"Promised who? Grigori Bianco? His daughter is nothing to

him but a piece on a chess board."

"I promised her mother."

Artemis took this in for a moment, his eyes the color of ink, hiding any hints as to what he was thinking.

"Let me protect her. I ask nothing else of you." Matteo was not one to beg, but here he was, voice quavering.

"I will do my best. Now go dry off."

Matteo understood that he was dismissed so he turned on his heels and marched confidently back toward the storm. He didn't want to look back and risk revealing his worry or anger to Artemis. He'd been in many compromising situations due to his work, but this felt personal. For the first time in many years, he was truly scared. Not for himself but for the girl he had begun to care so much about.

"And Matteo, my boy?" Artemis called out. "Not a word of this to Avira."

But Matteo made no promises.

He let the door slam in Artemis' face.

Chapter Thirteen

I f Nicolo hadn't told Avira he had sisters, she would have guessed on her own quickly enough. He knew exactly what to do. From the washcloth, he'd somehow found a way to heat up, to the warm flask of tea, to the new pants and cotton towels he brought her. Nicolo was as caring as he was quick-witted. He brought a small pail of warm water for her to use to clean up as well and then promptly excused himself while she put on the new pants.

"What do we do with these?" she asked, holding up her blood-stained pants.

"I told one of the ropesmen I cut my leg real bad and he offered to launder it for me."

"And he believed you?"

"Well, he didn't ask any more questions and that's all I can ask for. I'm sorry this happened, but I'm not mad at you for keeping the secret."

Avira was more relaxed now that she wasn't lying in a puddle of her own blood.

"But I can't help but be a little curious what yer runnin' from?" Nicolo didn't make eye contact and Avira could tell he was nervous to ask the question. She hadn't expressly stated she was running from someone, but it had to have been somewhat implied.

"I come from money," was all she could say.

"Why run from money?" He sounded shocked which made Avira remember that Nicolo likely hadn't had a cent to spare. His father worked the skies, and he hadn't mentioned what his mother did but with so many children, she couldn't imagine they were well off.

"Well, I wasn't running from that part at all," she corrected. "My father had arranged my marriage and the prospects were looking bleak."

She couldn't tell him the whole story. That her father had refused to allow her any shares in his trading empire, the empire that owned this very ship, and she had vowed to take him down. She didn't dare say that she found the very foundations of the sky trading routes to be repulsive. They only ever served to exploit.

"But enough about me. You've learned too much about me

today. Tell me about your village."

Nicolo's body softened at the idea of his home. He sat down next to Avira on the bed and sighed. "Well, it's rather far away these days."

"Is it beautiful?"

He nodded vigorously. "In my mother's kitchen there is a window that overlooks the mountains. They are so tall. It's hard to believe they're even real. I grew up in their shadow but still, sometimes you can't help but wonder if they're just a scene from a painting."

"Is your mother a good cook?" Avira didn't know why she asked. She'd expressly set out to not learn these kinds of things about her crewmates on The Apollo. But here she was.

"She's terrible, really. The garden is where she shines though. She can grow a squash the size of your arm. Her strawberry plants only make fruit in July, it's so cold up in the hills that we barely get any flowers before midsummer. But those berries are like taking a bite out of heaven."

Avira giggled at him, his joy was truly infectious. She wondered how he did it, how he kept such a spring in his step despite working away high above the ship all night every night.

"It's true. Someday, you've gotta come visit in the summer. I'll show you."

"I always eat strawberries with sugar," Avira said. Nicolo looked scandalized.

"You'll never want to do that again after you try my mother's strawberries. I swear it to you." They both laughed. Their joy was palpable and earnest and rare. For a moment, Avira forgot all of her anxieties. But a sharp cramp stabbing through her stomach brought her back to earth.

Nicolo noticed her wince and squeezed her arm tight. Then he whisked away the bucket of warm water and the soiled pants. The sun would have been out by now if it weren't for the rain. But Avira hadn't slept a wink so she figured it might be a good time to take a nap. She needed some rest before her next shift in the kitchen. Naps hadn't always come easy to Avira, but with the smell of rain wafting in from all around, she soon found herself deep in a dream.

She was wearing a wedding dress. It was funny when she was a little girl, she'd never been able to fantasize about her wedding gown the way her friends all did. She'd been to weddings, of course, and seen the white lacey gowns women got to wear. One of her cousins had looked like a gigantic pastry in a dress with so many layers of lace. Avira had given herself a headache trying to figure out where her legs would fit under there. In the schoolyard, Avira's friends used to daydream about what their wedding gowns would look like. But Avira had always stayed quiet, staring into space and daydreaming about all the adventures she could have if she never married.

This dream dress was everything Avira didn't want in a gown. It was massive, and she felt like a lace doily. Her sleeves were punctuated with gigantic puffy orbs of material, and her head felt heavy. Why did her head feel so heavy?

The answer came as her hand floated up to push a bug out of her face. It wasn't a bug, it was her hair. Long again, stick straight and dark as ebony. She realized only now that she didn't miss her long hair at all. Many girls in Alvanii had envied how shiny it was, but Avira always found it in the way.

She was standing in front of a mirror in her bedroom at home in Alvanii. She twirled for her reflection, taking in the way her hair framed her face. Her mother had said she had a heart-shaped face, which apparently ran on her mother's side. Avira liked that her face looked more like her mother's than her father's. Her father was not an unattractive man, but she had never learned to love the parts of herself that reflected his face back in the mirror.

"I am so proud of you, little one," a voice cooed from behind her. Avira swiveled around to see her mother who was wearing her best dress, a floor-length golden gown with gaudy beading all along the neckline.

"You look so pretty, Mama."

"Your father picked it."

This was typical of her father. He never liked to see Cristina out of the house in clothes he hadn't specifically approved of beforehand.

"And enough about me," her mother spoke gently. "You're the bride! I am so happy for you, Avira. You've found love for yourself. A woman can ask for nothing more."

"Why would you be happy for me?" She spat at her mother, unwilling to accept the reality crystalizing around her. "Mother, I do not love Gavriel. You know that!"

Her mother's face darkened for just a moment, "You will learn to love him, my dear. There is no other option. Marriage is like that."

The dream dissolved away, and Avira was awake, sitting straight up in bed. She could feel that she'd bled through the cotton rag, so she replaced it with a clean one Nicolo had tracked down. She barely thought about the bleeding as she cleaned herself and fussed with her hair to make it look a little more boyish. There was such a fine line between looking like she had bedhead and looking like a young man.

She finished tidying herself, washed her hands to the very

best of her ability, and made her way toward the kitchen. She noticed her hands were still shaking, likely letting out extra energy leftover from her terrible dream.

The rain had slowed but not stopped all the way. She used the ropes to traverse the deck just in case she was to slip, but she felt that maybe she didn't need them. There hadn't been a clap of thunder for hours.

When she got to the kitchen, Matteo was already there working away.

"How late am I?"

"I'm not angry," he said and smiled at her as she walked in.

"One hour? Two?"

"Don't worry about it, Cesario." She winced a little, hearing him use her false name.

Matteo gestured to the bread dough that was rising in the corner and Avira set to work rolling it out and braiding the loaf. She liked this part of baking bread the most. There's no need for bread to be aesthetically pleasing, but it was always fun to experiment with the strange shapes she could create.

"I know you like that part," Matteo said as he chopped another head of cabbage. "I saved it for you.

They hadn't been working for more than an hour before Diego stumbled in. Drunk, again.

"Cesario. Captains orders. Crow's nest," he spit at her. She didn't understand.

"What?"

"New assignment. New shifts." Diego was exceptionally drunk, perhaps the most liquored up she'd ever seen him.

"The crow's nest?" She knew there were the crow's nests perched high above The Apollo's deck. The shifts up there were rumored to be 12 hours long with no breaks. Since it only took six men, three by day and three by night, there weren't many hard facts about it.

"Why would he change positions?" Matteo sounded upset. Avira didn't know why. Of course, it was unfortunate to not have a shift with a friend anymore, but it's not like *he* had to learn a new job halfway through the voyage.

"When do I start?" Avira had a bad feeling in her stomach. She started untying her apron even before she'd heard Diego's response.

"Now," Diego growled.

Chapter Fourteen

It was as if Avira had vanished into thin air. Matteo hadn't had a chance to tell her he'd miss working shifts with her. And who was he to argue with the reassignment? In his gut, he knew it had nothing to do with "routine shift shuffling" as Diego had said. Artemis may be a good man, but he was also a crafty one. It had to be some kind of ploy to keep Matteo away from Avira in case she needed to be pawned off in the night.

He was used to only ever needing to care for himself. When he'd rescued children, it had always been a quick encounter. Many were babies who couldn't speak, much less form an intelligible connection with their rescuer. His job had always felt like a business transaction. But this wasn't like that at all. He cared for her.

Matteo wasn't used to caring this much. He'd spent so much of his life inside his own head that he hadn't bothered to connect with other people. He felt gratitude to his adoptive parents, but love was a stretch.

He hadn't been able to focus at all the night Avira was reassigned. He spent the whole shift scrambling for some way to convince Artemis this was a terrible idea. If Gavriel were to board the ship again, there would be no way for Matteo to protect Avira. The look of terror in her eyes when the glass window shattered was burned to the front of his brain. She'd been so scared.

Not to mention the crows' nest was known for being freezing cold. On the main deck of The Apollo, there was enough cover from the wind to keep things comfortable. The crows' nest was an unprotected basket in the middle of the sky. What if she caught a chill? She could die! He had to find her. Sleep was the smarter option, but his mind wouldn't rest until he knew she was all right.

The rain had died down, but Matteo still went to his bunk first to grab a blanket to bring up for Avira. Though the weather in Alvanii and Shaheen tended to be balmy and warm even in the winter, the skies played by their own rules. If there was enough moisture in the air, the wind brought with it freezing chunks of ice that pelted your skin bike bullets. Matteo had grown up in cold weather, he was used to it. He knew Avira was not.

With the rain gone, the web of ropes that crisscrossed the deck was now more of a nuisance than anything. He wrapped the blanket around his shoulders as a sort of cape. It was the darkest part of the night. Dawn was probably three hours away still. Little lanterns were hung from masts and ropes to light the deck, but it was still dim. The sky around The Apollo looked more like an unending void than anything. What was the point of a lookout if they couldn't see anything anyway?

Matteo quickly found three rope ladders, all marked with orange flags. One was at the front of the ship, another directly above the furnace, and another at the end of the ship. He assumed this was how watchmen got to their posts. But he was still at a loss for which post was Avira's. He didn't particularly want to climb a mile into the sky just to find himself face to face with some grumpy watchman hoping for his shift replacement.

He hadn't had long to contemplate the issue before a shadowy figure emerged from the darkness to his left. He recognized the man instantly as the tattooed man who had held him over the side of the deck upon his arrival. Figuring it was best not to surprise the man again. Matteo called out, "Malvolio."

Malvolio walked closer until a pang of recognition crossed his face.

"Kitchen boy," Malvolio grumbled. His breath smelled like fish, pickles and cheap brandy. Matteo forced back a gag, hoping it didn't show on his face. It felt impossible that Malvolio didn't remember the details of their first meeting. "What're you doin' up? Thought you had the night shift."

Matteo gestured cockily to the dark sky. "It's still night."

"Nah," Malvolio said impatiently. "Spend enough nights up here and you can tell."

"You sure are an expert on these things." Perhaps stroking the man's ego could be beneficial. "Say, I have a question for you."

"Hmmmph." The tattooed man looked suspicious.

"My friend Cesario just got reassigned. He was my friend in the kitchen. He loved cooking, and thought it was his calling in life. I thought I might bring along some bread for him to lessen the blow." Matteo was laying it on thick.

"Heard about that. Captain must've been angry to assign him to the front crow's nest like that. It's the coldest one, most dangerous too. I give him a week, tops."

"Dangerous?" Matteo had the information he needed now but his curiosity got the better of him.

"We've lost a couple of watchmen to raiders, always the ones at the front. They see everything first." Malvolio gave another grunt signifying the conversation was done and kept walking. But Matteo didn't mind the quick end to the conversation. He knew which ladder would lead him to Avira. He just had one stop to make first.

He popped his head into the kitchen, where Diego was passed out asleep as a stew boiled over. Perhaps this is what all the shifts that Matteo and Avira weren't on were like. Matteo found what he was looking for quickly, a little tin of tea leaves he'd found while cleaning once. Presumably, it was a secret stash of Diego's. He filled a pot with water and set it on the stove to boil, trying his best to be absolutely silent. There was a clay jar with a lid on one of the shelves that he snagged and once the water was hot, he filled it up and added the tea leaves trying to keep the amount unnoticeable.

Diego was still snoring when Matteo steeled away into the night. He'd cleaned up well enough that it would have been impossible to tell he was there. He left the pot boiling over, just in case Diego got suspicious that things were a little too clean.

Matteo tied the blanket around his waist and nestled the tea safely inside. He knew he'd need both hands free for the climb and hoped that the clay container wouldn't wriggle itself free and fall down onto the head of some unsuspecting ropesman. He found the ladder with the orange flag quickly, took a deep breath, and started climbing.

He was stronger now than he was when he'd climbed the ladder onto The Apollo a few weeks ago. His lungs had adjusted to the thinner air. Still, it must have taken him at least half an hour to get all the way to the top, where a tiny platform sat. The platform was aptly named, it looked almost identical to a bird's nest. There were two lanterns, one on either side and a collection of ropes tied directly to the platform. Right at the center, sat Avira. She was still wearing her thin tunic and pants. Matteo could see her shivering in the cold.

"Matteo?" she whispered in the dark.

Matteo felt his breathing hitch at the sound of her voice. His heart began to beat faster and faster as he said, "Is there room enough for two?"

"You should be sleeping."

"I was worried."

He didn't wait for a response before pulling himself up onto the platform. There was more light than he'd expected. All the way up here, the stars and the sliver of the moon were glowing so bright, it was almost like daytime. The balloon that kept The Apollo aloft shimmered in the dim starlight. The sun painted all over it had a deep glow to them.

As Matteo settled himself in across from Avira, he could feel the warmth of her body.

"I brought you a blanket." He untied it and held it out to her. Wordlessly, she took it and wrapped herself up in it. "I think it's wrong that Artemis didn't tell you about the change until halfway through your kitchen shift. You should've been given time to adjust your sleep schedule!"

Matteo could see from Avira's face that he was angrier about it than she was.

"I think it's kind of peaceful up here. Plus, nobody would be mad if I fell asleep."

"What if you fell? You'd die."

"That's what these ropes are for," she gestured to a rope that was fastened around her waist and then to the crow's nest itself as a sort of security line. "Here, you should strap in too."

"So, you want me to stay?"

Instead of answering, Avira wrapped a rope around his mid-section, tying a knot right at his belly button. He could feel his skin tingle with warmth in all the places her fingers grazed, like fireworks exploding beneath his skin. He sat for a moment in silence, letting the warmth bloom and then fade away.

"I brought you tea," he spit out awkwardly. He held the clay jug towards her.

"Did you bring cups?"

He deflated as soon as she said it. No. He'd forgotten cups. Only when she began to giggle did he realize she was giving him a hard time. She took the jug from his hands, unfastened the lid, and drank deeply.

"Thank you. I was getting cold. These shifts are long, you know. They start at sundown and don't end until dawn." She held out the tea to him.

"I wonder why he switched you," Matteo said, accepting the jug and taking a sip of the tea himself. He had to stifle a gag. It was over steeped. But Avira didn't appear to mind. In fact, he'd never seen her look so peaceful.

"It doesn't matter."

Matteo didn't know what to say so he just passed the tea back to her and let the quiet take over. At least, what he'd thought was quiet. As he sat in it, he realized that there were hundreds of little sounds in every direction. "It's like the night is singing to us," he said. And she smiled in agreement.

There was the sound of the ropes sliding against each other far below them. And the roar of the furnace, which sounded more like a hum from up here. Wind against the balloon made a whipping sound, like a cane flying through the air. If he closed his eyes, Matteo thought he could hear a harmonica or a flute song far below them.

"I love being able to see all the stars," Avira interrupted.

"They mean things, you know?"

"Don't tell me you believe those old stories." Even in the lantern light, Matteo swore he could see her rolling her eyes.

"It's true," he snapped. "In Veronii, they read the stars of every newborn baby to tell its future. I'm told it's never wrong."

"And did your stars say you would become the most insufferable man to ever live?" The way she said this made Matteo's stomach flip flop a little.

"They couldn't read my stars. I'm adopted. I don't even know my birthday."

Avira looked embarrassed. "It's just an old wives tale anyway."

"Is that what you believe?" Matteo couldn't help himself. "What a sad existence, to not think there is any magic in the world."

"I didn't say that! I just... I meant that... I just don't believe that it should be as important. I never have. I don't understand all the pressure we place on the Goddesses and on the stars when really, it's men who choose the way the world works. Men get to choose the paths their daughters and wives walk, so why would we lie to ourselves and pretend that —"

And then he kissed her.

He couldn't help it. He'd been listening to her, of course, but the way her eyes had lit up when she started speaking passionately had undone him. It was no longer the sparkling reflection of the lanterns that he saw in her but the brilliant light from within her. She *was* brilliant. She shone like a star. And Matteo could no longer pretend like she was just some kitchen boy he'd met chopping cabbages. She was Avira Bianco and he was falling in love with her.

He expected her to pull away, to stay in character as Cesario. But even she appeared to have forgotten herself. He melted into her as their lips pressed together. He closed his eyes after a moment. He hadn't wanted to because he was so afraid that he'd open them, and it would all be a dream. But when he opened his eyes, she was still there. Wrapped in his blanket. Her mouth hanging open ever so slightly as though she was searching for her next words.

"I don't think my stars designated that," he said, hoping that if he spoke first she wouldn't find a need for words, and they could kiss again. But instead, he saw tears welling up in her eyes. They were big fat tears that eventually freed themselves and began making long trails down her face.

"Oh, Matteo," she choked out, "I've been lying to you."

"I don't care!" he said because he didn't.

"I am not who I say I am."

"I just said I don't care."

"I am not even a boy." As she said this, Matteo realized what she meant. Her false persona had never fooled him but, now that he considered it, it would be quite jarring to kiss a fellow kitchen boy only to find out he was a noblewoman.

"Who are you then?"

"I'm afraid to say." The fear radiating from her eyes made Matteo's stomach flip over again. He didn't want her to be afraid. He wanted her to trust him.

"I want to know everything about you," he could hear himself begging. "Please."

"My name is Avira Bianco. I am a nobleman's daughter from Alvanii. You are the only person in the entire world who knows I am here. Matteo, I care for you. But I cannot tell you how important it is that you do not tell a soul."

And then he realized something that made his heart sink. She had just told him everything. She'd revealed a secret that he, more than anyone, knew would be deadly to reveal. But he could never tell her *his* secret. In what world could he say he'd been hired by her father to find her and bring her home? Even if his plan was to never return to Alvanii, to disappear into

Shaheen and spend his life protecting Avira. She could never know. But she was not stupid. She'd figure out his identity eventually, and then what?

"Avira-" he began, hoping words would follow. Her face broke into a massive, glimmering smile.

"It feels so good to hear you say my name!"

And then she was kissing him again, and for the shortest moment, all of his worries melted away.

Chapter Fifteen

Avira had kissed before. Once, when she was a schoolgirl, her friend Marta dared her to kiss their friend Leisel right on the lips. Leisel, who was a blonde girl with pointy cheekbones, kissed back. Avira had kissed boys too, but Leisel was her first kiss. It had been the only one that really meant anything until now.

She couldn't help but wonder if this was Matteo's first kiss. He was a good kisser; passionate, and kind. But the excitement in his eyes when they finally pulled away was enough to make her wonder. After the kiss, all of her secrets just tumbled out. She wanted to tell him, anyone, really, who she was. And Matteo had been her companion for this entire journey, she didn't even trust Nicolo as much as she did him.

Avira's heart fluttered a little when she thought of Matteo. But she'd dismissed it as a schoolyard crush up until the moment his head popped up in the crow's nest. He'd *found* her. It felt like a magical fairytale love story, the kind her mother had been so enamored with.

She didn't regret telling him her name was Avira Bianco. But she had hoped in the back of her mind that he would not know the weight of her last name. She'd hoped that she could melt into anonymity and bring Matteo along with her.

"Grigori Bianco is your father, then?" he asked, his nose touching hers.

"In a sense," she mumbled

A gust of wind ripped across the sky. Avira shivered and noticed that Matteo was doing the same.

"Here, share my blanket." It was more of an instruction than a request and he happily obliged.

"Avira." It felt more and more strange every time he said her name. The first time it had been romantic, passionate even. She didn't feel like Avira anymore. Of course, she didn't feel like Cesario either. Sure. She wanted him to know her. But she barely knew herself. It felt fast, forced, and wrong.

"Why did you run?" Matteo's dark eyes were intoxicating. He looked into her, and it felt like he saw deeper than she wanted him to.

"I was betrothed to a man I could not marry. I wanted a life that my father could never provide."

"I don't understand."

Avira didn't know how else to explain it to him, so she stood up. Clinging to the crows' nest guard rail, she held her hand out into the wind. She checked the stars and where they were positioned just to be sure before pointing a finger directly to the South.

"See that there?"

"All I see is night."

"*Beyond* the night, Matteo. Beyond the horizon, there is so much world. I knew I would die if I didn't see it."

Even if the only listeners were Matteo and the vast night sky, saying all of this out loud set forth a sort of release within Avira. She'd not thought this out so clearly before she left, but it all felt so obvious now. She would have died if she didn't get to see the world. It would have killed her.

"And once you've seen it, what will you do?"

Avira's head snapped towards Matteo like he'd just awoken her from a dream, "You are suggesting that it is possible to *finish* seeing the world. I have to disagree."

"I care for you, Avira." Matteo looked nervous to speak, "I don't have a dime to give you. I can't fund your travels like a rich man could. But I will never hold you back."

Avira snapped her head back to Matteo. She'd been lost in

the stars. "What are you doing, proposing marriage? You only just found out I was a woman."

The light was dim, but she swore she could see him blush.

"Oh, no! No, no, no. I only wish to know if you care for me too."

"Of course, I care for you, silly boy. I kissed you, didn't I?"

Matteo nodded in affirmation.

"Good. Because I'm about to do it again."

He visited her every night after that. On the second night he came, Avira worried out loud that he would exhaust himself. She'd worked the first six hours in the crow's nest alone while he finished his kitchen shift. Avira didn't want him to miss all of his sleep. After all, while her shift was one twelve-hour spurt, he had two six-hour shifts in a day—so much less time to sleep.

"If I went back to my bed I'd only dream about you."

On the highest point of The Apollo, she didn't have to worry about whether her disguise was fooling anyone. She could exist, occupying the space that she occupied. She no longer had to police her own laugh or worry it was too feminine. And she could be with Matteo.

Well, not *be* with Matteo. She sensed that perhaps he cared far more for her than she for him. But his friendship meant the world, and kissing him wasn't bad. She'd begun to look forward to the second half of each shift. She and Matteo would sit together until dawn, sharing stories of Veronii and Alvanii and their respective families.

She told hilarious stories about the housemaids. Matteo's favorite was one where Yasmina decided to hide all of Grigori Bianco's left slippers as a prank.

Other stories were sad. Matteo told about his school matron forcing him to cut his Shaheeni curls off because they didn't "fit the dress code." He told her about his brother Julio and the way they'd fought, he even told her about the fight that caused him to finally leave home. Though, on the off chance Avira had heard of Julio De Luca, Matteo changed the names.

"I was the only sibling smarter than he was. He saw me as a threat, not a brother. What he failed to understand is that I never wanted my father's title. I never wanted the money. I just wanted a family."

Avira tried to ask more questions about Matteo's childhood and family but every time she got close to any sort of real answer, he closed up. Eventually, she gave in. He didn't want to share his past with her. She would have to settle for the things she already knew about him. He was kind. He was loyal. He was head over heels for her. For now, that could be enough. "Growing up Shaheeni in Veronii must have been hard," she said.

"As a child, I never felt that way," he said, "but as I got older, I wondered what my life would have been like if my mother had not died in the gardens that day. I wanted to know where I came from. That's why I signed up for this crew, more or less."

She saw a twinge of something in his eye. Not precisely uncertainty but certainly a divorce from his usual unfettered confidence.

"More or less?" Avira asked, desperate for an explanation of the uncertainty that suddenly plagued Matteo. He was usually so confident.

He sputtered for his words. "Oh, well... I think all boys long for adventure. Girls, too, for that matter. Look at you!" He ran his thumb along her cheek and kissed her again. Avira couldn't help but wonder if he was kissing her to stop her questions. Either way, she didn't believe him. He'd come on board The Apollo for a different reason. She was afraid to learn what that reason could be.

Chapter Sixteen

Every moment Matteo didn't spend wrapped up in Avira's arms in the crows' nest or working in the kitchen with Diego, he spent laying on his bed staring at the wooden planks above him listening to his heart pound. The drumming in his chest had reached a crescendo the moment his lips had touched Avira's, day after day, it had refused to quiet down.

He spent half of each night in the kitchen and the other half with Avira, leaving only a few hours for sleep. But his mind was so wrought with thoughts of Avira that he couldn't bring himself to rest. He replayed each moment with her in his mind over and over. She'd absolutely enraptured him.

One night in the crows' nest, four or five nights after their kiss, Avira and Matteo had watched as a looming fog had rolled in, wrapping the ship like a blanket. It was such a dense fog that Matteo could barely see his hand if he held it out in front of him. When dawn had come and Matteo had made his way down the ladder, Avira had worried he'd fall.

"Don't worry, I'm getting better at the rope ladders up here, I promise."

"It's not your skill I'm worried about, it's the fog. Please, just go slow."

He secretly liked that she felt the need to worry about him. He'd lived so much of his life feeling like not one soul on earth truly cared for him. But Avira cared, she showed him she cared in a thousand tiny ways.

"You should be careful too," Matteo told her, kissing her on the cheek and soaking in the scent of her hair. "I've heard that smugglers like to use the fog as cover so they can board ships. Keep an eye out, okay?"

Worry filled Matteo's mind every second he and Avira weren't together. He knew that lookouts were frequently in the most danger of anyone on board a ship. He cursed Artemis for putting her in such an unsafe position.

When he reached the deck of the ship, he noticed that everything was eerily slow and silent. The usual hustle of the ship had been stalled like the ropesmen were ants moving their way through honey. It was so silent that you could hear a pin drop. Matteo made his way to his bunk, determined to find a little bit of sleep. He knew he needed it. He was growing clumsy in the kitchen from lack of rest and Diego was starting to notice it.

"Catch," Diego shouted as he tossed a cabbage at Matteo. When Matteo failed to catch it, the cabbage had broken and shattered across the floor. "You're getting slower, I think." Diego had sneered at Matteo before taking another swig of the brandy he kept in a flask on his hip the same way soldiers kept swords.

Matteo curled into his bed, his head resting on the thin mattress. He'd forgotten to pack a pillow. He didn't mind at first. His arm made a perfectly fine pillow. But after all these weeks in the sky, he was beginning to consider using his sweaty, grubby boot as a place to rest his head through the night. He was growing desperate.

Lying face down and burying his face in his arms, Matteo tried to steady his breathing. A memory of Avira crept into his mind. She lit up like fireworks when she talked about maps. She'd told him a little bit about the map she'd drawn on her bedroom floor. Matteo, of course, couldn't tell her he'd already seen the map. If he could tell her that, he'd also tell her that he thought her cartography work was exceptional.

Her shift in the crows' nest was likely almost over, something that brought him some peace. He didn't like knowing she was up there all alone in the fog. Unable to sleep, Matteo rolled back onto his back and pulled the golden medallion Cristina entrusted him with out of his pocket. He twirled the chain over in his hand. It was pure gold and far heavier than Matteo would have expected. The longer he looked at it the more details he noticed, from the tiny garnets in the falcon emblem's eyes to the opal inlay along the edges of the pendant. It had to be worth more money than Matteo could even imagine.

Perhaps he could sell it. Then he and Avira could flee into the desert and start a new life. He wasn't sure if it was enough to completely fund their adventures but maybe, if he found the right buyer, they could use the money to buy a small home in Irajmi, far across the desert where Grigori Bianco would never find them. Matteo had no loyalties in Veronii or Alvanii. He had his brothers and sisters, but his brother Julio had made it clear that he was no longer welcome in the De Luca household. What was stopping him from simply starting over? The two of them could start a family, sell maps in a little shop, slowly and silently undermine Grigori Bianco from afar. It didn't feel like all that crazy of an idea. He just had to find a way to sell the pendant without Avira knowing what it was or that it was a gift from her mother.

Another lie. In his youth, Matteo had prided himself in being an honest man. Now he was anything but. Love does strange things to people.

The clang of the bell shook Matteo from his daydreams. He sat straight up and hurled himself from his bed. He knew now that the bell could mean only one thing once the voyage had begun. Someone was boarding The Apollo, he was sure of it. His heart rate doubled in speed. All he could think about was Avira, likely still alone in the crows' nest. It could have been her who had spotted the visitors. If it was Gavriel, or another Bianco ship, she ran the risk of being recognized.

Matteo helplessly tried to calm himself, throwing open his cabin door and sprinting down the hall. Her shift was due to be over not long ago. Maybe, just maybe, she was safe in her room. The hall was completely empty. The crew knew that the bells meant to shelter in place.

"Avira?" The words burst out of Matteo as he ran towards her room. He wanted to check there first before sprinting up the ladder to find her. If it was a crew of raiders who'd boarded the ship, he was putting himself in danger just by being outside of his room. Matteo didn't care though. He had to protect Avira. He got to her room and banged on the door, "Avira."

The door swung open, and a strong arm flew out, grabbed

Matteo by the shirt collar and pulled him into the room, slamming the door behind him. Matteo had just barely choked out another desperate cry of Avira's name when the arm flung him into the wall. Matteo felt his head crack against the wooden planks so hard his skull rattled.

He found him face to face not with Avira, but with a red-haired boy who looked to be just a few years younger than Matteo. The boy's nose was flaking from a bad, unhealed sunburn and his hair was slicked back with either sweat or water, Matteo couldn't tell what. He looked like he was from the hills outside of Veronii. From his lanky frame to his pale skin, he looked like half the boys Matteo had known in his youth.

The boy had Matteo pressed against the wall, one hand against his neck and one elbow in his stomach. It was an uncomfortable position and Matteo was surprised at how stuck he was. The boy was strong, he had the sinewy lean muscles of a ropesman. Matteo knew Avira had a roommate. He couldn't for the life of himself remember his name though.

"You better have a damn good reason for throwing that name around." The ginger-haired boy spat into Matteo's face as he spoke. Matteo tried to recoil but the wall kept him from moving even an inch. At first, he didn't understand what the boy was saying to him. What name? Then it all hit him at once.

He'd grown so used to calling Avira by her real name that he hadn't even bothered to use her false one. He'd been shouting *Avira* for one and all to hear. If he'd been able to move his arms, one of his hands would have certainly flown to his mouth in horror. But all he was capable of doing was gasp.

"What do you know?" The boy held his face uncomfortably close to Matteo's as he snarled.

"About who?"

"About the girl." So, Avira had told her roommate about her true identity. Or at least, he knew she wasn't a kitchen boy, that was for sure.

"I could ask you the same question." Matteo tried to remind himself that he was a detective. It wasn't the first time someone had pinned him to the wall over sensitive information. He should have considered himself lucky, at least his assailant this time was on the same team as him.

"Avi and I are friends. We look out for one another. You two worked in the kitchen together, right?"

"Right." Matteo's neck was beginning to ache, he wasn't quite choking but the boy didn't exactly give him much space to inhale.

"Did she tell you who she was in the kitchens, then?"

"Yep." Matteo felt that, considering how protective of her

this boy was, it was wise to leave out all the kissing they'd been doing. This encounter was already too long for his taste, he wanted to find Avira and make sure she was safe and warm and out of the fog.

"I heard the bell. I got worried."

The boy's face softened. "I would have worried too, especially if she were still up in the lookout like that."

"So, she's not up in the lookout anymore?" Matteo asked hopefully.

"She came down about ten minutes before the bells rang. She went up to the kitchens from here. She said she wanted to say hi to the kitchen lead, Dorian or something."

"Diego," Matteo corrected absentmindedly. For a moment he felt thankful that Avira was safe. Then the jealousy set in. What was she doing going to say hello to Diego and not to him. He tried to push down the unhappiness that brought to him by reminding himself that Avira probably thought he was asleep.

"She's locked down in the kitchen?"

The red-haired boy nodded.

"And she's out of the fog?"

The boy nodded again.

"I need to go check on her. I won't be able to relax until I do."

The boy pressed his elbow harder into Matteo's stomach. He didn't have to say a word.

"Fine. I'll stay."

It was, of course, the smarter choice to wait out the lockdown here, just in case there was some imminent danger. He couldn't protect Avira if a raider cut his throat and threw his body overboard into the fog, that was for certain. The red-haired boy let go of Matteo, releasing him from the wall and holding his hands up. He wiggled his fingers as if he were saying, *okay, I'm done hurting you now.*

"I'm Matteo." Matteo stuck out a hand to shake and the boy returned the formality.

"Nicolo."

"You're from the hills outside of Veronii, aren't you? You have a village accent."

Nicolo sat down on the floor and Matteo did the same, they might as well get to know one another. They were the only two people on the entire ship who knew Avira's secret. Matteo suspected Avira had told him more than she'd told Nicolo about the circumstances of her escape. She likely wasn't throwing around her last name. Matteo felt a twinge of confidence. Nicolo might know Avira's true gender, but he didn't spend every night kissing her and sharing stories and blankets with her.

Nicolo nodded. "My village is south of the city. High in the hills. It's called Mynos, maybe you've heard of it." Matteo hadn't heard of the village, but he nodded anyway. There were hundreds of tiny communities tucked away in the cliff sides. It would be practically impossible to remember them all.

"See, I'm a little confused by you," Nicolo said. "You look like you're from Shaheen, right down to the curls and the nose ring. But you've got a Veronan accent, you sound like you're from the city, upper class if I know anything."

Matteo was impressed. Nicolo could be a detective in his own right. "You're right!" he said excitedly. It was fun to have someone correctly guess his origin. "I was adopted. I called Veronii home until I was fifteen."

"What happened when you were fifteen?"

Matteo snorted, trying to play off the anxiety that question gave him. He didn't want to talk about it. Nicolo could clearly read people well though because he dropped the topic instantly. They spent the next ten or so minutes talking about what foods they missed most from home. Nicolo gushed about all of his family recipes, things that made Matteo's mouth water. The idea of fresh strawberries in sugar made him weak in the knees. Matteo felt that he would take a knife to the thigh just for a bite of Veronan roast chicory root. Eventually, a whistle echoed out across the ship signaling it was safe to come out of lockdown. Nicolo opened the door and poked his head out. Another ropesman was doing the same.

"Did you hear?" the other ropesman asked. "They're saying it was a false alarm. All of our lookouts have gone senile, got too drunk and thought they saw a ghost ship. Nope. Just some birds in the fog. Ridiculous."

Matteo bid his goodbye to Nicolo. They shared an understanding that the moments they'd just shared were to be kept secret, especially from Avira. She didn't need to know Matteo made his way up to the kitchen. Fog still dripped from every inch of the ship like a thick silver mold. Matteo felt like he was going to disappear into it and pop out on the other side of the planet if he wasn't careful.

Sure enough, Avira was in the kitchen, just as Nicolo had said. She sat casually on the counter and chatted with Diego who was chopping up a cabbage. Matteo stood in the doorway for a minute just watching her. She didn't look ill at ease at all. He'd half expected her to be cowering in the closet. Her shoulders were relaxed, and she had her legs kicking up and down goofily. She didn't look like a lady of high birth at all. She looked shamelessly and flawlessly herself. Diego said something Matteo couldn't hear and Avira let out a loud laugh, punching him on the arm. Diego was truly an artfully good liar. He didn't give even the smallest hint of knowing Avira's true identity.

Matteo couldn't bring himself to barge in on this moment. He turned around and disappeared back into the fog. She fit in so well up here in the sky, even in a disguise she looked so free. How was he supposed to ask her to run away with him? He couldn't rip her away from this life, could he? But, knowing what he knew about Artemis' plans to sell her out, he couldn't let her stay either. He needed to think, so back to his bunk he went.

Only when he reached his room again did he realize that somewhere between the bell ringing and now, his heart had steadied and slowed to an easy, rhythmic *thump, thump. Thump, thump. Thump, thump.*

Chapter Seventeen

On the seventh day of Matteo's visits, dawn came earlier than expected. The fog that had kept The Apollo in the dark for the last few days had dissipated as though it were a dream. The air was starting to feel warmer, even at night. It was balmy on Avira's skin. They were traveling farther south each day. Soon they would be in a land where there were no winters at all. Sunrise from The Apollo had not yet gotten old. But, as Avira and Matteo cuddled under his wool blanket, she noticed something.

It was nothing more than a speck on a cluster of clouds above their heads. But it appeared to be moving downward, growing every second, coming closer. It was too small to be another ship, though Avira knew the Shaheeni people had invented small sky ships and even gliders that only transported two or three people. This must be some bird, but The Apollo was supposed to fly high enough that birds didn't reach it.

"Matteo," she whispered, though she didn't know why. "Do you see that?"

She pointed a finger toward the shape.

"Is it a ship?"

She shook her head. All they could do was watch as it slowly grew, the shape becoming clearer. It was a bird, a large red one with glistening wings.

"A falcon?" She barely had time to ask this before the bird began to nose-dive straight for them. She pressed her body against the guard rail, trying to be as small a target as possible. Matteo did the same. Avira pressed her eyes shut as if it would somehow protect her. But just as she expected a rush of pain, there was silence.

She opened her eyes to find the bird perched on the railing across from them. It sat still, blinking back at her and Matteo. It cocked its head sideways.

The bird was a bright burgundy color with streaks of gold running through its feathers and wore a little jacket.

"It has a little coat?" she said in disbelief.

The coat was engraved with what looked like a silver wave. Not sure what to do, she stretched her hand out, and the bird floated down. It dug its sharp claws into her wrist, which hurt devilishly, but she didn't have time to shoo it away before her eye caught a large silver tube fastened to its back.

"It works for someone," Matteo said grimly. Avira opened the tube, which had a tightly sealed lid. She emptied it into her hand. The contents included a note on thick brown parchment and a golden medallion. She recognized the medallion instantly.

It boasted the insignia of her father, a golden falcon. But this medal was stained with something brown and sticky, blood.

"All my father's men wear this medallion. " She looked at Matteo, searching for answers, but he was equally confused. He'd opened the letter only to find illegible scribbles. They looked like another language though Avira couldn't for the life of her figure which one.

"Is it Shaheeni?" she asked.

"I can't tell."

The bird flew back onto the perch, looking sideways at Avira and Matteo again, and then flew away, diving nose-first into the sunrise.

Avira looked at the medallion again. She wanted so badly to know what it meant and could only figure out two options. One, her father's men could have killed someone and sent along the medallion as a message. But the bird didn't look like one of her father's. Perhaps someone had killed the medallion's owner and wanted that message to be passed along instead. It was impossible to tell without reading the letter.

"I have to take this to the captain," she said firmly, "He'll know what to do."

"Avira, no. Let me do it."

"Why would you do it?" her voice came out harsher than she'd meant. "Crow's nest is my job, isn't it?" She could tell Matteo was worried so she added, "I can take care of myself. I promise. Now, you stay here okay? Keep a lookout until my replacement returns."

She shoved the letter into her pocket, wrapped the medallion around her neck and disappeared down the rope ladder.

She had to talk to Captain Cascella.

Chapter Eighteen

Until he was eight years old, the Winter Lights Festival in Veronii had been Matteo's favorite day of the year. The entire city would glow with candles and floating lanterns that glistened on the snowcapped hills. The holiday had started out as a spiritual one but, over the years it had morphed into a children's festival that made even the most elderly members of the city feel young again.

On the longest night of the year, light was sent into the sky as a gift to Aurora, the patron of the sky, in hopes that she would soon bring back the sun. Lanterns floated above the city like a dazzling new set of constellations and candles were placed upon the frozen river to make the ice glitter as well.

The main town square was decorated with lanterns and lace, and everyone dressed in white to reflect as much light as possible back towards Aurora as a symbol of their love and devotion. Matteo's adoptive father, a high up member of the clergy, was always charged with symbolic duties of some sort or another. The family didn't see him for most of that week as he was in the Basilica deep in prayer. This left Matteo's adoptive mother responsible for her gaggle of children who were all giddy and anxious to run wild through the city and explore all the magic of the festival night.

There were vendors selling candied plums and dried peppers on the square and live music and dancers with flowing white skirts on every corner. One stall was giving away free cups of salty, steaming escudella. The smell of the fresh cooked veal, pasta and onion coming from the soup made Matteo's mouth water uncontrollably. It was like the whole city of Veronii, which usually felt quite dull, especially for a child, came alive. Toy sellers lined the streets and, at the city center, a giant dance was always held for young men and women of the city to court one another.

The Winter Lights Festival when Matteo was eight had had a particular magic about it. A blizzard like none other had come the night before and not let up. The streets were filled with snow and the wind blew massive snowflakes every which way, but that did not stop the citizens of Veronii from coming out in spades. They took it as a sign that Aurora was witness to their prayers. The entire evening felt particularly holy.

Matteo's brother Julio, who was five years his senior, had been placed in charge of looking after him and keeping him from running too far. Julio had held Matteo's hand so tight it hurt. When his other brothers and sisters were given lanterns to decorate and send up into the sky, Julio did not allow Matteo to join. Matteo didn't understand why. He wanted to take part in the fun, just like all the other children. Julio never quite saw Matteo as family. This was the day that Matteo realized that.

"Please Julio! Let me decorate a lantern."

"There aren't enough for you. Calm down."

Young Matteo had stuck his tongue out at his brother. "You just want to go to the square and dance with girls."

Julio pinched his ear. "Shut up, Matteo."

The snow was coming down heavier and heavier by the minute and Matteo had to pull his

fur hood over his face so much so that his eyes were covered just to see. He felt like a little snow bear roaming the streets. A smell floated into his nose. Roasted seeds and chicory roots. The woman selling it gave him a little wave and Matteo dug in his heels, trying to get Julio to stop. But Julio just kept walking.

"Can I get some roast chicory root? Mother gave you money to use for me."

"No, Matteo. It's my money. I chose what we buy."

Without thinking, Matteo jerked his arm away from his brother and gave him a gentle push. The street was so icy, however, that Julio fell hard on his face. Matteo didn't stop to see if his older brother was alright. He turned and ran as fast as he could. He didn't want to be with his older brother anymore. He wanted to decorate a lantern with the rest of his family. He wanted roast chicory!

Matteo ran and ran until he was sure he had to be close to where he'd left his brothers and sisters, but the snow threw off his sense of direction and he soon found himself lost. Everyone looked the same, clad in pure white they barely stood out against the snow. Matteo ran hard into an older woman garnering a sharp yelp and a scolding from a young, blonde man. Matteo kept running.

Suddenly, an arm caught his. He turned around and found himself face to face with a gorgeous, dark set of eyes and nothing else. The person holding his arm was clearly a woman, but she was dressed in shapeless flowing white robes and a scarf over her head that covered everything but her eyes. She had loving eyes, a mother's eyes. She was worried about him, clearly. She spoke to him in a language he didn't recognize.

"Please let me go," Matteo had asked, unable to hide the childish fear in his voice. The woman spoke again, louder this time. Matteo could hear her perfectly well. It was her language he couldn't grasp. She sighed and shook her head.

"You are Shaheeni," she said, still gripping his arm with all her might. "What are you doing here?"

"I'm of the De Luca family." Matteo straightened his back and spoke with pride just like he'd seen his brother Julio do. The woman shook her head at him. "Who are you?" Matteo asked.

Before she had a chance to answer, Julio emerged from the crowd absolutely furious. He'd removed one of his fur gloves and was clutching it to his forehead which was gushing blood. Matteo's stomach fell. Julio must have hit his head in the fall.

"I'm going to kill you," Julio growled. Matteo pulled himself free of the woman and tried to run but Julio caught him.

"No, Julio. I'm sorry. I didn't mean to."

But the damage had been done. Matteo was not allowed to attend another Winter Lights Festival and his brother still sported a scar across his brow where he'd hit his head.

That was the first time Matteo truly felt different than his siblings. The seed had been planted. The woman was right. He was not like Julio, not like his mother or father. He didn't know who he was, where he'd come from, or why he'd wound up in Veronii. As he grew older, he dedicated himself to finding the answers to those exact questions.

He'd taken the Bianco case as just another job, just another path to finding what he really wanted: answers to why he existed. But then he'd met Avira and his heart had done with the rest. But when the time came, when the falcon arrived on the horizon and Avira had to choose between him or her disguise on board The Apollo, she'd chosen the latter. She hadn't even kissed him goodbye.

Matteo knew he should be worrying about other things. The old Matteo would have been worried about those things. The blood-stained Bianco medallion was meant to send a message. But all he could think about was how she'd just left.

The mornings they'd spent up here together had fallen into a lovely sort of pattern. He'd come straight from his shift bringing a jug of tea for her. They'd share the tea, tell stories, and watch the stars until dawn began to break, and then he would pack up the tea and the blanket, kiss her goodbye, and make his way down the rope ladder. It was vital that he did not wait too long before starting his descent, or he might run into the rutty old man who was Avira's shift replacement. It was easy to imagine how awkward it would be to meet someone halfway down a rope ladder that barely had space for one.

It would be an awful and awkward negotiation about who would move out of the way for the other to pass.

Matteo wanted so badly to follow Avira. But starting down the ladder now felt desperate. She was probably already sitting across from Artemis. It felt so strange that Artemis knew exactly who she was but pretended as though her disguise worked perfectly.

Matteo pouted like a child who'd been told no to a toy. He held the empty tea canister between his knees and crossed his arms. It was one thing to be alone but quite another to feel utterly useless.

He, too, was curious about the letter in the mysterious language. It was not a Northern Language at all, the characters looked like little triangles and loops with very little consistency. He'd tried to teach himself the Shaheeni language as a boy, but it never caught on. Still, he knew enough to feel quite confident the letter was not written in Shaheeni at all.

As Matteo sat, waiting for Avira's replacement to arrive (he was late, by the way), he set his eyes on a patch of clouds about a mile ahead of The Apollo. It had a strange shape, more rotund than most of the clouds he's seen. As they grew closer, he saw it was shimmering in the morning light. Matteo squinted his eyes, trying to figure out why the cloud looked so different.

That's when he realized it wasn't a cloud at all. It was a trick of the light. About a mile in the distance was a massive skyship, not quite as big as The Apollo but certainly a rival. This ship was unlike anything he'd seen in Veronii or Alvanii alike. It had massive sails instead of metal wings. The sails stretched all around the ship, covering what he could only assume was the wooden body of the vessel and the balloon that kept it aloft.

These sails, which Matteo had mistaken for clouds and sky, were a glittering silver and blue color. It was almost wholly camouflaged against the sky.

He was still squinting his eyes, trying without much luck to conceptualize how large the ship in front of him was when the falcons started circling. There were at least one hundred muscular birds flying in a massive loop from one ship to another. They were like some omen of death that existed only in storybooks. All the birds wore the same little coat that the messenger falcon had worn. It appeared that someone had taken the time to train the birds. They were as disciplined as soldiers.

In Veronii, the wealthy sent messages via dove from one household to another. Most of the city had been built right into a rocky cliffside, so it was hard to move from one villa to another any way other than by foot. The rocky cliffs of Veronii were keeping sky ships from making port anywhere near the city center. Sending messages ahead of time was more than just good etiquette. It was a necessity. But these birds had a more menacing aura than the doves that flew around Veronii night. Those birds felt like messengers. These falcons felt like soldiers ready to plow into battle at the snap of their master's fingers. But who could their master be? Matteo still could barely make out their ship with all of its camouflage.

Falcons were the symbol of The Bianco family, but he knew ships in the Biaco fleet were required to show gold as their color. So, who could these ships belong to?

He wondered if anyone else had seen it, and then he kicked himself for wondering that. Of course, nobody had. A bell was fastened to the side of the crow's nest. It was never to be rung unless the ship was being boarded. If Matteo rang the bell, the other lookouts would hear and begin ringing theirs, triggering the bells on deck and signaling the crew's lockdown.

Matteo stared at the bell. What were the odds this ship was all a figment of his imagination? He had no proof it meant harm, except for the armada of predatory birds that he swore were getting closer with each swoop.

If he rang the bell and nobody boarded the ship, it would be investigated, and he'd have to explain why he was in the crow's nest instead of Avira. He didn't want to put the girl in danger.

That's when he saw the gliders. Or at least, he thought they must be gliders. They were about six feet long, with a sail and a small balloon at the base to keep them aloft. There were two of them, moving surprisingly quickly. The sea of birds parted, the vessels cutting their way through like swiping blades. Each glider held two people dressed in flowing blue robes. They didn't look armed, but that didn't stop Matteo. He rang the bell.

Someone was coming for The Apollo.

CHAPTER NINETEEN

Avira had never descended the ladder from the crow's nest so quickly. Her heart was pitter-pattering like bumblebee wings. She had a mission, a task, and she was going to make an impact. For the first time, maybe ever, she felt like herself. She imagined how impressed Captain Cascella would be with her. Perhaps she'd get a promotion.

As soon as she set foot on the deck, she was running, clasping the letter in her knuckles so tightly they were white. She couldn't tell if the thump thumping in her ears was her feet on the deck or her heart drumming along.

She reached the door with engraved golden sun and knocked furiously. A tattooed man swung the door open. She wracked her brain for his name, but it wouldn't come.

"What's yer business?" he growled.

"I need to see the captain. It's important."

"Name?"

"Cesario."

"Last name?"

"I'm the lookout. A falcon brought me this letter. Please, it might be time sensitive."

The tattooed man sniffed a bit, which seemed to pique his interest. After a long moment, he opened the door wider and motioned for Avira to walk down a long dark hallway with a green velveteen carpet.

At the end of the hallway was another door with three suns that looked as though they had actual gold poured into the carvings. She knocked on this door, for some reason more gently than she had the first one. It opened, and she walked in, her eyes adjusting to the dim candlelight.

She could make out the silhouette of the captain, stretched out like a cat across a sofa, a glass of wine in hand.

"Sir, I have a letter for you. It may be urgent—"

"Well, if it isn't Miss Avira Bianco."

Her blood ran cold. "I don't know what you're talking about, sir."

"Don't lie to me, girl. It's not very ladylike. What would your father think?" Artemis smiled. His teeth shone as white as opals, even in the dark.

"Who told you? Matteo?" There was a crack in her voice as

she spoke. She'd trusted him. And he'd turned her in? All while kissing her so passionately. Her eyes were growing hot, and her face was burning, tears would come soon.

"I thought…" Artemis motioned with his hand for her to come closer. "…you said that this letter was urgent. Give it here."

She handed him the letter, and he glanced it over, his smile fading into more of a smirk.

"Do you know what language this is?"

"No, sir." She barely had the words to respond to him.

"It's the language of Shaheeni nobility. Very few speak it, and even fewer can write it. Do you know what that means?" Artemis barely waited a second for Avira to answer. It was clear she could not. "It means this letter is from Queen Adipe of Shaheen and from the looks of that medallion, she's here to retrieve you."

Avira could feel herself shaking violently, not a shiver like when you're cold, but more of a panic, like her bones were about to cave in on themselves from anger, from anxiety, from pure terror.

"Oh, quit your quivering, darling. I think you'll like Queen Adipe quite a lot. She and I don't like your father any more than you do. In a perfect world, this little relationship you and I have could be more of an alliance than anything. And the boy your father hired? Don't worry about him. He's head over heels for you. I figure we'll send him along to keep you company."

What did he mean? Who worked for her father? Nicolo, maybe, but he felt too genuine to lie. She wanted to close her eyes and think things through, but Artemis kept talking. This man seemed incapable of shutting up.

"You are a tricky girl, Avira. I'm so impressed with how far you've made it all on your own. But don't you think it's time to be a part of something just a little bit bigger?"

Avira didn't have time to respond or even think about what he was saying before the doors to the cabin flew open. This seemed to surprise even Artemis, who whipped his head sideways, scowling for a moment before his face finally dissolved into a despicable smile.

"Well, if it isn't the Queen herself." Artemis stood and strode across the room towards the door. Avira tried to take in the scene.

Standing in front of her was the most beautiful woman she had ever seen. Her skin was the color of cinnamon, like Matteo's. Her hair was braided with jewels and strands of pure silver woven into it. The braids fell on top of one another and ran across her forehead before being tucked under what looked like a gigantic silvery blue scarf that covered much of her body. The woman had a silver ring in her nose with a chain that stretched up to her ear where a sapphire was fastened as a sort of earring. Her eyes were the size of walnuts and a color she'd only seen once before. She looked strikingly like Matteo.

The woman wore no crown, but her blue gown and precious jewelry made it clear enough to anyone that she was a Queen. And not a broke noblewoman who'd burned all their money on liquor like Avira was so used to seeing in Alvanii. This woman seeped power from every pore. But most glorious of all were the two swords, one fastened to each of her hips. They glinted as though they'd been sharpened just moments before. The woman took Artemis in her arms.

"Artemis Cascella, you scoundrel." Though her words were harsh, she sounded as loving as a mother with a child. Her voice was thick with an accent Avira couldn't quite place. "And this must be the Bianco girl, yes?" Adipe didn't wait for a response. "She is beautiful, Artemis. You didn't tell me she was beautiful, far prettier in person than in her portraits." And with a glance at Avira, she added gently, "I love your haircut, darling."

Artemis and Adipe began conversing quickly in a language Avira didn't recognize. They seemed excited. Every few sentences, they paused to look at Avira and then promptly returned to the conversation at hand.

Behind Adipe stood two women in dark blue drapings. They each held a long staff with a sharp silver blade at the end. Half of their faces were covered with sheer veils. Only their eyes peeked out. Avira couldn't be sure, but she thought that, from the way the two women's gazes were fixed, they couldn't understand what Artemis and Adipe were saying to each other. They must have been speaking in the noble dialect of Shaheeni then. Avira was surprised that royal guards weren't taught it.

Adipe took another glance towards Avira, looking her up and down.

"She's so young, Artemis," Adipe said, switching for just a moment to words Avira could understand. Artemis just gave a stubborn shrug.

"Girl," Adipe called to her. "How old are you?"

"Nearly seventeen."

Adipe clicked her tongue and shook her head from side to side in response.

"It's the best we've got isn't it?" The woman said.

Avira felt a rage explode within her. "Will one of you please explain to me what is going on? If I am to be some chess piece, then I deserve an explanation as to how." She was shouting, but her voice kept cracking, revealing the fear that had twisted up within her.

"Oh, I am so sorry, my lady," Artemis cooed, almost sarcastically. "Did I offend? Would you like me to start at the beginning?"

"Yes," she said firmly, trying to hold her ground.

"Once upon a time," he started, triggering a round of giggles in Adipe and her guards.

"I am serious."

"I can tell."

"Artemis," Adipe interjected, "don't patronize her."

"You ruin my fun, Adipe. See, Avira, I've known who you were since you set foot on this ship. I assigned you to the kitchen because Diego, my oldest friend, was the only one I trusted to keep an eye on you."

"Diego knows?" Avira thought back through every one of their exchanges. He hadn't shown a single sign of knowing her real identity, not even when drunk. Perhaps the intoxication was all an act too.

"Of course, Diego knew, as did my bodyguard, Malvolio."

"What about Matteo?"

"You'll have to ask your father about that. He came looking

for you days after you showed up. Sweet boy, don't you think?"

It took Avira a moment to piece together the complete puzzle. Her father must have hired Matteo. He didn't care for her at all; he was a henchman. The tears were falling now, making slow rivers down each cheek.

"Artemis, what did you do? You made her cry!" Adipe was beginning to remind Avira of her mother. Perhaps she had children of her own. Her voice was so soothing it almost hurt.

Adipe walked slowly to her and reached out her hand to wipe a tear ever so gently from her cheek. Her hand was covered in deep red geometric tattoos that stretched from her fingertips and ran underneath her robes.

"I know it is scary now. And I know it is hard to trust me, but I will not hurt you, Avira. I want you to be free, but I need your help first."

Avira gave a pitiful sniff sending snot flying up her nose and into her throat choking her. She coughed. The whole image was disgusting.

"My people are being exploited at the hands of your father. I know you know this. We've built a blockade for all sky ships and sea vessels and are halting all trade until our demands are met. Your father is a poor loser, he is not taking this well. He's accused me of kidnapping you, and I cannot prove him wrong.

So, I hope to prove him right. If we return you to Gavriel on our own terms, my people may finally find peace."

Avira could tell already that Adipe was a remarkable ruler. Her voice was cool and calm, Avira almost believed her.

"I know it is not what you planned for your life, Avira," Adipe continued. "I want you to live all of your dreams. But this is my last resort. If it does not work, then my soldiers will have to go to battle, and I fear we will not win. They are fathers, daughters, husbands, and mothers. I cannot ask them to die for our country if there is another option."

Avira finally found the courage to speak, "But if you turn me in, I will have to go home to Alvanii and be the lady of the court, and I cannot do that."

"And I will not let that happen. The Shaheeni will owe you a great debt, Avira. We will find a way to rescue you."

"How?" Avira could hear the defeat in her voice. She didn't want to give in, but she was so exhausted.

"I don't know, yet," Adipe whispered.

"Do I have any other options?" Avira looked to Artemis.

"You could go with Matteo." He grinned as he spoke, "You and your little boyfriend could live a life on the run. I'd even pitch in a glider if you chose."

No. Avira couldn't trust Matteo anymore. He was a toy of

her father's. She never wanted to see him again, much less live on the run with him. What sickened her more was that even one hour ago, she may have said yes to this. She was so stupid.

"Okay," Avira mumbled. "I will go."

Just as Adipe let a small smile cross her face, a loud chiming sound broke out across the deck.

"What is that?" Artemis shouted.

"The bells, sir," Malvolio said, poking his head into the cabin. "Adipe's ship must have been spotted."

"How?" Adipe shouted. "You said the only crow's nest in view of my ship would be empty."

Avira's heart sank. "It's not empty."

"The boy?" Artemis looked furious, a vein on his temple popping out in an angry silhouette. Avira just nodded.

"I'll have him dealt with." Artemis stormed out the door.

"Come, Avira. We don't have much time." Adipe took her hand and walked quickly towards a massive wardrobe in the corner of Artemis' cabin. When Avira looked confused, Adipe said quickly, "A ship as big as The Apollo has many secrets, dear one."

Adipe pushed open the wardrobe doors to reveal a platform sticking off the ship's side with two gliders sitting like sleeping pigeons.

Adipe boarded one glider, and her guards boarded another.

"Have you flown one of these before?"

Avira shook her head. Adipe grinned.

"Hang on tight then," she said, and, with one strong push, hurled the glider, with Avira hanging on for dear life, into the sky.

Chapter Twenty

Matteo had to ring the bell for a minute straight before he heard a response from the other two crow's nests. Once they started ringing, the whole ship erupted with sound. By the time he looked back, the figures on the gliders had disappeared entirely. He could still see the shimmer of the ship in the distance, and there were a few falcons still circling, but, by and large, the morning was peaceful. Peaceful, except for the now deafening dings coming from the deck of The Apollo.

If the shift replacement had been on the rope ladder when the bells began to ring, Matteo assumed he would have made his way up to the crow's nest for safety. But, on a cursory peak down the ladder, Matteo couldn't make out anyone. He figured it was best to assume he'd be alone up here for a while. So, he settled in and fixed his eyes on the horizon, never daring to take them off the ship.

Every moment felt like an eternity.

And then he saw them. Two figures riding together on a glider back towards the ship. It was as though they had already come and gone. But he could have sworn there had been more than one glider. Two, at least.

He was still processing what he saw when someone dropped from above him and tackled him to the floor of the crow's nest. He didn't have a moment to cry out before a silk cloth was shoved in his mouth to shut him up, and a rope was tied around his wrists.

He tried his best to wriggle free, which incited a sharp jab to the stomach from one of his attackers. He could see from the corner of his eye that they were women. Still, they were stronger than any man he'd met. They spoke to each other in a language he recognized as Shaheeni. It was not as though recognizing the language helped him much, though. He still couldn't understand.

Matteo thrashed again, trying to throw the woman off of him. She was working hard on the knot around his wrists. Both women wore sheer veils over the lower halves of their faces, making them even more intimidating. It left only the intensity of their eyes to indicate if Matteo was about to die.

"Oi, you," she said finally. "If you stop being such a pest, this will be easier for all three of us."

The other woman, sitting on a glider that hung suspended in the air about six feet above them both, shouted down to them. "She's not gonna let up, you know. If you want, we can knock you out. Might make it easier on your ego, getting beat up by a couple of ladies."

He tried to shout through his gag but choked on his own spit. Both women laughed. The one who tied him up threw a length of rope up to her partner. Matteo noticed the smell of jasmine flowers on his captor's hair, but he didn't have much time to think about it before she threw him over her shoulder and began to climb. She climbed quickly, not fazed by the entire grown man she wore on her back like a backpack.

"Should I drive like a maniac? Scare him so bad he pees?" the woman piloting the glider asked.

"Adipe wants him alive, Rihane." The other woman shrugged. They looked a bit disappointed but shoved off, sending the glider into a near-immediate freefall.

"Don't worry!" he heard the pilot shout over the wind. "I won't kill him!"

Chapter Twenty-One

Adipe landed her glider as softly as a feather. Avira had been frightened at first because it looked like there was no ship for them to land on, but she realized soon after that Adipe's ship was so well camouflaged that it simply *looked* like part of the sky.

"Genius," she muttered to herself impulsively.

"I call her, The Mirage." Adipe chuckled, giving Avira her hand, and helping her off the glider. "I like to think it's a witty name, considering nobody ever sees me coming."

Upon closer inspection, Avira saw that the entire body of the vessel was decked in swirling silver and mother-of-pearl inlay. It reflected light in all directions, causing The Mirage to blend perfectly with the sky.

Adipe's landing pad, which Avira assumed was private, just like the one leading off of Artemis' cabin, led to a large suite, even more lavish than Avira's mother's chamber back home in

Alvanii. It was fit for a queen.

In the far corner, behind a translucent screen, Avira could see the silhouette of a servant preparing a bath. The servant popped her head out from behind the screen and bowed deeply for her queen.

"Your bath is ready, Your Highness."

Adipe chuckled again. "Thank you, Fela, but the bath is not for me." And with a quick wave of her hand and what Avira could've sworn was a wink, Adipe nudged her towards the tub. Avira hesitated.

"Whatever is the matter? Have you not bathed before?"

Avira couldn't speak. She hadn't had a bath since leaving home and lost track of how many days ago that was now. She'd stopped bleeding a day and a half ago, but her whole body still felt hot and sticky.

"You look like you're going to cry, little one," Adipe said with a pout. "Get in the bath. Fela here will take excellent care of you, and I will be back shortly to help you find something to wear, eh?"

She could only nod as Fela whisked her behind the screen and gently began removing the boy's clothes she'd grown so comfortable in. Fela took Avira's hand and helped her into the water, which was perfectly warm and felt silky from all of the soaps and perfumed oils that had been mixed into it. Avira could pick out the smells of frankincense and lavender as well as a few things she couldn't recognize.

Letting her entire body sink down into the water, Avira could feel her muscles relaxing in ways they hadn't for months. She was used to being bathed by a servant, so Fela's presence didn't feel bizarre at all. In fact, Avira found Fela was a welcome friend.

"You have such beautiful freckles, miss."

Avira's cheeks swelled with a smile. She'd rarely heard her freckles called anything but "spotty" and "annoying."

Avira let her face and hair dip below the water, submerging her entire being. It was quiet underneath the water. Back in Alvanii, mothers would tell their children stories of the Goddess Salicia, who controlled all water on earth. The intention was to keep the children from swimming in their mother's lilypad ponds, but it frequently worked double to make them afraid of bathing too. Avira had never been afraid of the water. She loved the way it made her body feel weightless and far away.

She wasn't sure how long she let herself float there. But Fela had long since finished soaping Avira's body and hair and excused herself to go do other things. Perhaps what Avira needed most of all was this moment alone. She felt as though, rather than water, she was submerged in her own thoughts.

Thoughts of Gavriel, whom she would be seeing soon.

Thoughts of how stupid she felt for letting Artemis get the better of her.

Thoughts of her mother, who she would be happy to see, at least.

Any time a thought of Grigori Bianco appeared in her mind, Avira quickly made it disappear. She couldn't think of him now. She wasn't strong enough.

But she did think about Matteo. She thought deeply about him. Without a doubt, she had cared for him, in some sense. She hadn't exactly loved him. But she had trusted him. And the fact that his entire persona could be a lie didn't sit well with her. Of course, her father had assumed she'd be aboard The Apollo. All those days earlier, when she thought she'd evaded him, he'd already stuck a private eye on her.

Avira wondered what the deal they made could have been. Half his weight in gold for the safe return of his daughter? She couldn't rule out an assassination plot either. Her father wasn't exactly a sentimental man. She wouldn't put killing his own daughter before she could cause more trouble past him.

Avira emerged from the water with a huge gasp, her mind still swirling. She could feel her cheeks were hot, as though she'd been crying. But all the tears had washed away.

She heard a door open and shut and a few sets of brisk footsteps.

"But, Amma!" a young voice called out from the other side of the screen.

"I won't have any more conversations on this, Miri." She heard Adipe and noted an unfamiliar tone in her voice. She was much more severe than usual, maternal, in a sense.

"What will our soldiers do when the plan fails, Amma? What then?"

"So little faith in your mother as a diplomat. I should scold you." Adipe clicked her tongue. Avira slowly pulled herself from the bath, trying not to make a sound. There was a silky blue robe sitting next to it on a stool, and she slipped it on before tiptoeing out into the main room. She was eager to make her presence known in case Adipe had forgotten. She didn't want to be taken for an eavesdropper.

Adipe gave a massive smile upon seeing Avira.

"Avira darling, you look so relaxed. Lovely." Avira curtseyed deeply, not wanting to appear ungrateful to her host. "There is someone I want you to meet. This is my daughter, Mirjana."

Adipe gestured to a young girl who couldn't have been older than fourteen. She had Adipe's gentle face and kind eyes, though Mirjana's eyes were fixed firmly on her mother.

"Don't change the subject, Amma. I could care less about whoever your new girlfriend is." Mirjana had bite to her voice. She was, in some facets, a child throwing a temper tantrum. But Avira could tell that underneath the fire was a powerful young woman who would someday fill her mother's shoes.

"At least let us arm a militia. Please. We need to be ready. What if Bianco launches an ambush on the capitol? We will have no protection. People will die."

Adipe was doing a remarkable job of staying calm while under fire from her daughter. "I think you will care more about my 'new little girlfriend' when you learn her last name. Avira, why don't you introduce yourself?"

Avira curtseyed again, realizing at the last minute that her robe was at risk of gaping open and exposing her chest to the Shaheeni royal family. "My name is Avira Bianco."

Mirjana's mouth dropped open.

"She is my secret weapon." Adipe smiled and then pursed her lips into a tiny frown. "But she isn't much of a weapon at all dressed like that. Come, we'll find you a new dress. I don't have any hoop skirts. I'm sure you'll understand how demeaning I find dressing up like a pastry."

Avira did understand. She dutifully followed Adipe to a

massive walk-in closet that was stocked with robes in colors and textures that she hadn't even imagined could exist.

"Try these on," Mirjana said, getting in on the fun. She threw a pair of baggy green pants to Avira. They were unlike any pants Avira had worn, the perfect intersection of pretty and practical. Adipe quickly settled on a cream-colored blouse to go with it and a silky green scarf to wrap around Avira's cropped hair.

"You're going to give me to Gavriel looking like this?" Avira asked. "It's brilliant! He'll never marry me then. He might not even recognize me."

Adipe clicked her tongue again, something Avira had mostly seen her do to her daughter.

She felt her heart fall. Of course, she'd have to dress like a lady again when the time came for her to go with Gavriel.

As Avira gazed in the mirror, she posed for herself. She didn't look boyish, but she didn't look feminine either. She walked the line perfectly. She felt more like herself than she had maybe ever.

"But until then, I think you look fantastic." Adipe smiled proudly at her work. "We will arrive in Shaheen at nightfall. Mirjana, did you speak with the prisoner?"

Mirjana grumbled.

"I thought you wanted to be Shaheen's finest warrior? But you can't even do an interrogation? Perhaps Avira should go with you to win over the boy?"

It wasn't long before Avira pieced together who they were speaking of. She couldn't protest any louder.

"If it's Matteo, tell him I never wish to speak to him again," she said firmly. Mirjana skipped off towards whatever kind of interrogation she'd been so reluctant, to begin with. The child appeared to love the drama of it all.

Avira tried to be tough, to make her face look strong like Adipe's, hoping to send the message that now was not the time. But she knew she was breaking down a little. Thankfully, Adipe let it go.

As Adipe was leaving, Avira could swear she saw a regretful look in the queen's eyes. But it vanished quickly, as did Adipe. Leaving Avira, yet again, alone with her thoughts. She was growing tired of them.

CHAPTER TWENTY-TWO

The women who'd taken Matteo were high-ranking Shaheeni guards or soldiers, who had not taken much time for niceties. After a few loop-de-loops, the woman piloting the glider gently landed on what appeared to be an even more lavish ship than The Apollo.

It was somewhat hard to tell, though, because in every direction the light hit the ship, a glare was reflected back into Matteo's eyes, and he had to look away. He'd heard rumors of the excellent camouflage of the Shaheeni warships but had never imagined that they were perfectly invisible, even to their own crew.

The women walked him swiftly across the deck and led him down a spiral staircase to a prison cell. He wasn't surprised. It's not like he assumed the women kidnapped him to take him to a bed and breakfast. But as they slammed the iron door to his cell and tossed a loaf of stale bread, Matteo realized he'd entirely forgotten to devise an escape plan.

In his old life, saving children from their captors in Veronii, Matteo had grown good at finding the weak spots of a jail cell and escaping quickly. But none of those prisons had been in the sky. Besides, he had no idea why the women had snatched him up from the crows' nest so rudely. He was suspicious that it had something to do with Avira. Perhaps this was phase one of Artemis' plan to turn her over to her father. Avira would be far easier to give back to Gavriel without Matteo there to protect her.

Even now, he could feel the cool metal of Avira's mother's pendant resting against his leg. He'd kept it safely tied to his belt so it could be with him at all times, in case Avira caught him in a lie and he had to explain himself. Wearing the necklace around his neck was far too obvious, so he'd secured it safely to his belt buckle.

Matteo heard footsteps on the spiral stairway above him. They didn't sound like the guard women this time, far too light and rapid. They almost sounded like the footsteps of a child. Matteo impulsively reached his waistline for a dagger, but he was unarmed. He hadn't carried a weapon in his time on The Apollo. He had no way of protecting himself, so he silently prayed to Aurora that he wouldn't have to.

"Awww, are you praying?" A shrill voice called out to him mockingly. He didn't respond. He was still trying to understand who this adversary was.

"Please, Goddess," the voice continued. "Don't let the child kill me. It would be so humiliating."

The dark room obscured the figure, but he could make out that she was small yet muscular. Perhaps a teenager?

Before he had time to think more, the mystery girl planted a foot squarely on the bars of his cell, letting out a thunderous ringing.

"Your little girlfriend says hello, by the way," she taunted.

"Who are you?" said Matteo.

"Hey. I'm the one asking the questions here."

After a moment of what Matteo could only assume was thinking, she said, "But I reckon you can know my name at least before I humiliate you. Princess Mirjana of Shaheen." The girl bowed deeply as though waiting for applause. She gave a little hmmph when they didn't come and continued with her amateur interrogation.

"My mother tells me you're from Veronii. I've never been. I hear it's nearly impossible to fly a glider there," she said and shrugged. "Why would I go? I'm a woman of the sky you know."

Matteo couldn't help but laugh. This was no woman standing in front of him. She was clearly a girl. She wore a pair of flowy pants and a tight muslin wrap around her chest leaving her shoulders and collarbones bare. In the dark, he couldn't tell what color her pants were, but he could tell they were expensive and embroidered with something sparkly. She wore her hair in two thick braids running from the crown of her head and down to the small of her back. He couldn't be sure, but it looked like something was sparkling in her braids too. If you'd have asked him, before, to describe the Crown Princess of Shaheen, he would have been surprisingly accurate. Except this girl was nothing like Veronan nobility. She was fierce, and a bit ornery.

"I'm going to be a great warrior someday, you know. I'll fly my troops into Veronii and conquer the city for Shaheen. That will serve them right for exploiting my people for so long."

"If it's the exploitation you want to fight," Matteo said, realizing he'd barely spoken at all since she'd arrived, "Then start with Alvanii. The Veronans live simple lives. You'd get bored."

"Oh, hello there! This is far more fun when you talk too." Mirjana sat down on the floor across from Matteo, the bars the only distance between their two faces. "But you interrupted me. My mother says you are from Veronii. So then, why do you look Shaheeni, huh? I'm confused. I'm also confused why a *simple* Veronan would take work from a man as evil as Grigori Bianco. Your story doesn't add up, boy."

There was something comical about this child calling him 'boy.' But the rest of her questioning was anything but funny.

"I was found in a rich family's garden when I was a baby. I've never been to Shaheen though I've always been taken for Shaheeni. I don't even speak your language."

Mirjana laughed in his face. "You are a man of poor fortune, then."

"You could say that."

"My mother demands to know whose side you're on. Veronii? Bianco? Artemis? Shaheen? When the chips are down, who will you fight for?"

"Avira." He didn't even have to think. "I'll fight for Avira."

Mirjana narrowed her eyes. She looked like she had dozens more questions to ask him, but instead, she stood up rather not so regally, and turned on her heels.

As she left, she threw over her shoulder, "She knows who you are, by the way. The Bianco girl. She knows whom you work for. And she told me she never wishes to speak with you again."

It was like the princess had shot an arrow clean through his heart. Artemis must have revealed the secret to her. He could hear Mirjana giggling as she ascended the stairs.

Matteo felt himself crumple down in his cell.

Chapter Twenty-Three

The center of Adipe's cabin held a table with a giant map of the sea. It was not quite as detailed a map as the one Avira had taken from her father, but it got all the main points correct. In the commotion of going with Adipe, Avira hadn't been able to grab a single personal belonging. She likely would have only taken the map, the rest of her life in Alvanii felt less and less sentimental now. But she wished she could pull it from her pocket and impress Adipe with her knowledge of the trade routes her father frequented.

Avira was particularly interested in the corner of the map where a little inlet along the Alvanii coastline was drawn over as though there was land there.

"Adipe?" Avira asked. "This land here. I think there might be an error."

Adipe raised an eyebrow sceptically, "My cartographers are the best in the world.

"I only say so because my father has a port on that bay. It's called the Bay of Khul. There's a beach there and I used to visit it as a child."

Avira pressed her finger into the map, "I think that your cartographers made a mistake."

Adipe inhaled sharply. Avira didn't want to offend her, she simply wanted to make sure the queen had as accurate of information as possible. Avira walked across the room and grabbed a quill. Wordlessly, she handed the pen to Avira.

"Fix it," Adipe said. Avira did as she was told, closing her eyes so she could remember the lines and inlets in as much detail as possible. When she was finished she handed the quill back to Adipe. She felt herself wishing she had her stolen map with her. Then she could show Adipe and prove she knew what she was talking about.

"Don't you think it's funny that we have ships that can sail through the skies, but we don't even really know what the world beneath our feet looks like?" Adipe said suddenly. Avira, who had been focusing wholeheartedly on the map, blinked up at her and tried to find something witty to say in response.

"I wouldn't necessarily call it funny," said Avira.

"But it is ironic, isn't it? The skies are something we all share but maps like this one—" Adipe gestured to the table in front of them. "—are only for those who can afford it."

Avira agreed wholeheartedly but she'd been caught so much by surprise, that she felt like an idiot trying to agree. So, she just nodded and returned her focus to the map.

There were six dotted lines leading from Alvanii to Shaheen, each varying slightly. Adipe ran her finger along the one at the direct center and explained, "This is the route The Apollo is following. See, it leads us right to the heart of Shaheen. In a day and a half, it will run right into our blockade."

"Will you let it through?"

"Yes, as an ally. I have drafted a trading charter of my own for Artemis."

"What about my father's other ships?"

"There are already five ships stuck at the blockade. I've received word from one of my patrol boats that an entire fleet of Bianco warships is coming to join them."

"What do you mean 'patrol boats?'" Avira couldn't hold in her curiosity.

"Well, your people are afraid of the water. They think Salicia will drown them and never even taught their children to swim. My people worship both goddesses as equals. We do not fear the water."

If the Shaheeni had boats on the water, they could easily

monitor all sky traffic from below without ever being noticed by sky ships.

"Your people are wise," was all Avira could say.

"I know." Adipe smiled.

The two then continued to go over their plan for making a successful handoff. Once in Shaheen, they would dress Avira as close to Alvanian clothes as they could find and send her via glider up to Gavriel's ship. She would be escorted by a Shaheeni guard, likely one of Adipe's two personal bodyguards. Before leaving, Gavriel will be forced to sign a treaty cutting the Bianco trade routes through Shaheen in half. Once Avira was back in Alvanii with Gavriel, a fleet of Shaheeni guards would airlift her out in the night.

"Wouldn't that cause another war?" Avira worried.

Adipe shook her head. "If we play our cards right, they won't know it was us."

As the plan took shape, Avira began to feel less and less like a chess piece. Adipe listened to her ideas and criticisms. Avira felt no doubt that she could make a life in Shaheen if she so wished. Women were respected there. But her dreams took her further. She had always been astounded by how many of Alvanii's greatest adventurers spent their lives flying ships in a straight line from Alvanii to Shaheen and never looking farther. She wanted more than that and Adipe, more than anyone she'd met before, appeared to understand.

Adipe gestured towards the sofas where a hot pot of fresh tea waited for them. She poured them each a cup and sipped gently.

"I didn't always want to be queen," Adipe said. "I was a princess. I knew someday my duty would be to lead Shaheen, but I didn't want to rule. I was obsessed with how terrible all of our maps of the world are. Have you heard what they say about entire cultures to the South, the East, and the West that we haven't even found yet, much less put on a map? I wanted to travel, to see all there was to see."

She gave a little shrug.

"We don't always get what we want, Avira. But sometimes the things that are handed to us wind up making more sense in the long run. I like it when things make sense, don't you?"

Adipe's big brown eyes wandered up to meet Avira's. Avira could only nod.

"I'll fix another pot of tea. This one has gone cold," Adipe said, and wandered off. Avira couldn't help but notice that the tea in her cup wasn't cold at all. Adipe must have just needed a break from the conversation.

It was hard to imagine Adipe not being a queen, with her

natural grace, elegance, diplomacy, and cool temper.

Avira continued to study the map, running her fingers along each route and wondering how long it had taken for maps as detailed as these to be made. As she tracked the route Adipe had told her The Apollo traveled on, something struck Avira.

"Adipe, is Artemis going to help us?"

Adipe just shrugged. "Artemis helps *himself.* Perhaps he will stay to aid in the fight but I doubt it. Once he has his new charter, he'll be as distant as a sunrise." Adipe made a little gesture with her hand to indicate The Apollo disappearing into thin air.

"But what if he turns on us? He knows the plan. What if he tells Gavriel it's all a setup? What if he spoils the ambush so Gavriel can sink your boats?"

Adipe frowned. "Tell me, little one, why is it that you cannot trust a soul? I trust Artemis. As slippery and obnoxious as he can be, I choose to trust him. Why is it you find that impossible?"

Avira didn't know why. She'd been born with a silver spoon in her mouth, and, despite her father's bad nature, she'd lived a charmed life. Still, she felt safer on her own. Perhaps it felt more realistic for somebody to betray her than for someone to stay and prove her wrong.

After all, she'd even been wrong about Matteo. And she'd *kissed* Matteo.

Avira didn't have to think too deeply about this, though, because only a minute later Mirjana came blurting into the room. This, Avira gathered, was the girl's usual means of making an entrance. Adipe, who had been silently swirling her tea around in its little clay mug, was clearly startled by her daughter. She gave a little grunt but quickly composed herself.

"The boy is insufferable, Amma. I say we throw him overboard." Mirjana flopped herself down next to her mother.

"Rubbish," said Adipe, who didn't seem to buy her daughter's whining.

"Oh, no. Mirjana might be right. The boy can be insufferable. He doesn't know when to quit." Avira was trying hard to win over the girl, but she was ineffective.

Mirjana pointed a long finger at Avira and said, in a rather accusatory voice, "He loves her, Amma. I think he loves her."

Avira felt her fists clench. It wasn't as though she was actually about to punch a crown princess in front of a queen. More so she needed somewhere to put all of the tension that had risen within her just at the mention of Matteo.

Avira spat, "He betrayed me. He works for my father. How is that love?"

Mirjana put her hands on her hips defiantly. "Do I look like I know anything about love? I asked him whom he fought for, and he said he'd fight for you. It's terribly romantic, isn't it, Amma?"

Adipe raised an eyebrow. "It's not romantic if she hates him, Miri."

"Oh, but you don't hate him, Avira? He's so devoted!"

"I don't know how I feel about him," Avira said, wanting terribly for this to all be over. "He works for my father. What am I to think of that?"

Avira didn't want to tell Mirjana the rest of what she was thinking. But she couldn't let go of the fact that he had lied to her. He'd looked right into her soul and made the choice to be dishonest with her. She couldn't forgive him and she absolutely couldn't let herself love him. She would never love a liar.

"Well, he didn't seem to have any loyalty to your father when *we* talked."

"Mirjana, you mustn't meddle in things that aren't about you. I'm sorry, Avira, my daughter, hasn't seen much romance in her life, so even small things excite her."

Avira felt like protesting. Matteo didn't feel like a *small* thing, not necessarily.

"It's all very confusing for me."

Mirjana shot up from her mother's sofa and stuck her fists on her hips.

"I have an idea."

"You do seem to have many of those," Adipe groaned.

"Send the boy as her bodyguard."

Adipe's other eyebrow raised to match the one she'd already flexed. This resulted in a sort of wide-eyed look of shock across her face. "Something tells me that is a bad idea."

"Think about it, Amma. If the boy is truly loyal to Avira, we might as well use him as bait instead of one of our own. What if the plan goes awry and Gavriel stabs them both to death immediately? Then we haven't lost one of our guards."

"Any of our guards would happily die for the cause."

"But what if they didn't have to! Plus, then we're rid of him. He looks Shaheeni, Amma. Nobody could ever tell the difference."

Avira felt compelled to chime in. "It won't work," she said. "He works for my father. They'll know who he is."

"Do you *know* that? We're handing you over to Gavriel, not your father."

Avira felt like it was safe to assume Gavriel had met Matteo and would recognize his face instantly.

"The good isn't worth the risk, Miri," Adipe said, clearly trying to pacify her daughter.

"You could at least leave the choice to Avira!"

Two sets of dark eyes fell onto Avira, sending a chill up her spine.

This was one choice she didn't want to make.

Adipe set her cup of tea down gently and rose from her seat. She crossed the room and placed her hand on Avira's cheek. Mirjana watched, not looking confused at all by this.

"Avira, I am not ignorant that I have taken every choice from you to save my people. I will leave you this one. Who escorts you to Gavriel is up to you."

Avira could feel her eyes getting hot, partially from anger and the thoughts flooding her mind. Thoughts of the boy who'd stolen a bag of lemons from below deck on The Apollo to make lemonade because he knew that would cheer her up. The boy who'd climbed a mile into the sky to bring her tea in the crows' nest. The boy who'd seen right through her unfriendly facade somehow became her friend. She didn't want to do this without that boy. But that boy could have all been a lie, a trick, a mirage.

"I need to talk to him."

Adipe nodded in response and, with a wave of her hand,

summoned Fela to show Avira her way to the ship's jail.

"We arrive in Shaheen in an hour. Is that enough time?"

"I hope so," Avira said, forcing a smile. She noticed how Mirjana and Adipe watched her leave and couldn't quite place the emotions she saw on their faces. They looked nearly identical.

As the door closed behind her, Avira realized that the emotion was pity.

CHAPTER TWENTY-FOUR

Matteo counted the footsteps that crossed the deck above his head. Some were loud and collided with the wood, making a resounding *thunk, thunk.* Some could barely be heard at all. From the noise of the footsteps, he'd deduced that most of the crew had to have been women. There was a lightness and grace to most of the noise above him. While The Apollo had constantly rumbled with sound, this ship cut through the sky like a hot knife in butter. It was no wonder it snuck up on its rivals; even Matteo had been fooled.

Steps on the spiral staircase startled him out of his thoughts. He couldn't see who was coming down, but he hoped it wouldn't be Mirjana again. It was humiliating to be held hostage by a child, even if that child would someday rule a significant section of the Southern Continent.

He craned his neck to try and make out his visitor. There was a flash of green pants in the corner of his eye. He didn't recognize her until she was right in front of him, eyes narrowed, lips pressed together.

"Avira," he breathed and pressed his body into the bars, reaching for her.

"Don't touch me," she said as she stepped away from him. Her face was sober, but he couldn't help but notice how she glowed, even in the darkness of the jail cell. "I know whom you work for, Matteo De Luca. How dare you lie to me."

Avira was cold as stone. She wanted an explanation.

"I'm not like them, Avira. You don't understand. I don't work for him anymore."

"Am I supposed to congratulate you for sending your letter of resignation? How could you pretend like this? Playing a game like you had no idea who I was. I trusted you. Don't you understand how much that means to me?"

Matteo couldn't speak. He opened his mouth and closed it again, trying to string together words into a sentence that even began to capture what he wanted to tell her.

"The only way you are different from Gavriel, from my father, is you pretend to be good when you aren't. At least they know exactly who they are and don't act like anything different."

Her voice was steady. It hadn't cracked even once until she

said, "Matteo, I let you kiss me, and you still lied."

"I'm sorry."

"I don't care!" she was screaming now, letting specs of spit fly into his face. "Was it worth it? Did you get what you wanted from me?"

"No," Matteo whispered in response.

"Of course, you never did get me into bed with you, did you?"

"That's not it, Avira." Without thinking, he shoved his hand through the bars at her. She backed away, a look of disgust on her face. But then she saw the glint of gold hanging from his hand. A sparkling golden pendant with a falcon at the center, the falcon's outstretched wings carved with hundreds of tiny brush stroke details, its eyes two diamonds.

"That is my mother's."

"She made me promise I'd protect you from any harm that came your way. She knew it meant she might never see you again, but she didn't care. I promised her and I wanted so badly to keep it. So, no, I did not get what I wanted from you, from *this*. Because you are here, kidnapped by the Queen of the Shaheeni to be carted back to Alvanii like a prized sapphire."

Avira's face scrunched up. She let the necklace fall into her hand where she stared at it for a long, silent moment.

"Do you know why my father's symbol is a falcon, Matteo?"

He shook his head.

"Because he thinks they look fearsome. But you know, Adipe uses falcons as her messengers because they are wise, graceful and loyal. It's ironic isn't it, that something so brilliant can be heralded simply for how it looks?"

Avira was no longer talking about birds.

"Don't you want that too? Don't you want to fly free like a falcon?"

"That's just it, Matteo," she said without making eye contact. "The most helpful falcons are the ones tamed and used for the good of others, the ones who work in partnership with a falconer. Maybe that's what's supposed to come of me. I want to do this. I want to do something bigger. I can't spend the rest of my days hiding. I just don't understand why you lied to me for so long."

"Avira," Matteo said, getting as close to her as he could. "If I'd have been honest with you, you'd have snapped my neck."

Avira blinked at him. She relaxed and stepped closer to the cell, close enough to run her hand down his cheek, resting it on his shoulder.

"I always believed my adventures would happen alone. But here you are. Strange."

he tensed up again and turned to go, keeping the pendant in her closed fist.

"Avira, wait." She stopped to look back at him as he spoke. "Your mother would want you to wear that."

Wordlessly, she slid on the pendant and left. The air felt so much heavier than it had before.

Avira knocked gently on Adipe's cabin door. Fela opened it with a smile and escorted Avira back to the sofa where Mirjana was talking at a mile a minute about a novel she'd read from Alvanii that was 'positively heinous.'

Adipe poured a cup of tea for Avira, not speaking at all until Avira said softly, "Let Matteo escort me. He'll be helpful."

And, sipping their tea in near silence, the three women all relaxed into their plan.

Chapter Twenty-Five

Not even an hour later, two guards came in to let Adipe know the ship was docking at her palace. It was no surprise to Avira that Adipe had her own private shipyard available to her at all times. She was, however, surprised when she, Adipe and Mirjana made their way to the deck of the ship. Shaheen looked nothing at all like she'd expected.

Avira had imagined Shaheen was a small city-state wrapped on three sides by a desert and bordering the sea. She'd heard stories about the rocky Shaheeni beaches, the luxurious bathhouses, and fragrant markets that dotted every corner. She knew Shaheen was grande. But the city that lay before her was more opulent than she could have ever dreamed of. Shaheen was built on a towering cliffside. The city stretched out in all directions, with tall villas and lush gardens visible from the sky. Avira let her mouth drop open as she balked.

"It is beautiful, isn't it?"

"I thought my father was exploiting you? Using all your resources so you had none left!"

"He is." Adipe sounded somber even through her pride. "Imagine what my city could look like if we were allowed to keep all of our wealth rather than just the sliver your father leaves for us."

"Where does it all come from?" Avira said she still had not found where the city ended. It appeared to go on forever, past the horizon—an unending city.

"The Goddesses have always blessed us—riches from the sea and friends to the South. I used to pray that we could have alliances with Alvanii and Veronii too, but—" Adipe clicked her tongue.

Instead of a rope ladder, they stepped onto a large wooden platform with ropes on each end. Two guards then lowered the platform from the ship's deck to a circle of stones in the center of what appeared to be a palace garden. There were fruit trees and flowering shrubbery. Mirjana nearly immediately disappeared, muttering something about wanting to see if any letters had arrived from her friends while she was gone.

Falcons darted everywhere above them, many of which looked as though they were carrying letters on their backs. Avira stared at them, mesmerized.

Adipe told Fela, who Avira had learned was the queen's most trusted lady's maid, to find Matteo and pull him from his prison cell. He was to be bathed and dressed in traditional Shaheeni clothing before being brought before the queen to be given his orders.

"Is it true," Adipe said, "that he looks like a true-born Shaheeni boy despite being raised in Veronii?"

Avira nodded her head and agreed that it was pretty odd. She blushed a little, remembering the night she and Matteo had made lemonade together and she'd pushed him too hard for the details of his childhood.

Adipe and Avira were escorted from the garden into the palace, which was the most illustrious building Avira had ever seen. It hardly felt like a home, but rather a grand temple. Each hallway was the size of a city street, wound around in circles decorated with intricate mosaic tiles.

At the end of one of the hallways, a great room with two massive mosaics, at least two stories tall, towering above a golden throne decorated in sapphires.

"Are those the goddesses?" Avira stared at the mosaics that stretched up the wall. She'd never seen the goddesses depicted like this, so incredibly human. Aurora, the goddess of the sky, reached out a hand toward her sister, Salicia. Her hair was done in such detail that you could see it evaporating into clouds. She was nearly naked except for the pink and orange scarves she wore wrapped around her body in intricate knots. Against the darkness of Aurora's skin, the scarves almost looked like a sunrise.

In the mosaic, Salicia held her hand to meet Aurora's, but they could barely reach her. Whereas Aurora showed nearly every inch of skin, Salicia was covered from the top of her head to the tip of her toes in blue robes and scarves. Her hair was covered though small white whisps peaked their way out. She was crying, blue tears running down her cheeks. Avira strained her eyes to see, but she thought that the tears might be made of sapphires.

"Why is she crying?" Avira asked.

"Because she cannot reach Aurora."

"They're close sisters, then?"

Adipe snorted. "Who told you they were sisters? No. They are in love. But they cannot be together, or our world will lose balance. That is why when the skies are angry, so is the sea. They watch one another and respond to one another. They are one."

Avira's heart felt fuller than it had in days. She'd never been taught about Salicia, the goddess of the sea, past the fact that she was fickle and not to be trusted. It felt different to know Salicia's heart was a heart in love.

"They cannot hold one another so, instead, they protect each other. It is beautiful." Avira couldn't tell, but she thought she could see the glitter of a tear in Adipe's eye. She didn't ask, though.

"Come, I will show you to your suite."

"Oh, I don't need a suite! I've been in a shared bunk for the last month. I can handle it a little longer."

"Nonsense!" Adipe silenced her. "You are a hero. We will treat you as such while you are here. Besides, I had one of my maids shop for an entire new wardrobe of gowns for you to pick from."

Avira hadn't missed gowns at all. She was so fond of the pants that she hadn't immediately understood why Adipe'd bought any gowns. Then she remembered that she had to wear *something* when she was presented to Gavriel, and it was probably for the best that she looked like a proper Alvanian woman.

Just as Adipe began walking away from the throne room, Fela came rushing in with someone at her heels. The boy who trailed behind her was unrecognizable compared to the one Avira knew.

Matteo's curls had been braided close to his head in little rows with small beads tied in. The beads weren't jewels like Adipe's, but they still glittered in the light. He wore a long silver kaftan that went down to his knees, matching silver trousers beneath that, and a pair of white sandals tied to his feet with various knots. He looked absolutely, indisputably Shaheeni.

Matteo bowed deeply to the queen, who said nothing in response. Avira half expected some of the queen's quick wit or banter to accompany Matteo's introduction, but Adipe was standing in silence, her dark eyes locked on Matteo.

"What is your name, boy?" Adipe asked, the tone of her voice severe and stern.

"Matteo De Luca."

"Is that the name your mother gave you? De Luca?"

"No. I never knew my mother. My adoptive parents called me Matteo, and I took their last name."

Adipe gave a knowing *hmmm*. She looked deep in thought, clearly knocked off her feet by the boy. Fela seemed to notice and quickly took control of the situation.

"Madame, would you like me to show Avira to her room?"

Adipe nodded. "Leave the boy with me. We have things to discuss."

Fela scurried away, and Avira followed her closely, saying nothing to Matteo, who kept his eyes locked on Adipe. Once the two of them were down the hall, Fela turned to Avira and asked, "How does the queen know that boy?"

Avira shook her head. "She doesn't. Not that I know of, at least."

Fela gave a confused sigh and sped up her walking. Almost to herself, she said, "It was like he took the air right out of her lungs."

Chapter Twenty-Six

Matteo had been planning to stay by Avira's side for the rest of the day. But the queen appeared to have a different plan in mind. She whisked him out of the throne room and into a study with massive open windows looking out onto the garden. In the garden, a family of peacocks strutted around. It looked like something out of a storybook.

"Would you like some tea?" the queen asked him, pouring tea herself rather than waiting for a servant to come to do it for her. The tea she was brewing didn't look the way Matteo was used to. It was far darker in color, and its leaves had expanded to almost fill the pot. Seeming to notice his apprehension, Adipe said, "It's called pu'er. Artemis gave it to me as a gift from his travels in the Far East. It's quite strong."

She poured him a cup, no longer seeming to care whether he wanted it. Her hands were shaking a bit as she poured.

"Have you been briefed on your duties protecting the girl?"

"I have." Matteo took a sip of his tea, which was still a bit too hot, and burnt his lips as he drank. She was right, it was intense. It felt like liquor going down.

"She has chosen to put her life on the line for our people. I can only pray you would do the same for her should something go wrong."

Matteo tried to ignore the queen's use of 'our people.' He didn't even speak Shaheeni. It felt wrong to claim them as his own.

"With all respect, I'm wondering what the danger is for her. We're giving Gavriel what he wants, aren't we?"

Adipe shook her head. "He is a violent man. He might act out in anger if he suspects he's being lied to. We've sent him a letter claiming to have captured her. If he learns that she is doing this of her own free will, or worse, that we hope to free her from her father once she's back in Alvanii, all will be for naught."

"And when you free her, won't they assume it was you? Doesn't that just put you right back where you started?"

"Maybe. I hope not. But if we are at war again in three months, at least we will have time to prepare."

Now it was Matteo's turn to shake his head. It felt like a far too risky plan to throw Avira right into the center. But he'd been given his orders, and he felt there was little space for him to argue.

A peacock in the garden had become fixated on pulling a golden plum down from the tree's boughs. Matteo watched the bird pull the branch as far down as it would go and then tried to reach for the plum, letting go of the branch and sending it flying back out of reach.

"I must admit, Matteo," Adipe said, "I did not wish to speak with you purely about our plans for tricking Gavriel Castillo. He couldn't be further from my mind right now."

Matteo caught the woman's eye. There was a glint of gold in her stare that he hadn't noticed before. "What do you mean?"

"Tell me everything you know about your birth mother."

"I already have."

"No, there must be more. Did she leave you with any clues to who you were?"

"I'm sorry. No."

"Does the name Hamida Al Amir mean anything to you?

Adipe sounded desperate, her voice breaking more and more with each word. Matteo even considered lying to her for comfort, but he did not know what she was talking about.

"Please," he begged her, "I don't know what you mean.

"I mean..." Adipe took a long deep breath. "I have seen your eyes before. I know your eyes. I have only ever seen such deep, stormy eyes once."

"Who is Hamida Al Amir?"

"She was my best friend. And, in many ways, she was the greatest love of my life." Adipe poured herself another cup of tea.

"My mother and father ruled together as king and queen. Their dearest friends were named Selene and Akram. Akram was my father's closest advisor. They had two children, twins named Hamida and Alonso. They were exactly my age and my closest friends. I never had siblings. It is customary for the Shaheeni royal family to have one child and one child only. Hamida and Alonso were as close to family as I had.

"As time went on, I learned that my mother and Selene were planning for my marriage to Alonso. He would be my husband, and I would lead Shaheen as the sovereign queen. Only after I learned of my betrothal to Alonso did I realize the depth of my love for Hamida. I wanted her ruling next to me, not her brother."

Adipe giggled as though there were a thousand memories flooding back to her and rushing over her like a river.

"I like to think she wanted that too. But I will never know. One day I woke up and Hamida was gone. She'd taken a glider and gone to see the world. Her mother and father worried for fifty days and fifty nights until finally a letter arrived on a falcon saying she had made it safely to Alvanii and she'd fallen in love with a wealthy merchant. I was crushed. I made my mother move my wedding to Alonso so we could be wed sooner. I thought if she got word of our marriage, she'd come home. I thought perhaps I could see her again if I just gave in and married Alonso. But she didn't return. I married Alonso and a few days later a falcon arrived with a note for me saying she was pregnant, and they would be making a life for themselves in Veronii with their child."

Tears were welling up in Adipe's eyes.

"I never heard from Hamida again. I thought perhaps she'd just ignored me for twenty years but now I see. This boy in front of me, a Shaheeni boy raised in Veronii with Hamida's eyes? It cannot be a coincidence.

"Alonso died of a fever when Mirjana was small, but I've never minded being alone because I prayed that someday Hamida would come home to me. Now I see that can never be. But Aurora brought you to me."

Matteo could feel his face heating up. All his life, he'd wanted to know who he was and now it was being handed to him, and he didn't know what to say.

"How did she die, Matteo?"

"I don't know."

She shrunk down into Matteo's arms, and he did the best he could to comfort her. He could feel his kaftan growing damp from her tears.

"I am so sorry," was all he could say. "I am so sorry. I am so sorry."

Adipe snapped her head and looked straight into his eyes, "Do not apologize! You are here now. My Hamida's son has come home to Shaheen, which is a beautiful, *beautiful* thing."

Chapter Twenty-Seven

Fela showed Avira to her suite, where a hot bath and a pot of tea were waiting for her. There was a wardrobe filled with six gowns, each one wildly different. Trying on six different Alvanian dresses, with their frilly lace and impossibly large hoop skirts, didn't interest Avira at all. So, she flopped herself down on the sofa and stared out the window of her room into the gardens. She did this for a long time, letting the world turn around her.

A cluster of jasmine flowers hung right outside her bedroom window. Avira wanted so badly to reach out and pick it. She kept going back and forth as to whether or not she should. It was doubtful that anyone would be too angry with her. But it felt cruel to kill the flowers just because she thought they were beautiful. She stood and walked to them, taking the stem in her hands and pulling ever so slightly, but the flowers wouldn't come free. Avira took this as a sign.

Since she was already standing up, Avira figured she might pursue the dresses Adipe had brought for her. One of these would be the dress she wore to meet Gavriel.

She shuddered at the thought of him. He was handsome in the way a lion is a handsome beast. His eyes were intense but not like Matteo's, that held so much care and thought, his eyes were intense like a snake's.

The first dress was a burnt orange color. She pulled it on and struggled with the long and fluffy sleeves. She felt like one of the exotic flowers Adipe had kept stocked in her gardens.

Avira knew that all of these dresses required a corset, but she chose not to worry about one since that required assistance from at least two servants, and she didn't feel like talking to anyone. Besides, if she was to spend a month married to Gavriel while awaiting rescue, she would have to wear a corset daily. Avira figured it was worthwhile to soak up every last moment she could in her trousers.

Strangely, she felt more nervous about returning to her life on Alvanii for a month than she had about leaving that same life forever to journey on The Apollo.

It was almost funny now how quickly her great adventure had come and gone. She could only pray that Adipe would be true to her word and save her from Gavriel when the time was right. Avira didn't particularly enjoy feeling like a damsel but what choice did she have?

The second dress she tried on was her favorite of the lot, though she knew she could never wear it for Gavriel. It was a deep blue, and while it had the unmistakable hoop skirt of Alvanian fashion, it was clearly designed by a Shaheeni seamstress who didn't much care for tight clothing. She took it off quickly, knowing the lack of shape in the bodice would be a turn-off for Gavriel. And, at this point, the only real weapon she had against him was what she wore.

The third dress was bright yellow and made Avira's pale skin look sickly and green. She didn't even bother to tie the bodice up all the way before deciding against it.

Dress number four was a brilliant red and covered in beads. It was so gaudy that Avira, with her short hair and simple face, looked like she was being eaten alive.

She was still wearing the red dress when a knock came at the door.

"Come in," Avira called out as she tried to get the bodice on straight. She wasn't confident that she didn't have the whole thing on backward.

"You look so beautiful!" Mirjana's voice startled Avira.

"Is that how everyone in Alvanii dresses? It's incredible."

"I'd personally much rather we all wore pants like yours."

Mirjana had stars in her eyes. "I'd love to wear a dress like that someday. You look like a princess from a storybook."

Avira didn't feel like it was a good moment to point out that Mirjana was actually a princess. Instead, she held out a hand and said, "Would you like to try on one of these? I don't need all of them."

Avira went to the rack and pulled the yellow one down. She felt it would look stunning with Mirjana's dark hair and eyes.

"You can slide it on right over your trousers. And I'll help with the corset."

Mirjana looked positively elated. They slid the dress over her head, and Avira got to work lacing up the back. She was far more coordinated when helping someone else put on a gown than when putting on her own. When they were finished, Mirjana ran to the mirror and did a spin.

"I can't believe people really get to dress like this every day," Mirjana squealed a bit as she spoke. "When I am Queen of Shaheen, I'll hold massive stately balls so I can wear gowns too. I'll invite you, if you like. My mother's all but given up on alliances with Alvanii, but I like to think there's still hope. There are noblemen in Alvanii and Veronii. You must have some royal family."

"Yes, but they spent all their money years ago. Now they rely on men like my father to support our economy."

"So," Mirjana pressed, "if you think about it, you're practically a real-life princess too!"

Avira laughed. She honestly couldn't remember the last time she'd giggled like this. It had to have been days ago, if not weeks. Perhaps it was with Matteo, but she couldn't pinpoint a time.

"What? What's so funny?"

"It's just that you really are a princess, Mirjana. Sometimes I wonder if you forget that."

Mirjana just shrugged. "Princesses in storybooks are never lonely. I feel lonely all the time. It's customary for the royal family only to have one child and, if you think about it, that makes sense. They don't want anyone going to war over the crown. But, I don't even have a single cousin or child my age to play with. I feel more like a prisoner than a princess."

Then something caught Mirjana's eye. "Oh look! Jasmine!" She ran to the window where the cluster of flowers bloomed and plucked it without thinking. "Avira, will you put this in my hair?"

Smiling softly, Avira did as she was told. She tucked the jasmine in with Mirjana's braids.

"You look beautiful, Miri."

Mirjana's face changed again as though she'd suddenly remembered something significant.

"I didn't come in here to play dress up." Mirjana hiked up her skirt and began, almost comically, trying to find the pockets of her pants. She was searching for something but every time she shifted her body, the dress bubbled up in a different direction creating more obstacles.

"Damn this Alvanian fashion. It's absurd," she muttered under her breath, which made Avira smile again.

Finally, Mirjana found what she was looking for and pulled it from her pocket. She straightened her skirt and extended her arm to Avira. In her hand was a small knife. It had a thin blade and a golden handle decorated with tiny flowers sculpted of gold.

"I wanted to give you a bigger one, but I worried my mother might notice it was gone. This was my first dagger. My father gave it to me to protect myself against bad men."

Avira gave a knowing nod. She took the knife from Mirjana's hand. It was heavier than it looked.

"I know you're not *supposed to* kill Gavriel. I know we're supposed to sign a treaty with him. But if he tries to hurt you Avira, please don't let him."

The child's eyes had a glimmer of maturity that Avira had never noticed before. Avira set the knife down and embraced her in a hug.

"I won't let him hurt me, Mirjana."

"Promise?"

"Promise."

Mirjana pulled away, a little smile on her lips.

"What do you think," Avira said. "Should I wear this dress to meet him?"

Mirjana shook her head and returned to the shelf where two dresses sat untouched.

"What about this one?"

Mirjana held in her hands a slim-fitting, sky-blue gown. It hadn't looked like much on the rack, but Avira could now see it had silver threads woven in to make it sparkle. It reminded her of The Mirage.

Avira slid the red dress off, and Mirjana helped her tie up the bodice of the blue one. It fit perfectly. Instead of puffing out like a pastry, it stayed close to her hips until her knees and became loose fitting. Its long sleeves trumpeted at the ends and stretched to the floor. It wasn't a typical Alvanian style, but it looked phenomenal on Avira's petite frame.

Avira started grinning as soon as she looked in the mirror.

Partially from joy and partially from how absolutely ridiculous her hair looked.

"What are we going to do with my hair?"

Mirjana scrunched her nose. And then she clearly had an idea and bolted out of the room. She returned a few minutes later with Fela and a jewelry box filled with silver hair baubles. One was a thin circle that sat perfectly on top of Avira's head. It popped against her dark hair perfectly

"You look absolutely stunning, Avira," Fela said with a complimentary nod toward Mirjana.

They had just finished putting together the look, Avira feeling more girly than she had in years when a firm knock shook the door. Mirjana opened it up wide, revealing Matteo.

"Where's Avira?"

"She doesn't want to see you, remember?

His voice was urgent: "I *need* to talk to her."

Avira stepped forward, putting herself in his line of view. She saw his mouth drop open and realized this was the first time he'd seen her in a gown, much less a dress that she felt beautiful in.

His dark eyes darted from Avira to Mirjana and then back to Avira. She felt a pull within her. She wanted to wrap her arms around him and ask for his advice. She clenched her fists tightly, not wanting to give in to the softness she felt for Matteo. She could not be soft or delicate or fragile. Not today. Not tomorrow. Perhaps not ever. There was no longer space for that in her life and she didn't particularly mind that.

"What do you want, Matteo?" The moment she spoke, her voice cracked awkwardly.

Where were those voice cracks when he was pretending to be a boy back on The Apollo? They would have come in handy.

"Can we talk?"

"No." Avira gritted her teeth, painfully aware of Mirjana and Fela's eyes watching her every move. Mirjana wanted to believe in their love story. But Avira could not give the child her fairytale ending.

"Now, now," Matteo begged, "I see you have company. You look beautiful, by the way."

Avira shook her head. Matteo took her hands in his, his skin surprisingly soft upon hers.

She felt the familiar feeling of a heat flickering through her body, radiating out from the places where he touched her. She gritted her teeth, begging herself to be stronger.

Matteo leaned in, his nose pressed into her hair and his lips just brushing her ear. She could feel the warmth of his breath like a summer wind.

"Meet me in the garden at midnight," he whispered.

"Don't beg, Matteo. The time for begging has long since passed-"

Matteo squeezed her hands even tighter, this time so tight she let out a small gasp.

"Meet me at midnight."

He wasn't begging. He was commanding. It was so unlike him to do so that Avira

stepped back, pulling her hands from his. She gave a silent nod, promising without words that she would be there. And he turned on his heels and left her standing in the doorway, jaw slacked and hands empty.

She turned back around, her eyes wide like a doe's. Fela took her hand and walked her to the chair. She sat, hunched over in her seat like an old woman, not worried about wrinkling the satin of her gown, and hung her head in her hands.

Chapter Twenty-Eight

Midnight came and went, leaving Matteo standing alone beneath a magnolia tree that bloomed with the radiance of a sunrise. There was a bench beneath the tree, but he couldn't bring himself to sit. He walked in slow, silent circles, wearing a path through the grass from the pattern of his stride.

It had to be ten after midnight by now, of course, he couldn't be sure. He couldn't stand the thought of going back to his rooms, of admitting to himself that Avira would not be coming to meet him. Next to the bench, Matteo had hidden a small bag he'd stuffed with as much as would fit. He'd managed to snag a few oranges and lemons from the kitchen, some money, an extra tunic and a scarf to keep his face safe from the sands and the wind of the desert should he need. Most of what he owned had been left behind upon The Apollo. And the only thing he truly cared to bring with him was an ebony haired girl who did not appear to be coming along.

After what felt like another hour of waiting, Matteo slammed his fist into the trunk of the magnolia tree as hard as he could. He felt the crack of his knuckles and the heat of blood across his dry skin as petals fell from the boughs above down onto him like sick, starlit confetti.

"Matteo?" A voice called through the garden. He looked up, desperately searching for the owner of the voice. He'd have known it anywhere.

"Matteo, what is wrong with you?"

Avira strode out of the darkness wearing only a silver silk nightgown and a dark blue wrap around her shoulders. She looked as dainty as the flowers that filled the garden, but her eyes were stern and dark, filled with fear.

He ran to her. He couldn't help himself. He wrapped her in his arms and held tight, breathing in the smell of her hair and the softness of the air all around her.

She did not hug him back.

"What did you need to talk to me about?" She pressed her hands against his chest and pushed him away, forcing him to step at least an arm's distance back.

Matteo opened his mouth to speak but no words came out. He didn't know where to begin, what the best words were to say what he needed to tell her. They'd felt so clear in his mind just moments before but now they were about as clear as honey and twice as murky.

"Matteo?" The apprehension in Avira's voice scared him. At any moment she could turn around and leave him there. She didn't have to come out to the garden. She could go at any time.

"Run away with me." His voice was barely a squeak, as soft as a little mouse.

"What?" It wasn't clear if Avira was asking this because she didn't know what he said or because she didn't understand why he would say it.

"Run away with me," Matteo said again. "My bags are packed. We could go now and have Shaheen behind us by dawn. I don't have much money but I think there's enough for us to charter two camels and get across the desert. We could go to Irajmi, escape your father for good."

Avira sucked in her breath, her hair floated around her head like a halo caught upon a warm breeze that rushed through the garden. It was like the garden was gasping alongside Avira.

"What makes you think my father won't find us in Irajmi?"

Matteo furrowed his brow.

"We could travel to the end of the earth in any direction, he would find us eventually. And then he would kill you. He'd gut you right there in front of my eyes and then he'd make me marry Gavriel anyway. There is no use running from him."

"You don't believe that!" Matteo protested. He was suddenly aware of the blood dripping along his fist. The pain felt a million miles away now.

"My father is a powerful man."

"The Avira I love doesn't believe that."

Avira snapped, "The Avira you love is a figment of your imagination. She is a dream. She will be gone like morning mist as soon as you come to your senses."

Her words hurt Matteo more than the gashes on his hand. They twisted in his stomach and burned in his ears.

"I am offering to abandon everything for you, Avira. My work as a detective, the only family I've ever known, I would give it all up if you would just go with me now."

Avira cocked her head sideways, looking somewhat like a bird. "What do you mean *family*? You don't have a family." If she felt bad for saying this, Avira didn't show it. Her face was stoic, her jaw locked tight.

"It doesn't matter. What matters is that this doesn't have to be our story. We can go, tell a new story. Live a new life!"

"It does matter, Matteo! I want to know what you're talking about. It's not fair of you to tell me you're leaving every-thing behind for me and then not explain what that means."

"I'm Shaheeni!" The words burst from Matteo like an ex-plosion. "My mother was part of the royal family. *I am* part of the royal family. But I'd give that all up if it meant I could live a life with you, if it meant you didn't have to go up there and give yourself to Gavriel tomorrow. You are not just a piece on a chess board, Avira."

"You think I don't know that?" Avira's words were ven-omous. She began pacing around the garden, walking in the same futile circle Matteo had become so familiar with only minutes before.

Without warning, she stopped in her tracks, turning to him with an unmistakable fire in her eyes. "You're related to the queen." Avira stomped the ground and gestured to the palace all around them. "She trusts you. She sees you as *family*. And you would betray her for me? You would walk away from all this just for some Alvanian heiress who doesn't even love you back. I knew you were a coward, Matteo, but you're a traitor too."

It was rare that Matteo saw any semblance of her father in Avira. But this was one of those rare moments. Staring into her eyes as she ripped right into his soul was like looking into the eyes of Grigori Bianco himself.

"You love me back," was all Matteo could bring himself to say. "You do."

"Even if I did, Matteo, how could I ever trust someone like you to be loyal to me? You'll abandon your people when they need you most. What makes you think I could trust you? There is no love without trust."

Matteo kicked the grass in frustration, boiling over with emotion. "Don't you understand, Avira?" He shouted. "I would chase down the stars for you!"

Avira looked around the garden, her eyes sad, her lips pulled together in a stern frown. Tears has begun to well up in her eyes. "You cannot ask me to love you if I cannot trust you. It would be like asking a flower to grow with no sunshine."

Matteo instinctually reached out to touch her face. She pulled away quickly, stepping even farther away from him.

"If you know what's good for you, you'll stay." She whispered to him.

"I don't know if I can watch you give yourself to Gavriel like that."

"It's not permanent. Adipe will come save me."

Matteo let a laugh escape his lips. "So, you'll trust her with your future but you won't trust me?"

"I guess not."

And with that Avira turned and walked back inside, leaving Matteo alone once again in the garden. He felt the muscles in his throat tighten. He wanted to hit the tree again but just as he pulled his fist back to strike, every ounce of energy escaped his body. He deflated. And finally, he sat down.

An hour or so passed, perhaps even more. Matteo heard something stirring in the garden next to him. Footsteps, perhaps. He didn't care. He could tell they were not Avira and if it was not her returning to apologize for crushing his heart, he didn't want to see. He kept his head hung low until, at some point, he became aware of a calming presence next to him. Then, the sound of doves cooing filled his ears. He looked up, confused and curious.

A woman he barely recognized had taken a seat next to him and was throwing seed to the flock of doves that had gathered at their feet. She wore dark robes and a veil over her hair. Her eyes were dark like an ocean at night and her lips were thin and raw as though they'd frowned more than they'd smiled in her lifetime.

"I'm sorry," Matteo said. Though he wasn't sure why. She was the one who had chosen to sit next to him.

"I couldn't sleep," the woman said confidently, "I always

feed the doves when I can't sleep. Here." She handed him a fist full of birdseeds. He stared down at them, unsure of what to say. Who was this woman? Some kind of apparition? A ghost of the palace?

"You're supposed to throw them." She made a gesture to the seeds that Matteo still had clamped in his sweaty fist. He did as he was told and a wave of doves hopped over to his feet.

"I'm Matteo."

"I know who you are." She tossed another handful of seeds, and the doves slowly landed back on the ground and returned to their feeding.

"What's your name?" Matteo didn't much feel like sitting in silence with this woman. If she didn't talk to him, he might as well go. He again caught the scent of jasmine on her hair. Wondering how she made it smell so sweet, he decided to stay.

"What's your name?" he said.

"Rihane."

"Rihane," Matteo repeated back to her. It was fun to say. "What does it mean?"

"What makes you think it means something?"

"I was just wondering. Matteo means 'Aurora's Gift'. My adoptive mother picked it for me."

"It sounds Veronan."

"It *is* Veronan."

Rihane snorted at him. And that's when he recognized her. She was the guard who had taken him from the crow's nest of The Apollo. Not the one flying the glider, she'd been the one who tied him up. She pulled her knees up close to her body, rocking a little. Matteo couldn't tell, but it was almost as though she didn't know she was doing it.

"Rihane is our word for the tiny flowers a basil plant makes. It means 'delicate' and 'feminine.' Like a little flower. I think it's funny because I turned out not to be delicate at all. Not even a little bit."

"I could have told you that."

Rihane smiled, clearly remembering how she'd practically hog-tied Matteo just a few hours ago.

"I was supposed to be the girl's escort, you know. It was supposed to be me protecting her from Gavriel Castillo."

She sounded angry. Matteo raised an eyebrow in question.

"If I'd died," Rihane said somberly, "it would have been an honorable death. If I'd lived, I would have been rewarded handsomely. I could have fed my family for months."

"Don't you get paid well as a guard?"

"Well enough. But I have twelve younger brothers and sisters. There's not much money left after that."

"You can have my reward," Matteo said without thinking. "I don't need it."

"You only get the money if you live."

"So?"

"Don't die."

Rihane tossed another handful of seeds to the birds.

"So, how are you going to get the girl up to the Bianco ship tomorrow night? You don't have a glider. You don't even know how to fly one."

Matteo hadn't thought of this. When he shrugged, Rihane gave him a scandalized look.

"Seriously? You don't know how to fly a glider."

The smile on her face was equal parts determined and mischievous. She tossed the rest of her handful of birdseed and looked at him.

"Meet me on the cliffs outside the palace at dawn. I'll teach you."

"I don't need a teacher." Matteo tried to protest but it was futile. Rihane had stood.

"Let me do this for you. Let me feel like a hero."

A warm breeze floated through the garden, the smell of saffron, rose and rainwater filled Matteo's nose.

"Okay. You can teach me."

Rihane took his hand and shook it firmly. "Don't be late. A good student is never late."

Chapter Twenty-Nine

Avira returned to her room, unsettled right down to her core. Her mind was buzzing with information, questions, worries. Every move she made felt frail. She sat on her sofa and pulled her knees in close, pressing her head between them and squeezing as tightly as she could. It wasn't tight enough. Her ears rang. She tried to focus on the in and out of her breath but every time her mind got quiet, another thought rang out like a gong within her skull.

Matteo was somehow related to the Shaheeni royal family. Matteo wanted to run away with her. Matteo loved her. She wasn't sure how she felt about Matteo. She could have said yes. She could be gone like a spring rainstorm by now. But she told Matteo no. *Matteo, Matteo, Matteo, Matteo, Matteo.* Why on earth did he matter so much to her? It didn't make any logical sense.

But then again, none of this made sense. All those weeks

ago, when she'd fled her father's villa in the night, she had been determined to never set foot on another Bianco vessel. Now she was preparing herself to do exactly that for a kingdom of people she hardly knew at all. Who was this new Avira and what did she do with the headstrong girl who wanted to inherit her father's company?

She kept her head in her knees for a long time, growing accustomed to the humming in her ears and the pounding of her heart. She was so accustomed to it, in fact, that she didn't notice Fela the first time she said her name.

"Avira?" A voice called out through the maze of her thoughts. Avira looked up. Fela blinked back at her, her almond shaped eyes betraying the worry she so clearly felt.

"I'm sorry."

"I came to collect your dishes. I didn't expect you to be awake."

"I'll be alright, really. You can go."

Fela shook her head and sat down next to her. "I don't believe you. You don't look like someone who wants to be alone."

"I don't know who I'm doing this for, Fela. I don't know what I'm fighting for."

"Is it so wrong to be fighting for yourself?" Her words

echoed with truth.

"If I were fighting for myself, I'd have run away again. I wouldn't be giving myself over to the very man I would rather die than marry if I were fighting for myself. I don't know who I'm doing this for."

Fela ran her hand along Avira's back gently, it reminded her of the way her mother rubbed her back to help her sleep as a child. "You believe in our cause, and you see that you have the power to help us in a way nobody else can. You could ignore that power, keep it for yourself, but you believe in helping others."

"You make me sound far more altruistic than I feel." Avira sniffed and wiped a gigantic ball of snot from her nose. "I barely know a thing about Shaheen. I haven't even been beyond the palace walls."

Fela's face lit up, an idea had clearly struck her like a bolt of lightning. "What if I could change that?"

Avira sat up, curious as to what Fela was about to propose. Fela grabbed her hands. "Come with me. All you have to do is promise you'll be back by morning."

Not twenty minutes later, Avira was walking out the back gate of the palace along with a few other servants who's shifts had just come to an end. Fela had rubbed some soot on Avira's hands to make her look grubby and given her some dirty old servants' clothes to wear into the city.

"You won't see much at night but maybe, just maybe, it will help you see what you're fighting for."

Avira hugged Fela tight and held on for longer than she should have. "Thank you."

As she wandered the streets, she realized how dark they were. The buildings were taller than the villas in Alvanii and the streets were far more cramped. It felt like she was making her way through a maze. She passed some apartments and plenty of closed down shops, figuring she must be walking through some kind of market. It makes sense that the shops would be closed but she still coudn't help but daydream about what the different merchants sold.

After a while of walking, she came to a grove lit with torches, a fountain sparkled in the middle. The fountain, rather than having statues at its center like those in Alvanii, was decorated with calligraphy and mosaic tiles in bold patterns. Avira stared at it for a long time, taking in the different shapes. It was like it depicted nothing and everything all at once. From one angle it looked like a flower garden, from another it looked like clouds and golden sunshine. The longer she looked, the more she saw.

Shaheen was just as beautiful as her father had always said, but as she watched the water sparkle in the torchlight, Avira realized that it was just another city. It was a place that people called home, just like Alvanii and Veronii. Shaheen was not a diamond glistening across a sea for her father to come and collect. It was not a pearl in an oyster that just needed harvesting. It was a home. It was a place where hundreds, maybe thousands of people, woke up in the mornings, made tea for their mothers, maybe fell in love, read books, dreamed about the world, and had their hearts broken just like her. Of course it was worth fighting for.

A commotion in a dark corner of the grove startled Avira out of her meditations. She looked up to see two pale men in familiar golden uniforms arguing with another man, this one clearly Shaheeni and not older than fourteen. A boy, really.

"What are you doing out this late at night?" One of the men growled at the boy.

"I'm on my way home," the boy squeaked, "Please let go, you're hurting my arm."

The men were Bianco soldiers. What were they doing here?

Avira ducked down behind the fountain and watched. She wanted to shout, to go up and slap the men across the face so the boy could go free, but she was too scared they'd recognize her. She hated herself for hiding like this. She was no hero, clearly.

A shrill voice echoed across the grove. It was undoubtedly a woman's voice.

"Let go of him!"

The Bianco men paused and looked up, a woman in dark robes with her hair covered in a red scarf stood at the other end. She made large strides towards the men and the boy.

"That is my son, let go of him."

"He was stealing!" One of the soldiers tried to argue. He was met with a slap across the face. A breeze blew the women's robes a bit and Avira realized that the woman was massively pregnant.

"You and I both know you have no authority here. Shaheen is still under Queen Adipe's rule. Would you like me to report you to her guards? I'm sure they'll make quick work of you." The woman scowled, her voice was almost a hiss like a cat.

The men excused themselves and disappeared into the darkness of the alley. The woman brushed the boy off. Avira could just barely hear her say, "Get out of the streets. They aren't safe this time of night. Now run along. Your mother will worry."

The boy sprinted away, disappearing into the dark. Avira let herself exhale, sure that there was no way the woman could hear her. She was thankful someone else had chased away the soldiers. The woman made her way back to the part of the grove that she appeared from. Avira didn't even realize she'd been seen until the woman stopped in her tracks.

"Who are you hiding from? The Bianco men are gone. No thanks to you, I'd add."

Stunned, Avira stood. She realized how silly she must have looked. It was so useless of her to hide in that boy's time of need.

"Close your mouth. You look like a fish." The woman gave a smirk. "Now come along, let me make you a cup of tea before I send you home too."

Avira didn't argue. She did as she was told, following the woman as close as she was able.

"My name is Layla," the woman said. "What's yours?"

"My name doesn't matter." Avira tried to play it off but she was met with a dry look from Layla that made her blood run cold. "Avi. I go by Avi."

"Nice to meet you, Avi. This is my shop. I sell spices."

The woman opened a door that Avira hadn't seen until just then and it swung inward from the alley revealing a small spice shop. It was decorated with gorgeous quilts and the room smelled of incense and pepper. Along the walls, hundreds of glass bottles of spices in all shapes and sizes were lined up. One spice caught her eye, something she'd only heard about. It was a small brown seed in the shape of a flower; star anise. A large wooden bowl sat at the center of the room.

To Avira's surprise, a pot of tea was already prepared. As though she'd read her mind, Layla said, "I was about to sit down for tea when I heard the soldiers. I couldn't sleep."

"I understand that." Layla poured Avira a small cup and they sat on the carpet at the center of the floor.

"You're not from here, I can tell."

Avira chuckled. "What tipped you off?" She didn't look even the slightest bit Shaheeni and she'd been gaping at the grove like she'd never seen it before.

"You're used to sugar in your tea. You winced when you took a sip of mine."

"That's what tipped you off, huh?"

"Among other things. Look, Avi, I'm sure you're just a cabin hand on one of the airships around here but you need to be careful. Don't wander the streets at night. Even for you, Bianco's men can be dangerous. Go back to wherever you're calling home for the night and stay there. Alright?"

Layla ran her hand along the edge of the large wooden bowl that sat on the floor between them. Her fingers were long and delicate, like the legs of a spider. Her pregnant belly bulged out, swollen and golden in the evening light. She was going to be a great mother. Avira couldn't help but listen to what she had to say.

Avira sipped her tea. It tasted fresh and cool in her mouth and ran down her throat like an icy hot river, tickling her stomach.

"This is delicious. You're right, I'm used to sweeter tea but this is really very good." Avira smiled as she took another greedy sip. "What's in it?"

Layla's smile was sly and silky like she knew every single one of Avira's secrets. Somehow, that was the most comforting thing about her.

"It's mostly mint," Layla said with a grin. "A few other spices in there too but I won't bore you with details."

"You didn't need to help me back there."

"I know that. You should have known better than to walk the streets at night. This has always been a safe city but every day it grows more dangerous. People are afraid. Have you heard the rumblings?"

Avira shook her head, trying her best to look aloof. Layla swirled her tea around in her cup ever so gently. "I hate to say it but I am afraid too. I don't want my child to grow up in a country controlled by an evil man across the sea. I want my child to know freedom. I fear she never will."

"I'm sorry," Avira croaked.

"There is nothing you can do. You're just a street rat."

Avira nodded, trying to remind herself that this woman had no idea who she was. The more discreet she could be the better. It was hard though to believe. It felt like Layla knew more than she was letting on.

"Do you have a husband?" Avira asked, trying her best to change the subject. Layla raised a single eyebrow, it made a perfect angular arch across her temple.

"I did. He is waiting for me on the other side."

"But he couldn't have died long ago." Avira gestured to Layla's swollen belly. As soon as she spoke, she regretted her lack of poise. Bringing up someone's dead husband to shift focus away from herself was low, she knew this.

Layla's dark eyes cast down onto the polished wooden bowl, she sighed deeply, letting her fingers continue to run along the rim.

"Let me show you," Layla said.

She stood slowly and shuffled to the corner of her shop where giant clear jars of spices stood in a row. She grabbed a few jars and carried them over to the center of the room, laying them out around the bowl.

First, Layla rubbed her hands together and said a quiet prayer to either Aurora or Salicia, Avira couldn't tell. Then she opened a jar of a vibrant orange spice that Avira assumed was turmeric. Layla plunged her hand into the jar of spices, pulled out a thick handful of the powder, and tossed it violently into the wooden bowl.

As soon as the spices collided with the bowl, something amazing happened. The powder whirred to life as though an ancient wind had taken it in its grasp. The golden powder began to twist and spiral until it made the shape of a cloud, it practically glowed orange. Then, out of the cloud, the shape of a skyship became as clear as day. Avira's mouth hung open in awe. It was just like Diego's bowl on The Apollo. That was so long ago now. It was before The Apollo had even left port. Avira was a different person now than she was then, but she was still equally in awe of what she was seeing.

With a wave of Layla's hand, the cloud of turmeric faded away and only the shape of the ship was visible. She plunged her fist into another jar, this one filled with what looked like black pepper. She tossed it in the bowl and, just like the turmeric, it took shape. The pepper made human forms, the outline of a crew working on the golden skyship.

"My husband was a merchant on a skyship. He traveled the world with a small crew, bringing back spices for me to sell in the shop as well as other treasures. He was excellent at his work. We met in the market one day when I was very young."

Layla tossed a pale white spice that smelled like ginger into the bowl and the golden ship scattered, now magically taking the form of the Shaheeni marketplace Avira had wandered just an hour ago. The silhouette of a girl and a boy made themselves clear, they danced in circles around one another. The detail was so perfect that Avira could even make out the shape of Layla's nose and her husband's smile in the shape.

"I've never seen anything so magical," Avira murmured.

"We were lovers in secret for many years. He dealt with some unsavory customers and always tried to protect me. One day, he flew east to the forests of Carth where he found a grove of magical trees."

Layla tossed some green spices that smelled strong and tickled Avira's nose into the bowl. A wind burst through the market scene and a forest took shape, the golden ship tied to a tree as the black pepper form of Layla's husband chopped at another tree.

"These trees had wood that was said to amplify the powers of the goddesses. If used to make a skyship it would surely be the fastest, most unsinkable ship in the world. He sent some home to me and I used it to make this bowl for grinding my spices."

Layla waved her hands and the spices separated out making veins of green and gold and dark black in a swirling pattern in the bowl.

"Grigori Bianco wanted the secret to finding the grove of trees, but my husband would not tell him."

Layla added a mere pinch of something a deep burgundy color, paprika perhaps, and the whole bowl turned red like blood.

"We had married in secret, conceived a child together. We had dreams of a life that would never be, all because of Grigori Bianco and his greed."

As Layla waved her hands, the spices began to float again, each spice returned to its respective jar. It was as though Layla had the hands of a sorceress. Avira wasn't convinced that the wooden bowl was the only magical thing in this room.

"Bianco killed your husband." Avira hung her head. How many other husbands, wives, sons, and daughters had her father taken before their time?

"For months I dreamed of taking a knife and stabbing it through Grigori Bianco's heart so he could feel what it is like to have your love pulled from your chest like that. But after a while, I made peace. I do not want my daughter to be raised by an angry, bitter, violent mother. I must trust that, in time, the goddesses will bring vengeance down upon Grigori for me."

Avira stood up suddenly, blood rushed to her head and she felt faint. "I have to go."

"So soon? It's still dark out. The streets aren't safe."

The morning light was beginning to brighten up the city, Avira knew it would be dawn before she made it back to the palace, even if she hurried. "Thank you for your kindness, Layla. I have nothing to give you to repay you."

Layla shook her head, clicking her tongue like Adipe always did. "Before you go, take this." She plunged her hand into a smaller, deep red jar of spices. She sprinkled the contents of her fist onto a small piece of parchment paper and folded it tightly.

"It's harissa pepper. It will temporarily blind anyone who gets it in their eyes. If anyone bothers you on your way home, throw it in their face."

Avira placed the package in her pocket and gave a grateful nod. When she reached the door, Layla called out to her one more time.

"Make him pay for it, Miss Bianco."

Avira stopped in her tracks. Layla had known who she was

all along, and she'd still shown her kindness. Avira knew she should turn back and acknowledge the words, but she couldn't bring herself to. It was too much for her. She felt ashamed, more ashamed of her last name than ever before.

She did not turn back. Instead, she kept walking, back into the streets of Shaheen, back towards the palace, back towards her mission. *I will make him pay, Layla,* she thought to herself as the sun began to rise over the palace. *I promise I will.*

Chapter Thirty

At some point between returning to his room and the first whisper of dawn, Matteo fell asleep. It was a restless, dreamless sleep and, when he woke up, his head hurt from tension. He didn't know when he'd next get a restful night of sleep. All he knew was that the last night had not been it.

It had taken a little wandering for him to find the way to the cliffs. He'd assumed incorrectly that, if he found the throne room, the way to the cliffs where airships landed to see the queen would be clear. Instead, he wound up walking in a gigantic circle and finding himself in the throne room again. A guard who was stationed near one of the thrones snickered at him.

He shrugged. What did he have to lose at this point? It's not like he was ever going to truly gain the respect of the Shaheeni guards or soldiers when one night before he had been their prisoner.

"I need help finding the cliffs." The woman pursed her lips, clearly stifling another giggle. She pointed vaguely and he, eventually, realized what she meant. There was a gilded gateway at the far end of the garden with a window at its center revealing the sea. Matteo hurried to the cliffs, worried Rihane would reprimand him for his tardiness.

She was standing with her hands on her hips, two gliders resting on either side of her, staring at the sunrise.

"I'm sorry I was late. I got lost." He was out of breath from the rush and the sprint. He rested his hands on his knees trying to catch up with himself.

Rihane snorted with laughter, turning and casting her dark eyes onto him. "You're a bit useless, Matteo De Luca."

"I know." The words tumbled out between gasps. Perhaps it was not wise to admit to his own uselessness in front of one of the Shaheeni Guard's most competent soldiers, but he was too tired to try and defend himself. He was, after all, acting rather useless these days.

"I hear you were quite the powerful detective back home in Veronii. The guards spent all night telling stories about you. You've rescued infants, destroyed crime rings, some even say you've saved royal families from ruin. But here you are, useless in Shaheen. It's ironic."

Matteo scrunched his nose, frustrated. "Are you going to teach me how to fly that thing or are you just going to stand here and make fun of me."

Rihane handed him the glider. It was a simple enough design, a board with some steam technology strapped to the bottom to make it fly and a windsail attached to a thick mast. It was a little taller than him but surprisingly light. Rihane picked up her glider and rubbed her sleeve along a scuff in the polished metal.

"What are these things made out of anyway?" Matteo asked, lifting it up to test just how light it was. It weighed less than a book, less than a jug of water. It was shocking.

"Aluminum."

Matteo raised an eyebrow. "I've never heard of it."

"It's a special metal, it looks like silver but bends like paper. The Shaheeni military invented it. Which reminds me -" Rihane snatched the glider out of Matteo's hands. "If you leak any of this technology to your friends on The Apollo, I will personally cut your throat, Queen Adipe's orders."

Somehow Matteo doubted that Adipe had made any such order, but he didn't want to press his luck. He withheld his laughter at the idea of anyone on board The Apollo being his friend. The only person he cared for there was Avira and she'd practically renounced any contact with him at this point, at least it felt that way. Matteo gazed at the waves crashing on the rocky beach below. Funny, he thought, that the sea looked so peaceful from up in the sky and so brutal upon closer inspection. There was a metaphor there, but he was not smart enough to think of it.

Rihane gave him a punch on the arm. It was not a soft, playful punch like the one Matteo's friends had given him in the schoolyard. His shoulder throbbed a bit and he impulsively stepped back. "Are we going to stand here thinking about your girlfriend all morning or are you going to learn to fly this thing?"

"She's not my girlfriend."

"That wasn't my point." Rihane used her heel to kick a little lever on the bottom of her glider and it whirred to life.

"It's a steam engine," she explained. "You don't need it once you catch the wind, it just helps to get you going at first. Watch!"

Rihane took a few steps back and before Matteo knew what was happening, she began running, glider in hand, towards the cliff. She took four giant, graceful strides and then leaped feet first into the open air. At first, she plummeted down towards the water, but within seconds the sail of her glider had caught the wind and she was flying upwards, her back parallel with the waves and one arm dangling off the mast, gesturing at Matteo to follow her lead.

"I can't do that! I'm not ready!"

"You don't have to jump," Rihane shouted over the wind, she looked like an eagle swooping through the sky. "It's just more fun if you do."

"It doesn't look fun!" Matteo shouted, realizing how child-like he looked. Rihane was quite literally flying in circles around him.

"Sorry. I can't hear you over how much fun I'm having."

This girl was really starting to get on Matteo's nerves. He decided that was it. If he fell to his death, he wouldn't be the one to blame. He kicked the lever starting the tiny steam engine on the bottom of his glider as hard as he could and backed up as far as he had space to. Then, holding on tight to the mast of the glider, he started running. The wind whipped at his face. As he reached the edge of the cliff, his head got the better of him. What was he doing? He couldn't just hurl himself off a cliff and expect that to work. But it was too late, his body and the glider were moving too fast, and the momentum was too strong.

Tripping over his feet, Matteo hurdled off the cliff. He

didn't have a chance to scream or even breathe before he was flying through the air and falling toward the rock below. The stones looked even sharper from this angle. He wanted to close his eyes and wait for the sting of impact but he heard, from out of his field of vision, a voice calling out.

"Matteo! Straighten the mast!"

He did as the mystery voice told him, pulling the glider close to him and propping the sail upright so it could catch the wind. Within seconds, he was traveling up instead of down. He let out a surprised laugh.

"I'm doing it." The glider sailed up and up and up until the cliff he'd just been standing on looked small. "I'm doing it!" he shouted, knowing it was unlikely anyone could hear him over the whipping wind. He could see Rihane soaring about fifty yards above him, a massive smile on her face. She swooped in and out between rays of the sun. Matteo had trouble controlling the glider at first, he could only really go wherever the wind was taking him. But after some time in the air, he realized it was relatively easy to lean his body weight in one direction or another and fly that way. Every once in a while he hit a pocket where there was no wind, and his glider plummeted a few feet leaving his insides twisted in a knot. But he soon learned that there was always another stream of wind ready to take him in a new direction. He just had to be trusting enough to find it.

After two hours or so of flying, Rihane waved towards the cliff. "Are you ready to learn how to land?"

He had been so thrilled at the idea of flying that he hadn't even considered he would have to land this thing at some point. He shook his head vigorously.

"Let me put it this way, you're either going to land or you're going to crash, and I assume you prefer the former." Rihane had a way of arching her eyebrow that drove Matteo crazy. "Besides," she continued, "It's late in the morning already and I have to meet the rest of the guard in preparation for tonight."

Rihane caught a gust of wind and piloted her glider down and around Matteo, eclipsing him. Meanwhile, he was still struggling to stay in a straight line.

"Now the most important part of landing is to land on your feet. Smashing the glider into the ground isn't going to help you. You'll just destroy it."

Only when he whipped his glider around did Matteo fully grasp how high and how far from the cliffs he had flown. The bottoms of his feet began to tingle, and his hands began to sweat.

"I can't!" A memory hit him of when he was a child and he'd climbed up to the top of a tree in his adoptive family's orchard. One of his older brothers had tried to coax him down from the branches but he was too stubborn to climb on.

"The ground is a lot farther from your eyes than it is from your feet, Matteo!" His brother had tried to reason with him but eventually, he'd had to climb up and carry him down himself. That was a decade and a half ago now, he had to land the glider. He could feel his cheeks burning, he was embarrassed at how afraid he was.

"Just watch me do it. It will be alright."

Rihane, as gracefully as a bird, tilted the nose of her glider down and flew at the cliff. When she was close enough to touch the ground, she pulled the glider out from under her feet and landed softly in the dirt, both her body and her glider still upright. She had all the poise of a cat jumping down from a sunny windowsill after a nap. Matteo knew he was about to show just as much grace as an albatross. He sucked in a breath, deciding it would be a miracle if he could pilot a glider half this well with Avira on board, and pointed the nose down. He didn't pray often, but he prayed to Aurora to soften his landing.

It happened so quickly, before he knew it his feet were back on land. He didn't quite catch his balance upon landing. He had to let go of the glider and stumble forward a few steps, catching himself with his hands in the dirt and tearing the knees of his pants.

Rihane was jumping up and down. When he turned to check for her approval, she was just about exploding with joy.

"You did it. I can't believe you did it."

"Well, I only had one other option."

Rihane set her glider down and wrapped him in a tight hug. "I thought for sure you were going to kill yourself on accident, really." Matteo bit his tongue, not wanting to ask Rihane why she would bother trying to teach him how to use a glider if she thought he was going to die trying. Maybe this was all part of some big plot to get him killed and take his job of delivering Avira to Gavriel. It was doubtful though. From the look on her face, he could tell Rihane was genuinely thrilled to have helped.

"Now you have to remember, you'll be taking off from a sea ship, not a cliff, tonight. It will be harder to pilot with Avira on board but I think you'll figure it out. You're a regular prodigy."

"I have a great teacher." Rihane gave him a punch on the arm, he had a feeling this was her preferred method of taking a compliment. He wiped his hands on his shirt, trying to get the sweat to start pouring out of them. His heart was still pounding from the adrenaline, the excitement of it all was almost too much for him.

Rihane looked up from Matteo and her smile fell. "I should go," she said softly. Matteo whipped his head around to see Avira. She was rocking back and forth on her heels as though she'd been standing there for a little too long.

Rihane grabbed her glider and took long strides toward the palace walls. She looked almost sad, nose turned towards the ground. Matteo felt a pull in his stomach. Was Rihane upset that Avira had shown up? That didn't make any sense.

"Rihane!" Matteo yelled after her. She stopped and gave him a small smile. "Thank you," was all Matteo could muster.

She nodded and disappeared behind the palace wall.

"Were you flying that thing?" Avira asked gently.

"Barely." Matteo twisted his foot in the dirt. He didn't feel quite as excited about any of his newfound flying skills, not with Avira giving him such a strange look.

"Will you show me?"

Avira looked so curious that Matteo couldn't help but say yes, after all, he was still holding the glider.

"Do you want to go for a ride?" He said the words before he could really think through what they meant. He'd never flown with a second person on board the glider before, it probably wasn't a good idea. He couldn't even tell where this newfound confidence was coming from. Once again, he blamed adrenaline and lack of sleep. Both were powerful enough to drive a man mad, after all.

Avira gave her little half grin, the same one that always drove Matteo crazy. Perhaps, somehow, she'd forgiven him a little bit since last night in the garden. Avria reached out her hand and Matteo took it, holding tight for he didn't know when he'd next get the chance to.

"We'll need to get a running start," Matteo said, flicking the switch on the side of his glider with his foot as though he was an expert. He was decidedly not an expert yet but he didn't want Avira to know that. "We're going to jump, hold on to the sail, after a moment the wind will take us with it, okay?"

Avira gave a curt nod.

"On three okay?" Matteo and Avira backed up farther than he knew they needed to. He worried for just a moment about how they were going to land but tried to push that worry down. This might be his last moment with Avira ever. He wanted it to be special, magical even.

"One-- two--- three!"

They took off running, leaping off the cliff with twice as much speed behind them as Matteo had possessed when he was making the jump alone. At first, they plummeted twice as fast, but the wind caught them quickly and with a whoosh, they flew straight up.

Matteo was suddenly aware of Avira's scream. It was not a scream of terror, however, a scream of joy. She was laughing, cackling like a witch from a storybook.

"We're flying," she said with a laugh so loud and strong Matteo barely recognized her. He'd never seen Avira so filled to the brim with joy.

"I can't believe we're actually flying. How do these things work?" Avira asked. Matteo shrugged. He didn't honestly understand the physics of it, and he assumed it was stupid to pretend to.

Matteo shifted his weight, pressing his body into Avira to get the best angle, and the glider tipped sideways resulting in a giddy squeal from the girl. He pointed down at the white caps of the waves and Avira let out a gasp. "It's so beautiful up here."

Matteo looked at her, the way her cheeks stretched out as she smiled, her freckles practically glowing along with the rest of her with joy, the way her short hair flipped in the wind and her dark ebony eyes glittered. He felt that feeling within him again, the uncontrollable love he'd felt that night in the crow's nest.

He pressed his body closer to hers and she curved her body to make space for them. It was as though they were puzzle pieces that fit perfectly together. Avira turned her head and smiled at him, trying to say thank you. The wind was too strong for him to say anything back, so he let go of the glider with one hand and touched it to her heart.

Then an idea struck him. He pushed her closer to the sail and grabbed it tight with both hands. "Hey," he said into her ear. He'd meant to whisper it, but he had to speak loudly to make it over the wind. "Let go."

Avira raised an eyebrow skeptically, only letting go with one hand.

"It's okay. I'll hold on to you."

She did as she was told and, after a moment of hesitation, stretched her arms out like wings, running them through the wind. She began to laugh again, even heartier this time which Matteo didn't know was possible.

"Matteo, this is the most magical thing I've ever experienced."

Just as they spoke, the glider hit a pocket of air and fell at least fifty feet down toward the water. Avira squealed again, seemingly not worried at all about their deaths. She trusted the wind. She trusted Aurora. Matteo smiled to himself, aware that she couldn't see his face. He allowed himself to rest his head against her shoulder, taking in the smell of her hair and the sea. He wanted to live in this moment forever, such a rare moment of pure joy between them. Why couldn't this be their forever?

As the new jet stream, they'd found took them higher and higher, Matteo realized they were headed straight toward a cloud. Matteo instinctively closed his eyes though he wasn't quite sure why.

Flying through the cloud, the glider bounded around a little and Avira grabbed back onto the glider tighter than ever. As they burst through the cloud up into the blue sky above, for a moment the sun glistened in a way that was more radiant than Matteo had ever seen. It took his breath away. Then he heard Avira let out a sound he hadn't heard yet, it was one of pain, one of fear.

"Matteo, look," she said. He turned to where she was pointing and that's when he saw it. There were at least two dozen massive golden airships flying in formation straight toward Shaheen. "It's my father's army."

Even over the wind Matteo could hear the dejection and terror in her voice. "He came early." She pointed at a golden ship flying right in the center of the fleet. "That one is Gavriel's."

Something else caught Matteo's eye, a golden ship that made even Gavriel's ship look dull. It was painted with hundreds of suns and flying in formation with the rest of them.

"The Apollo," Matteo said to nobody but himself. When Avira realized why he said it, she deflated, resting her body against the sail as though her spine was no longer strong enough to take it.

"No. It can't be." Avira's voice cracked as she spoke. "Artemis would never. Adipe said he was her ally. Why would he betray her? She trusted him."

Matteo looked at Avira and could see tears streaming down her face. He didn't have words to say to her. He knew as well as she did what Artemis had promised but he was a pirate at his heart, would a lie really be so far-fetched?

"Come on," he said. "We should tell Adipe they're here."

Matteo tilted the glider down and they began their descent toward the cliffs. The wind and the waves and the air rushing past them suddenly felt far heavier, far quieter.

"It will be okay, Avira. We have a plan. Remember the plan."

Avira shook her head. They made the landing clumsily and quietly, nearly destroying the glider in the process. Avira didn't even blink. As soon as her feet were back on land she was walking toward the palace

"Avira, wait. Please wait for me."

She shook her head. "The time for waiting around is gone, Matteo. We have a job to do." Turning on her heels, Matteo could tell from the slouch in her back and the furrow in her brow that there was no reason with her. He stood alone on the cliffs for just a little longer, watching the clouds part to reveal the Bianco army in all its glory.

CHAPTER THIRTY-ONE

"Artemis betrayed us," Avira shouted as she practically broke down the door to the throne room with her foot. She stormed into the room, stopping only to reorient herself. Adipe was sitting around a small table studying a map. She was sipping a glass of lemonade. She clicked her tongue at the girl.

"What did I tell you about trust?"

"The Apollo is flying with the rest of my father's fleet. I just saw it with my own eyes."

"So, they're here." Adipe all but ignored Avira. She gave a wave of her hand and a few soldiers appeared out of what felt like nowhere. She whispered something in Shaheeni to one of the soldiers and then turned her attention back to Avira. "I don't pretend to understand Artemis or his plans. I just know that I trust him."

"Your blind trust will get you and the rest of your kingdom

killed," Avira spoke. Adipe shook her head. Her calm aura infuriated Avira.

"You poor girl," Adipe said. "You've been taught that trust is a bad thing. Trust is the most beautiful thing we have. Trust is the seed of hope and hope is what keeps human beings alive through the darkest of nights."

"I disagree," Avira said, defeated. She wanted to sink onto her knees and cry, but she didn't Fela took her by the arm and escorted her to her rooms. As she was leaving, she saw Matteo make his way into the throne room. He hung his head low.

When they got to her room, Avira didn't know what to say. Her blue dress hung on a rack in the corner.

Fela and Avira sat in front of the tall mirror in the corner of her bedroom. Neither girl knew quite what to say. Fela was working hard on Avira's short hair. She'd tousled it up and begun to twist little sections up and around the silver crown to keep it in place. The woman in the mirror was feeling less and less familiar to Avira. She didn't feel like an Alvanian lady. She barely felt like a lady at all. She just felt like Avi.

"I'm happy," she said, lying. Fela bit her lip, clearly holding back her true thoughts. "I really am happy. I'm happy that, if I have to spend the rest of my life as a quiet wife locked in her rooms, I at least got an adventure out of it. I got to see some of the world. I'm lucky." The shakiness in her voice betrayed her true feelings.

Fela shook her head. "Adipe's plan will work. We'll come to save you. She's true to her word. You have to trust that." She had finished on Avira's hair and was now working on lacing up the back of her dress. The pale blue material looked like the sky on a summer day. Avira tried to focus on blue skies and not her doubts about Adipe's plans.

"Tell me about your family, Fela."

"There's not much to tell if I'm honest," Fela said, shrugging. "I have a husband and a daughter. We live in the city. I get to go home and see them once every week for two nights."

Avira whipped around in her seat, "You have a child?"

"I was married by the time I was your age. We struggled to conceive but Aurora blessed us with a baby not too long ago." "Why do you still work for Adipe then?"

"Real people have to work, Avira." Fela gave her arm a gentle pinch and Avira blushed bright red all over. Where she'd come from, women didn't have many responsibilities. Once they gave birth they were expected to focus all attention on keeping up a home. Shaheen was different. Avira liked the differences, though she felt like a flaming idiot every time she discovered one.

"I believe in the power of a woman and her family. All I've ever dreamed about was being a wife and a mother. I get to live out my dreams every day. Working for Queen Adipe is an excellent bonus. She inspires me."

"Thank you for telling me this, Fela."

Fela smiled warmly. She motioned for Avira to get up out of her chair and do a spin. She handed the girl a garter that held in it Mirjana's knife and the small pouch of harissa pepper Layla had given her. Avira slid the garter up her thigh and under her dress. She tried hard to recognize the woman in the mirror, but she knew she likely never would. She was not like Fela. She did not dream of things like marriage and babies.

Men got to live out their lives in a thousand different ways. They could be generals or merchants or fathers or sky captains or bums on a street corner. Avira wished that she could have the same opportunity. Instead, she was a bargaining chip in the fight to prevent her father's war. Being a tool in Adipe's belt was the most important thing she'd ever done. She was proud of herself, sure, but sad that she might never find the chance to do more.

As though she'd read her mind, Fela asked, "What will you do once you're free of your marriage to Gavriel?"

Avira shrugged. "I want to be a cartographer, I think. I'd like to sail the world and make maps to sell. I love maps more than anything. I hope that, whatever happens, I still get to think about them every single day."

Fela pressed her forehead into Avira's, a Shaheeni sign of respect and love. "I will pray to Aurora for you, sweet Avira."

Avira basked in the sweet scent of Fela's perfume. She'd never smelled anything like it, orange and jasmine and frankincense all rolled up into one. She was beginning to feel like prayer was futile. Aurora had abandoned her, Matteo, and the Shaheeni people. She was supposed to be the protector of the skies. Where was she when her people needed her most? She'd vanished like seafoam on a sunny day and with her had gone every last bit of hope and trust Avira had left.

"Fela wait," Avira said just as they started down the hallway towards the throne room, "Will you do me a favor?"
 Avira hiked up the tumbling silk of her gown and ran back to her room. In the corner, there sat a small pile of jewels and baubles. At the bottom of the pile, sat the golden falcon pendant, her only remaining tie to the life she'd left behind in Alvanii.

She held the pendant up to the light and looked at the falcon's eyes shimmer. It was her mother's, she'd admired it since childhood. It was also worth a fortune.

"Fela, there is a woman in town, a spice merchant. She runs a little shop near the fountain. When I'm gone, will you bring this to her? Tell her to sell it. It's worth enough to support her and her child for a while."

Fela took the necklace in her palm and nodded solemnly. Avira was thankful that the maid didn't ask for any more explanation of why the necklace needed to go to Layla. If Aurora was not going to protect her people, then Avira would do everything she could to get the job done herself.

Chapter Thirty-Two

Adipe sat placidly on her throne, sipping a glass of lemonade. The clouds had parted to reveal the full glory of Grigori Bianco's fleet. It was formidable. Matteo sat on a small stool Adipe had requested for him next to the throne. He twiddled his thumbs, not sure what to say to the queen.

"Would you like some lemonade?" the queen asked, holding out a glass for him. Matteo shook his head. Lemonade made him think of Avira. He couldn't stomach that, not right now.

"I thought you were more of a tea drinker," Matteo said.

"I am." Adipe smirked. "But I wanted to have a bit of poetic justice. Alvanii is the number one exporter of citrus, and today I will be defeating Alvanii's greatest merchant baron without firing a single cannon. It's satisfying, don't you agree?"

Matteo chuckled. Adipe was filled with surprises.

"Do you think I'm crazy, Matteo?" Adipe asked out of the blue. She stirred her lemonade nervously with a crystal stir stick. Matteo watched the lemons and sugar floating around and around like a little cyclone.

"Why would you ask me that? Of course, I don't."

Adipe took a hearty sip of lemonade. "The girl thinks I'm crazy. She thinks I am out of my mind to trust Artemis, to believe Aurora will protect us. She thinks she knows something I don't."

Matteo rocked back and forth on the legs of the stool. He didn't particularly want to be in the middle of this conversation. "I don't think you're crazy," he repeated.

"Even after I told you that I believe we are family? You still believe that I am in my right mind? Fascinating."

"I'll admit, I don't know how to process all the things you told me yesterday. I know nothing of the woman you claim is my mother. I know nothing but Veronii and even there I never fit in. It doesn't matter if I'm part of the royal family. I still don't fit."

Adipe rested her hand on his knee, "I sense that your adopted family caused you great pain as a child. I promise you, as long as I am alive, I will never let anyone else treat you that way."

Matteo had purposefully shared very little about his childhood or his relationship with his adopted family. He wondered how Adipe came to such a conclusion. Perhaps she could read minds.

"I had a brother, Julio, back in Veronii. He is high up in the church."

Adipe shook her head. "The priesthood is overrated. I've been to Veronii on diplomatic trips before, I always found their interpretation of the goddesses quite constricting. It's like they forget that the goddesses are, in fact, women."

Matteo took this in. He was uncomfortable. He didn't know what to say to Adipe. She was not a stranger but simultaneously not a friend. He'd been willing to abandon her not all too many hours ago. Now she was speaking to him like he was a trusted advisor. His stomach churned with discomfort.

"If I gave you a bag packed with everything you needed to start a new life, would you take it? Would you go right now, go far away, to a place where Grigori Bianco could not touch you?"

Avira's voice echoed in his mind. *There is nowhere Grigori Bianco could not touch me,* he thought grimly, chewing on his lip a little too hard. He could taste the blood in his mouth before he even realized the pain.

"No. I would stay."

"For the girl." Adipe wasn't asking.

"Yes, I'd stay for the girl."

Adipe gripped his shoulder tightly and gave him a firm shake, clicking her tongue. "I remember the days when I loved your mother the same way you love the Bianco girl. I would have gone anywhere in the world for her, but I didn't. I wasn't brave enough to. Be brave Matteo."

The sun was beginning to set. Matteo didn't have a chance to respond. He and Adipe stared into each other's eyes. Before they could break eye contact, a commotion came from down the hall. Avira was ready for her departure. Fela held the train of her dress and escorted her into the throne room.

Adipe grinned from ear to ear when she saw Avira's dress. Fela had done some sort of makeup that Matteo couldn't place. It made Avira's eyes pop. He was less happy to see that they'd decided to smear a pink powder over her cheeks, hiding her freckles.

"A blushing bride," Adipe cooed.

Matteo noticed that Avira's eyes were pink like her cheeks. She'd been crying. He hated to see her cry. "Let's go over the plan one more time," Avira said emotionlessly.

Matteo gestured to Adipe's map which was still splayed out across the table. "You and I ride the boat out until we're directly below Gavriel's skyship. That should be about here." He pointed to an X on the map. "Then we take a glider from the ship and land on its Eastern deck, hopefully throwing Gavriel off the scent of the Shaheeni boats just below him."

Adipe continued for Matteo, "You hand over Avira. Gavriel signs the treaty. Once off the ship, Matteo sends off a flair that tells us to move back the blockade. The whole process should be relatively fast as long as everything goes to plan."

"And a month later, you send two guards to save me in the night from Gavriel," Avira finished.

"Foolproof," Matteo said. In reality, it was anything but. He could see ten and a half different ways it could go wrong, and almost all of them resulted in Avira being hurt. But, with a whole country relying on them, what could they do to stop it now? Avira was the most self-assured human he'd ever known. She wanted to do this, and there was no way to keep her from that. Still, Matteo's greatest fear was that the plan would work and Gavriel would open fire on the unprepared Shaheeni boats. Adipe had been stubborn in her decision to not prepare any military forces.

The sky was beginning to streak with gold and amber. Adipe, Matteo, and Avira left the throne room and took a massive staircase from the gardens down to the base of the cliffs, where a ship was waiting for them. "I will leave you here,"

Adipe said, hugging each of them.

Avira crossed onto the ship before Matteo. She had to hold her skirts high to be sure she didn't trip. "Matteo." Adipe grabbed his hand and pulled him into her. "You will always have a home in Shaheen. Know that."

He hugged her back. She smelled like jasmine, sandalwood, and salt. She smiled like a mother. He looked into her eyes, nodded quickly, and crossed onto the ship. It was only a few moments before they were clipping across the sea. When the boat first started moving, Matteo nearly fell over. He'd never been on a water ship before. It was different from being in the sky. Everything felt heavier, slower.

Looking up, he realized Avira must be having the same problem. She was looking a little green. He walked to her, and she raised her eyes from the sea to meet his.

"Avira-" he started.

She held a finger to his lips and shushed him. Then she grabbed his hand and held it tight until a shadow crossed above them that was far too dark to be a cloud. Avira looked up and scowled. The skyship above them was undoubtedly Gavriel's. It was decorated with the unmistakable falcon crest of the Biancos.

"Does Gavriel's ship have a name?" Matteo asked, trying

hard to distract Avira.

"Golden Boy," she responded, wrinkling her nose.

Matteo forced himself to laugh. "What a ridiculous name for a ship," he said, pushing his laugh out even harder. Eventually, Avira gave in. She laughed too. Laughed at the name of Gavriel's ship. Laughed at the water below them. Laughed at the absurdity of it all. For a minute or two, they just let themselves laugh.

"Matteo," Avira said suddenly. "Where would we be now if we'd left together last night?"

Matteo had to think for a moment, he wasn't quite sure. "Somewhere in the middle of the desert, I suppose."

"Riding camels?"

"Probably." Matteo couldn't think about his request for Avira to run away with him without cringing. He'd been a fool to ask that of her. He knew Avira, she was steadfast. When she made a choice there was no stopping her. He'd made a fool of himself.

Avira pressed her eyes closed, sighing sweetly to herself.

"What are you doing," Matteo asked, taking her hand.

"I'm imagining it: you and me in the desert on camels, the hot sand blowing on my face, the sweat rolling down my brow. I'm just imagining it. I wish it were real."

Matteo had nothing left to say. Thinking any further on the hypotheticals that would never be was only hurting him. He gripped her hand tight and walked her to the glider. They stood staring at it in silence for a long, slow moment. Matteo could only hear the constant *thump, thump* of his heart. The time had come. They had no choice but to take off.

CHAPTER THIRTY-THREE

Avira didn't want to go.

With the shadow of Golden Boy looming above her, every bit of her body felt frozen in place. She wanted to run. She wasn't a good swimmer, and the gown would surely weigh her down, but maybe she could jump from the boat and float.

There was this feeling in the bottom of her stomach that she couldn't ignore. She tried to close her eyes and imagine the plan working. She tried to imagine Gavriel taking her hand and signing the treaty, waving Matteo away. She tried to imagine the gigantic wedding in Alvanii that her mother was most certainly already planning.

None of it felt real. It didn't even feel possible.

"Are you ready?" Matteo asked. She couldn't respond. The panic began to rise higher and higher in her throat. She pulled him close, so their faces were barely an inch apart. She could feel her body shaking.

"Matteo, let's not do this."

"What?" he whispered.

Her eyes were growing hot. She tried to fight back the tears, but it took too much energy. They began to fall. Matteo tried mopping them up with his sleeve.

"I can't do it. I can't marry him. I can't go back. I'm not meant for Alvanii. I'll die there."

A tall woman in a dark veil walked to them. "Are you two ready?"

Avira shook her head furiously.

"We're running out of time," the woman pressed.

"This is all going to go wrong. I can feel it. I thought it would work. I'm an idiot." Avira began to sob. "Oh, I'm such an idiot."

Matteo pulled her close. She dissolved into him, the sleeves of her gown pooling around his waist.

"Avira, look at me." He lifted her chin, so her eyes met his. "It is not stupid to believe in the best in people. That's not stupidity. That's hope."

He pulled her in tight. He forced himself to count to ten or he could hang onto her forever.

Then, in silence, they walked to the glider. They were in the sky almost instantly, it felt too easy. Matteo's flying skills weren't perfect, but Avira felt confident in his ability to at least land them on board Golden Boy. Besides, what's the worst that could happen? He sends them flying into the sea and to their deaths? At least then she wouldn't have to go with Gavriel.

The wind stung her face. She'd hoped she could say something to Matteo before they landed, but it was far too loud for anything to be heard. Instead, she turned her face to look at his. He was focusing everything he had on piloting the glider. She tried to keep her message simple. She smiled at him. He smiled back. She gave the nod. He nodded back. And then she let go of the glider with one of her hands and touched her hand to her heart. She stretched her arm out and touched her hand to Matteo's heart.

She couldn't tell if he understood, but turbulence forced her to turn back around and cling to the glider even tighter.

Avira felt the familiar feeling of being on a skyship settle into her stomach as the glider landed. She hadn't realized until then how much The Apollo had felt like a home. Her very own floating villa.

Matteo stepped off of the glider first. He offered Avira his hand, and she picked up her skirts as she stepped down onto the deck. Only then did she look up and realize they had company -- lots of company.

At least fifty of Grigori Bianco's men had encircled them, swords at the ready. They all wore the standard golden doublet trousers set that looked so silly to Avira now, especially compared to the more practical clothes men on board The Apollo had worn.

At the center of the men stood Gavriel. He was taller than Matteo by a significant amount. Avira admitted to herself that he was handsome. He had sharp features and bulky shoulders. But she knew what was underneath all of the preening. Gavriel would do whatever it took to get what he wanted from life. That's why her father liked him so much.

Gavriel stepped forward, a fake smile plastered across his broad face. He extended a hand to Avira, and she dutifully took it. He pressed his lips to her fingers.

"My jewel. You've returned to me."

Avira tried her best to sound truthful as she spoke, "Please, Gavriel, do what they ask so we can go home and be married." She'd never fancied herself much of an actor.

"Who is this boy? A friend of yours?" Gavriel, still holding Avira's hand with one of his, made a grand gesture to Matteo.

"He's Shaheeni nobility. He's come to make sure you sign the treaty."

Gavriel shook his head. "What a shame."

And before Avira even had a chance to note the sarcasm on Gavriel's voice, he'd snapped his fingers and two of his men were holding Matteo up by his collar. The men held Matteo out over the open ocean but, unlike Malvolio, Avira knew that Gavriel would not hesitate before giving the order to drop the boy to his death.

She heard herself screaming before she realized what was happening. It was like, somewhere miles away, she could hear a young lady crying and begging for Gavriel to stop. It took a moment for her to understand that the voice was her own.

"You should know better than to lie to me, Avira," Gavriel whispered in her ear. "Tell me again, who is the Shaheeni boy?"

"Matteo De Luca," she sobbed. "Please, please, Gavriel, don't kill him."

Gavriel looked at her, his cat-like eyes locked on hers. He wiped her tears with one hand, but the hand still holding hers was twisting her arm backward. She wasn't strong enough to keep him from overpowering her.

"I'll let you choose, Avira. You can save the boy, or I can sign the treaty. Your call."

Avira snapped her head up to Matteo.

"Choose quickly, Avira," Matteo teased. "One...."

Avira thought about the people of Shaheen. They weren't

ready for an attack from Gavriel. It would be a bloodbath. She thought about Mirjana and how she'd begged her mother to prepare for war.

"Two..."

And then Avira's mind jumped from Shaheen to the night in the crows' nest with Matteo. When he'd climbed all that way to bring her tea. She thought of his eyes and the future she'd ever so briefly let herself imagine with him, a future where they could dissolve into the sky together.

"I'm getting impatient, Avira."

She opened her mouth to speak but didn't know what to say. She couldn't find the breath even to murmur a word. Gavriel blinked at her, feigning sadness. She turned away, refusing to look at him. Still dangling over the side of the ship, Matteo placed his hand on his heart and gave her a nod.

"Neither, then."

And before she could process another thought, Gavriel snapped his fingers, and his men let go of Matteo. She watched him disappear below the deck. It all happened so fast. She heard someone screaming in the distance, a young woman. It took a long time to realize she was hearing herself.

"No. No! What have you done?" she choked between sobs.

"Men, prepare for battle."

"What? What do you mean? What about the treaty?"

"This is what happens when silly little girls can't make up their minds, Avira."

Gavriel was pulling her by her arm now. She couldn't walk, couldn't breathe, couldn't think. He dragged her almost to his cabin before stopping, crouching down, and looking right into her soul.

"I'm so sorry about our betrothal being cut short, my dear."

"What do you mean? Are we not engaged?"

Gavriel shook his head. "Quite the opposite. With your propensity for running away, I convinced your father that I needed to marry you as soon as I found you. How do you feel about marriage at sea?"

Avira couldn't speak. She could only sob. Her body shook violently, like her soul was trying to pry its way out.

"Now go get out of that hideous dress." Gavriel shoved her into his cabin. "I have a wedding gown waiting for you."

In a different scenario, Avira might have realized that Gavriel was bruising her arm. His grip on her was so tight she could feel her heart beating where his fingers met her skin. He threw her down to the ground, where she landed in a heap. Her dress bubbled up around her, and she could no longer tell where her limbs stopped and the gown began. She didn't care much either, the tears were still streaming. Her head throbbed.

"Oh, shut up, would you?" Gavriel said, taking a swig of liquor from a dark brown bottle on his writing desk. "You're so ugly when you cry."

Avira wiped her tears. Outside the cabin, she could hear the men calling back and forth to one another as they prepared for battle.

"Avira," Gavriel chirped, "I can't understand what you're so sad about. This is the new order. This is the way the world works. Kingdoms fall. New leaders rise. Your father will rule Shaheen well. You'll be a princess!"

"Shaheen already has a princess," Avira spat. It makes so much sense now. There was never going to be a treaty. Her father didn't care about trade *through* Shaheen, he wanted to rule Shaheen himself.

Avira had more to say, but she didn't have a chance to say it. Gavriel had kicked her in the stomach so hard she couldn't speak anymore. Every thought that swirled around in her skull hurt. Matteo. Adipe. Mirjana. They were all as good as dead, and she couldn't do anything to stop it.

Gavriel took another swig of the liquor. He waved his arm at a wedding gown standing in the corner. "It's pretty, no?"

It wasn't pretty. Avira wasn't going to pretend it was.

"Avira, when we were children together, I thought you cared for me. Can you imagine how foolish I feel now, seeing you grieving this pathetic Veronan detective? He's gone, Avira. Dead. He died instantly when his body collided with the sea. You will need to accept that. I can't have you sobbing like this through our wedding night."

She moaned, the pain inside her rising up out of her body like a gust of wind.

"I mean, what could he possibly have offered you. Not money. Not notoriety. I did us both a favor." Gavriel crouched down and pulled Avira's face towards him, "Your father thinks you love me. By the time we get back to Alvanii, I expect that to be true. Do you understand?"

Avira started laughing a wet, sickly giggle.

"What?"

"You sure think my father is special, don't you?"

"I'm his second in command, you know that."

"Right. But if you were truly powerful you wouldn't need his daughter as a wife to seal the deal. Just like every other soldier my father hires, you are expendable. How does that make you feel?"

Gavriel huffed. "I don't need you."

"Then throw me overboard too."

"You'll love me. You'll learn to love me."

Avira stood, rising from her heap on the floor. Gavriel stood with her, and their eyes locked. She caught her breath, mustering every ounce of strength she had.

She kept her voice calm and balanced. "I used to think you were a monster," Avira scoffed. "But now I see you are just a pathetic little man with a pathetic little ship with a stupid name."

He slapped her. She didn't even flinch.

There was a clamoring outside Gavriel's cabin, and a man's voice called out for him. Gavriel grabbed Avira by the shoulder.

"I'm not done with you."

He threw her to the ground again and stomped out of the room, slamming the door behind him. Avira stood, once again not even feeling a glimmer of pain. If she made it to tomorrow, perhaps she'd have bruises for all this. But not now. Now she had work to do.

She began pulling at the strings of her gown until the bodice fell from her body and to the floor. Outside the cabin, there was some chaos going on, but Avira chose not to pay attention to that and instead focused every effort on getting the piling skirts off her body. Eventually, she wore only her slip. She reached a hand down to touch her thigh.

Attached to a lace garter was Mirjana's knife. It hadn't shifted at all in the action. Avira pulled the knife out from under her slip and hid it under her armpit. She didn't want to go face to face with Gavriel again unarmed. Beneath the knife was a small paper package. It was a bit sweaty from being against her skin so much but still good for its intended purpose.

Avira said a thank you prayer to Aurora and Salicia for Mirjana and Layla. She'd rarely prayed so much, but this felt appropriate. Avira had been too distracted even to consider bringing a weapon with her. Now she had two.

A crash sounded out on the deck of the ship. She considered going out to see what was happening for a moment, but she chose against it. Instead, she cut a long strip of fabric from her blue gown, which now looked like a dead animal lying on the floor. She tied the strip around her head to keep the hair out of her face.

She sat down at Gavriel's writing desk. A map of Shaheen and Alvanii was splayed out across the table. She put her feet up on top of it. And she waited.

After a few minutes, the door burst open. Gavriel was sweaty and angry. He stormed towards her but paused when he saw what she was wearing. Avira's stomach burned, she almost wanted to vomit thinking about being naked in front of

Gavriel. But Gavriel didn't need to be told twice. He marched to her and pressed his lips to hers so aggressively she was afraid their teeth would bash together. He ran his hand up her thigh as she forced herself to kiss him back.

Kissing him wasn't like kissing Matteo. There was no softness. No care or affection. There didn't need to be.

Because the next thing Avira did was pull the knife out from under her armpit and slam it as hard as she could into the side of Gavriel's head. She'd meant to stab him in the eye but wholly missed, slashing off a chunk of his cheek and what looked to be his entire ear instead.

"That was for Matteo."

She spit on him as she stood up, wiping the nervous sweat off her hands. Mirjana's knife was small but surprisingly sharp. Gavriel threw himself back in pain, wailing like a cat in heat. Avira stood up, briefly considering leaving him like this.

Gavriel cowered over, holding the side of his head and moaning. She took his hand ever so gently in hers, batting her long dark lashes.

He moaned, trying to wrestle himself away from her. Acting quickly, she took his hand and laid it open and palmed it on his desk. Then she slammed the knife down on the center of his hand, pinning him to the map, and spilling blood everywhere. For good measure, she ripped open the paper package of harissa pepper and blew it right into his eyes and the bloody wound on his face.

"But that was for me."

She didn't know how long that would hold him. All she knew was that she needed a head start. She ran, kicking open the door with one foot and hoping that she might get to the glider and escape. She'd get the hang of it eventually, and it was a better option than jumping to her inevitable death. Or she could snag a sword and force the men to free her.

As she stumbled out into the feigning light of sunset, Avira found herself face to face with Artemis Cascella. He held a long dagger in one hand and one of Gavriel's men by the hair with the other hand.

"There you are," Artemis said with his token grin. "I've been looking for you."

Artemis threw the man in his hand to the ground and grabbed Avira's arm. Together they ran to the side of the ship. He clambered up onto the guard rail, lifting Avira with him.

"What are you doing here?" Avira said, sure, they'd fall.

"Saving your life," he shouted as he grabbed her shoulders and hurled them both off the ship's side.

Avira didn't have time to realize she was falling before she landed with a thud on something rugged and sturdy.

Catching her breath, she looked at Artemis, who was already back on his feet. Avira tried to choke out a question. But all she had to do was look around. Standing all around her were familiar faces—the crew of The Apollo.

Chapter Thirty-Four

Artemis had long since stood and brushed himself off, but Avira was still sitting in her undergarments, staring at the sea of faces. It was eerily silent. She scanned every face she saw, looking for Matteo's dark eyes or glittering golden nose ring. But he was nowhere to be seen.

"Where's Matteo?" she said softly, hoping only Artemis would hear. Artemis turned and have her a look of pure, earnest confusion.

"How should I know? He went with the queen when you left."

"He was my escort up to Golden Boy. Gavriel threw him. You caught him, right?" Avira nodded her head furiously as she spoke, as though she were trying to convince herself that she was correct. She had to be correct. Otherwise Matteo was dead.

"If he fell he didn't land here." Artemis shrugged her off and turned back to his men who still ogled her, eyes wide and heads tilted sideways in confusion.

"You let Matteo die?" Avira already knew the answer, but she wouldn't let herself believe it. Not yet. Not until Artemis said the words. "Artemis. Did you let him die?" Avira could hear the roar of tears in the back of her throat. She couldn't stop herself. An eruption was coming from within her. Artemis' cool eyes scanned her. He shook his head.

"Like I said, if he fell, he didn't land here."

"No." Avira fell to her knees "No. No. No. No. No. No. He's not dead. He can't be dead. He didn't fall. He didn't die."

Artemis didn't say a word. He let her sob for a moment and then turned back to his crew. "Men. some of you may recognize this girl here. She's been on board our ship since we took off and — "

Avira didn't let him finish his sentence. She raised her hand high and, with every bit of energy she could muster, she slapped Artemis across the face. "How dare you save me and not him!"

Artemis, not even wincing at the pain of the slap, grabbed Avira by the wrist. "I didn't have to save you, Avira. I could have let you die. I could have let that wretched puppet of your father's have you. But I didn't. Show some gratitude."

Artemis's spit flew into Avira's face. She sucked in a breath and stopped her tears.

"Avi?" a voice called from the crowd. It was a meek voice, like the speaker was terrified to interrupt what was going on, but it was a familiar voice nonetheless. "Avi, it's going to be okay."

Nicolo stepped out from the crowd, beaming at her, his familiar kind eyes aglow with compassion. Avira wondered if it was probably fun for him to feel like the only one in on some big secret. If it was, he didn't show it.

"Who's Avi?" one man said.

"I thought that was the boy from the kitchen. What's he doing in a dress?"

"Are you sure that's a dress? Looks like underwear to me."

Artemis raised an eyebrow at Avira, rubbing his cheek where she'd slapped it, clearly expecting her to explain. She wiped her tears with the back of her hand, trying to ignore the thick layer of grime, mud, and snot that had caked her face. Looking down at her hand, she realized it was also covered in the wet, sticky, harissa pepper Layla had given her.

"It's true," she started, forcing back the hurricane raging inside her at the loss of Matteo. "Some of you may know me as Cesario, the kitchen boy. But my name is not Cesario." She paused for a moment, knowing she couldn't ever go back from this moment. "My name is Avira Bianco." A hush fell over the already quiet crowd. Any air they'd had left was now gone. "My father is Grigori Bianco. He is a bad man. But you already know this. His crest is at the top of each of your contracts. As we speak, he plans to destroy as many Shaheeni people as necessary for him to rule like a king. I'm sorry I lied to you all. But I had to escape him."

Artemis stepped forward. "Men, listen to what the girl says. Grigori Bianco owns each of you. But it doesn't have to be this way. Queen Adipe has offered me a new charter for The Apollo if we fight alongside her people today. We may not be warriors, but we can still make a difference. We can still fight."

Avira felt a smile on her lips. She'd never felt so glad to be wrong. Artemis had been hoping to betray the Bianco fleet this whole time.

"Sir, we don't have any weapons." Avira saw Malvolio step out of the crowd, his hands pinned to his hips. She couldn't help but think that it didn't matter if they had weapons if half the crew didn't want to fight.

"Who's with me?" Artemis shouted.

"What about our families back home? Will they be safe?" Nicolo asked. Avira knew he was thinking about his father, his many sisters, and that boy he loved back home, Benjamin.

"I'll see to it that they are."

"And will we all still get paid?"

"The Shaheeni royal family will reward you handsomely for your service to the throne. I'll see to that myself." She hoped it was true but she couldn't imagine Adipe being stingy, especially if The Apollo helped win the war.

That seemed to do it. The men started murmuring amongst themselves again, the general consensus being that if they get paid, they'll fight.

Avira tugged Artemis' arm. "Malvolio is right, Captain. We don't have any weapons."

"No." Artemis shrugged. "But we have at least two hundred barrels of Popping Pepper."

Popping pepper was well known to be highly combustible if heated up too quickly. Avira had heard stories of it being used to make bombs in a pinch. Avira realized she had nothing to offer these men. She knew nothing of war or weaponry. She'd been raised in a glass bubble. Her mind drifted to her bedroom at home, and then to the map she had painstakingly drawn out on her bedroom floor.

That was it. Her map. It had to have something useful for Artemis to use against Gavriel and his fleet, after all it was the most prized document in the whole of the trading empire.

Even if it wasn't useful today, maybe Adipe could make use of it in protecting her country in the future. Avira had to find her map. Avira smiled in the lantern light. She didn't feel like she was in the way anymore. She had a task to do. But first, she needed to check on Nicolo.

"I want every barrel of pepper we own on this deck now. We'll need torches too. If you're a ropesman I want you to work to make some slingshots. I don't care how you do it. It doesn't even have to be accurate. As long as it launches a barrel, it's good for me."

As Artemis barked orders, Avira pulled Nicolo aside.

"I'm sorry I didn't tell you. I wanted to protect you."

Nicolo flexed his face in a funny way before saying, "I was worried about ya, Avira. You didn't come back from your shift this morning. I thought you'd been caught lying or something."

He pressed his forehead into hers. She'd seen Veronan mothers do this to their children, it was a sign of familial love. Nicolo had been right. When he met her, he said that someday they would have no secrets at all. Now there were none left.

"Are you sure you're not afraid to go to battle?" she asked.

"'Of course, I am. But, hey, it'll be a good story to write home about, eh? Benjamin loves a good adventure story." Nicolo gave her a once over. "Now, come on. Let's find you a pair of pants before this gets interesting."

The two of them snaked their way through the underbelly of the ship back to their bunk, which looked exactly the same as it had when Avira left for her shift the day before. So much has changed since then.

Nicolo dug through his chest and tossed a pair of trousers to Avira. She tore the shift she'd been wearing until it resembled a loose shirt, and slid the trousers on.

Nicolo laughed at her outfit.

Avira looked in the mirror, and, for the first time, the face staring back at her looked familiar. From the loose-fitting top to the torn piece of the gown around her head, pulling her hair back and out of sight, to her practical pants with deep pockets.

She found her map quickly, tucked away for safety at the bottom of her chest. Nicolo didn't ask about it at all, but he didn't have to. Avira spread it out across the bead and smiled up at him.

"A map?"

Nicolo's eyes were wide. Avira realized that this must be the first map he'd ever seen. They weren't commonplace, especially among the lower class.

"It's the most comprehensive map of Shaheen, Alvanii or

Veronii that exists. I stole it from my father. Someday I'm going to visit every single place you can see on this map, Nicolo."

Nicolo's eyes grew wide. "Can I come?"

"When I have my own ship, you can be my second in command." She held out her hand for him to shake and he did.

She rolled up the map and shoved it safely into her deep pockets.

Above them, on deck, things were getting loud.

"This isn't your war, Nicolo. Why are you all fighting?" Avira asked.

"Because we trust Artemis, I guess. And because we trust you," he said nonchalantly.

Once they were back on deck, Avira was struck by the cacophony of sound and action coming at her from all sides. The ropesmen were hard at work, lacing up some slingshot out of tied-up shirts and dish towels. Diego taught furnace workers how to boil kitchen oil and launch it at enemy ships.

It was impossible to walk even six feet across the deck without being in somebody's way, especially as the deck began to fill with barrel after barrel of popping pepper. Diego saw Avira and waved her over. He was toiling over a vat of kitchen oil, and Avira assumed he wanted her help. Instead, he pulled her into a sweaty, smelly hug.

"I'm glad you're back, kid," he said into her ear. "Wish Matteo could've come with you."

Diego, whom Avira had rarely seen sober, looked like a candle that had been blown out. His cheeks were sallow, and his eyes were red from crying. Avira had never related to the old man more. "If he'd of known Gavriel's plans, Artemis would have been right there to save the boy. We all would. We were just a little too late."

If Avira was supposed to find that comforting, she didn't. So, what if Artemis was sorry for letting Matteo die. Matteo was only in this mess because of her. There was nothing that made her life more valuable than his.

He would have wanted me alive. The thought struck Avira like a clap of thunder. *He would have wanted to die for me. If we could bring him back, he'd do it again.* Even though it was true, Avira still shuddered at the though. What had she done to deserve the love Matteo had given her? She couldn't think of one thing she'd done to earn it.

"Matteo died to prevent this horrible war. I refuse to believe he died in vain." Avira ran her hands through her hair anxiously as she spoke. She hadn't felt this alone in weeks. Matteo's absence reverberated through her. She wanted him to take her in his arms and tell her it was all going to be okay. But he couldn't. She had to do that for herself now.

Diego clapped her on the back with his hand and gave her a gentle nod, then he returned to his work. Really, it was the only thing he could do. As the men all around her snapped into action, Avira felt a little useless. Nicolo was soon pulled into work on the ropes, his skills with knots were far too advanced for him to sit on the outskirts comforting her. She wanted to crawl into the closet in the kitchen and rock herself back and forth until all of this was over. But anytime she imagined doing that, Matteo was there too, holding her close and whispering sweet things in her ears.

Someone grabbed her arm. "Oi, girl. We need all hands on deck!" It was Malvolio. He'd clearly adjusted quickly to her new identity.

So, she busied her mind and hands, helping the ropesmen hoist barrels high above the deck. They were rigged to a simple pulley system that would trigger the barrel to launch violently forward if the rope was caught. Diego was tasked with pouring a ladle full of boiling oil onto the lid of each barrel before the men launched it forward as far as it would go. Since The Apollo was a trade ship equipped only with two measly cannons, these exploding barrels of spices would have to make do.

The Bianco Trade Network had begun to arm their ships

as battle ships in secret, just in case a situation like this were to break out. Unfortunately, The Apollo had been in the sky for half a decade before giving ships heavy artillery became common place. The crew of The Apollo was on the back foot, and they knew it.

"How do we know when the battle starts?" she heard one man ask his friend.

"Things start blowing up, I reckon."

Avira stole a glance over the side of the ship. Below them, there was a fleet of Shaheeni boats sitting in wait. The Apollo was still floating alongside her father's ships, waiting patiently to ambush the soldiers who thought Artemis' crew were their allies. It was brilliant, this plan of Artemis and Adipe's. It was almost free of error, except for the loss of Matteo. Avira didn't think she'd ever forgive them for that.

It was overwhelming: the smell of the peppers and the hot oil, the pounding in Avira's head and under her skin from Gavriel's bruises, the pain in her heart, the image of Matteo looking into her eyes just before he fell. Her mouth tasted salty from either tears or blood. couldn't tell which. She tried to press her hand against her split lip to help the wound clot up faster. Unfortunately, the leftover harissa pepper on her hand smeared into the wound causing it to burn and throb twice as bad. She bit back the pain, using as a welcome distraction as he tried not to to imagine all of these crewmen of The Apollo dying at the hands of her father and Gavriel. Thoughts kept breaking through her skull like a rapture.

She felt a hand gently touch her lower back again. Looking up, she saw Artemis' dark eyes. He didn't say a word, just pulled her into him. Avira had expected many things from Artemis Cascella, but not a hug. Night had fallen and the stars wrapped around the ship like a blanket.

"I'm sorry I slapped you like that," she croaked.

"I'm sorry I couldn't save him," was all there was left to say.

"Will there be fighting tonight, do you think?" she asked, almost hoping he wouldn't hear so he couldn't respond.

"Hard to say," Artemis said. "Soak up every second of stillness, every second of the night, every moment. It might be the last one we get for a while."

And, with his token smirk, Artemis disappeared into the night. Leaving Avira and the stars alone with each other. The anticipation burned.

Chapter Thirty-Five

Matteo didn't even realize he was falling.

Not at first, at least. He felt a gust of wind hit him, and then everything felt cold. He couldn't catch his breath and didn't understand why he couldn't breathe. The confusion was the most terrifying part of the entire ordeal. Then, all at once, it made sense.

They'd thrown him overboard.

He'd thought it would happen fast, dying, that is. But falling felt like an eternity. He refused to look down. He didn't want to know how close he was to the sea.

Eventually, he just closed his eyes and thought of Avira. Not the frightened woman he'd seen just moments before but the girl in the crow's nest who'd taught him about stars and maps and the shape of the world.

He didn't mind dying but he was sad he'd never get to hold her again. His heart ached knowing he'd never get to see the way her eyes squinted up when she thought deeply about something, or the way she bit her lip when she was worried.

He was thinking about her lips and her constellation of freckles when he saw something out of the corner of his eye. It was moving so fast he could barely make it out, a large dark streak in the sky falling next to him. He strained his eyes just enough to make out the shape.

Rihane.

She was in a full downward nosedive on her glider, falling parallel to him, one arm outstretched towards him. She must have seen him fall and rushed out to save him. Matteo reached his arm out to grab hers, suddenly all too aware of how close the water was getting.

Then Rihane let go of the glider completely, maintaining her balance by wrapping one leg around the sail. She grabbed Matteo with both arms and pulled him in close. Then she let go, dropping him with a thud on the base of the glider and pulling the nose of the glider up so quickly Matteo's head jerked back, hurting his neck. Better a hurt neck than a broken one.

As the glider slowed to a more elegant floating speed, Matteo looked up at Rihane. They were so close to the sea now that ocean spray was flying up and leaving a cool residue all across

Matteo's skin. He let his arms and legs relax, reaching a hand down and skimming it across the water. Rihane wore her smirk like a badge of honor.

"How's that for a hero, huh?" she shouted over the wind.

For a moment it was just the two of them, hanging in the air and smiling at one another. He was alive. She'd saved his life.

But reality set in all too quickly. It had all happened so fast, he realized that a mile above him Avira was defenseless against Gavriel and, even more sinister, Gavriel hadn't signed the treaty.

"Rihane, we have to get back to Adipe. Gavriel never meant to strike a deal. There will be war. The Shaheeni aren't ready."

She didn't look fazed. "Our warships are prepared. The queen knew this might happen. After you and Avira took off she gave the final command. We knew it was coming. I'm taking you to her now."

Matteo didn't understand.

"We're not stupid, you know. Not about war."

The Shaheeni and Gavriel Castillo were going to war. And there was nothing Matteo could do now to protect Avira, or anyone else, from that.

As Rihane landed her glider gracefully on the The Mirage, she explained to Matteo that they'd been preparing for battle all along, just in case. Mirjana had been left at the castle to keep things running smoothly there while The Mirage trailed Adipe's sea fleet just a little ways below where Golden Boy had been floating, unseen by the enemy due to its state-of-the-art camouflage.

They'd watched with bated breath as Matteo landed his glider on the deck of Gavriel's ship, soldiers at the ready in case of any foul play. Rihane admitted that getting tossed to his death wasn't exactly in their top ten list of expected outcomes but they'd considered it as an option. Rihane had been the first one to see him falling, it only took her a few seconds to launch herself into the sky after him. Matteo didn't say anything, but in his head he marvelled at Rihane's skill. The fact that she could pilot a glider so successfully without even a second thought, was hard for him to believe. Piloting a glider himself took every ounce of focus he had.

Rihane almost blushed as she admitted that she hadn't even considered once whether or not she should try to save him. She was simply hoping her superiors wouldn't be angry at her for abandoning post. "I couldn't just let you die," she said. "You're my friend. Besides, you're too good on a glider. It would have been a terrible waste."

Once they'd landed on the private landing deck of The Mirage, it was clear that Rihane had made the right choice in rushing to save him. The landing deck had a doorway that led directly to Adipe's chamber and the queen came rushing out as soon as the glider was still, her cheeks still glistening with the trails of tears.

She first ran to Rihane, saying something in Shaheeni that Matteo couldn't understand.

Then Adipe embraced Matteo in a hug. He'd never been hugged so much, or so tightly, in his life.

"I saw you fall," Adipe said, her voice still shaking and her face wet from tears. "I thought you were going to die. From that height your bones would have shattered instantly. I closed my eyes and prayed."

She pulled him in again and he let himself relax. But only for a moment before he pulled away. "What about Avira? She's still up there."

Adipe pointed to Golden Boy. The early evening light was nearly blinding in its brightness and from this angle, Matteo could only see a giant golden blob floating just below. The halo of sunshine made the ship look practically angelic.

Adipe had changed clothes. Instead of her usual regal robes and jewels, she was wearing a much more practical tunic and pair of pants. She and Rihane looked practically identical in their matching outfits. It must have been the traditional war garb of the Shaheeni. He had to admit, it was rather intimidating. As they flew through the sky on their gliders, the Shaheeni warriors looked like hawks themselves.

Matteo suddenly felt brutally underprepared. Not one soul in the sky or on the sea that day was afraid of what would come. Adipe had dressed for battle.

"Let me fight too then."

"No." Adipe was stern this time.

"No?"

"Someone needs to protect my daughter. If I die out here today with my people, she will need a guide. You must go be with her. Help her understand."

"I don't think Mirjana, of all people, needs any help understanding things-" Matteo started. But Adipe cut him off.

"Matteo, she is still a child. She sees the world through the eyes of a little girl. A very wise little girl, but a little girl all the same. She is wise but not worldy, passionate but not patient. She will need you."

"You're not going to die, Adipe," he protested.

"I may die. But Aurora and Salicia will protect Shaheen. They will protect you and they will protect Mirjana, and that is worth sacrificing myself for."

Matteo opened his mouth to protest again but Adipe was not to be argued with. "Rihane will take you back to my palace. I hope this is not goodbye, but if it is-" She brushed her hand along his cheek. "If it is goodbye, I trust you'll know what to do."

She pressed her forehead to his for another quick second.

Rihane boarded the glider and gave Matteo a look as though she were telling him to hurry up. He climbed on board and hung on tight.

"Thank you for bringing my Hamida back to me, Matteo," Adipe called to him. And then the glider began to descend, and Adipe disappeared from view.

Matteo and Rihane didn't speak until nearly the end of the journey back to the palace. Not until he finally asked her, "Are you returning to the battle?"

Rihane shook her head. "Queen Adipe says I need to stay alive for my little brothers and sisters. I'm assigned to protect you and Mirjana."

They landed in the garden and sprinted to the throne room where they found Mirjana pacing around the map, her eyes on the sky outside the throne room windows. It was a perfect view of the battle. It only took a glance to realize how outnumbered the Shaheeni were.

Mirjana didn't speak either. The three of them just watched in silence.

There were at least a dozen massive golden sky ships. All but one of which had falcon crests on their masts and balloons. They flew in a formation, close enough together that Matteo wondered what would happen if one ship went down. Would it domino the rest of them with it?

The Apollo floated a little below the rest of Bianco's fleet. It stuck out like a sore thumb. Matteo hoped Adipe was right, and Avira was safe with Artemis by now.

The Shaheeni had ten boats on the water, but their sky fleet was dwarfed by Bianco's. Matteo could barely look. If he strained his eyes, he could make out their silhouettes, but he didn't want to know just how outnumbered they were.

Falcons were circling like a gathering storm.

"What do we do now," Mirjana said, breaking the silence.

Neither Rihane nor Matteo could answer. They couldn't answer. Every answer felt wrong. Finally, Rihane grabbed Mirjana's hand.

"We pray," Rihane said, trying to sound calm.

"We pray?" Mirjana protested. "Why? That's ridiculous. This is war! Who does praying help?"

"It helps us," said Matteo. He kneeled down. Deep in his

memory, he recalled a prayer song from Veronii. It was a simple enough melody. He began to sing. To his surprise, Rihane and Mijrana joined him. They knew the melody, too, except they sang in Shaheeni.

Chapter Thirty-Six

The fighting didn't begin until well after midnight, in the darkest part of the night. Avira had convinced herself many times that the sound of a bell or the footsteps of a fellow crew member was the signal for the battle to begin. But, while each new noise came with a deeper pang of anxiety within her, it was beginning to feel like the battle would never come. Like Gavriel had hauled all these sky ships out here, the Shaheeni had prepared for war, and Matteo had given his life for a battle that would never happen. This infuriated Avira. She was ready to scream across the deck for someone, anyone, to just do something already.

When the noise came, a deafening rip through the sky that made the insides of her ears ring, Avira cursed herself for ever assuming any other noise could signal a war. For a moment, she was like a child again, frightened of the fireworks her father set off for her on her birthday. When the canon above them fired, the sky lit up for a split second, exposing every crewman's face. They were frozen in their expressions, some looking shocked but most looking stoic. Avira knew her face had already betrayed her fear. Nicolo, who was across the deck from her, gave her a small smile before hitching his foot into a loop and beginning his climb up towards the sails where more barrels of popping pepper had been hidden. It was eerily silent. Not one man said a word.

And then, all at once, like a gust of wind, every man jumped into action.

Diego was the first to start shouting, bellowing orders to the men holding hot oil to pour it slowly over the top of the barrels and give the signal for the ropesman to release. The oil was hot enough to eat through the top of the barrel and as soon as it made contact with the peppers, a deafening explosion was sure to come. It was nearly impossible to see where you were shooting, save for every so often when a cannon would go off on a ship directly above them, illuminating the sky for a moment.

Avira felt extraneous, running back and forth across the deck, not really doing anything. She brought one of the men a canteen of water and held ropes down for another one as he tied a complicated knot. The goal of the men on The Apollo was to blend in with the Bianco fleet for as long as possible and begin firing pepper barrels as soon as they were noticed. They'd hoped to aim directly at the balloons that kept the enemy sky ships aloft, but, in the dark, it wasn't possible to aim at all. They could be launching their limited ammunition into the abyss for all they know.

A cannonball hit The Apollo, and the whole ship rocked sideways. Avira grabbed for the rope closest to her. As the ship continued to rock, she slid across the deck. Some men stumbled but most held their ground, waiting for Diego's word. Avira prayed that the rope she held was connected to something or else she'd be falling through the dark night sky within seconds. Luckily, with a snap, the rope caught and held her tight.

"Fire!" Diego shouted. A dozen barrels of pepper flew through the sky, colliding with Bianco's ships. When the peppers exploded, the sound wasn't quite as loud as Avira had expected. Perhaps she simply couldn't hear well over the drumming of her own heart. The fire of the popping peppers, however, was unmistakable. They burned a hot, sickly green color. Ahead of them, Avira could see green flames spreading across the deck of a smaller Bianco ship. Once the flames overtook the balloon, she knew the ship would sink into the sea. One down, plenty left to go.

She thought she heard a glider streak by, then another, but she couldn't be sure. Most of Gavriel's canons were trained toward the boats far below the ocean. If the Shaheeni had prepared ships, it would have been useless to try and see them. While their camouflage was effective by day, it was insurmountable in the dark of the night.

Cannons and barrels of pepper exploded in all directions. A Bianco ship had tried to hit The Apollo a few times, but the flaming peppers were too much of a liability. A dozen green fireballs met every cannonball that rocked the ship in response. It felt like they were winning, or at least the most powerful ship in the sky.

That was, of course, until Adipe's ships began firing. Instead of fireballs. They shot cannonballs made of tiny, razor-sharp darts. When the Shaheeni weapons collided with a ship, every surface in a ten-foot radius was coated with the tiny blades. One dart wasn't enough to kill a man, but thirty darts could easily take him out of the fight.

The night itself only seemed to get darker as the hours raged on. Every so often, a ship could be heard falling towards the ocean though Avira couldn't be sure which ships were allies and which were enemies.

It was as though fifteen men had been given daggers, blindfolded, and locked in a dark room, and told to be the last ones standing. Everyone, even the most experienced of the crew, was flying blind.

"How long will this last, Artemis?" Avira asked.

"Until someone surrenders."

"And why has nobody surrendered yet? It's chaos."

"Nobody is going to surrender until they know who's winning, and we won't know that until dawn."

"So, it's just senseless violence until sunrise?"

Artemis nodded.

Shouts began to overtake the ship. The sound of sword clatter was caving in on them.

"What's going on?"

"We've been boarded." Artemis threw her a sword and began running towards the noise.

In the dim lantern light Avira could only make out about twenty men in golden uniforms. One of them had a bandage wrapped around his head. Gavriel.

Avira had never brandished a sword before but followed Artemis closely, knowing she had unfinished business.

"Where is she?" Gavriel was shouting at a boy as he was held by the collar. "Where's the girl?"

From behind and in the dark , Avira couldn't tell who the boy Gavriel had in has hands was until he spoke. "I'll never tell." It was Nicolo.

Gavriel spit in Nicolo's face and tossed him to the ground. He raised his sword. He was going to kill Nicolo, Avira knew it.

"Hey," she shouted at him. "I think you're looking for me." She couldn't let anyone else die for this war, not after losing Matteo. Raising her sword, she walked towards him. He smiled and she could see that there was blood on his teeth. One of his hands was heavily bandaged. Avira didn't exactly know what she was going to do. All she knew was that she couldn't hide anymore. Gavriel wasn't going to stop until he'd delivered her and all of Shaheen to her father. She had to end this.

Gavriel taunted, "Running away sure did you a lot of good."

"I'm done running, Gavriel."

Avira closed her eyes and ran towards him, sword out in front of her. Before either of them realized what she was doing she swept the sword across his stomach. He fell to his knees, as if he was bowing before her, holding his stomach. She could see the blood seeping into his hands. She couldn't look away.

Gavriel opened his mouth to speak but only a small trickle of blood came out, running like a river down his chin and dripping down onto the wooden deck of The Apollo. Avira swore she could hear the drop hit the wood, as though everything else around her had gone silent. She backed away slowly as Gavriel crumpled at her feet, her sword still tucked between his ribs. She didn't know if he was dead, but she didn't have time to check. She gave a hand to Nicolo, helping him off the ground.

"Is that the chap yer dad wanted you to marry?"

Avira nodded.

"Aint much to look at now, is he?"

Avira looked down at him. Perhaps in another life, she would be his wife, the heiress to all his riches. Not anymore. She could never be Avira Bianco again, and she didn't want to be. Looking out at the battle all around them, Avira could see dozens of dead men littering the deck, barrels of pepper exploding in one direction and canons firing in the other, and just above them, the fleet of her father's ships still flying in a perfect formation. She remembered being a child and seeing the pale-bellied geese flying in formation through the sky, on the way from Polislav to warmer skies for the winter. She and her mother had made a game of counting the geese. An idea sparked inside her head.

In an instant, she'd grabbed Nicolo's hand and had him running with her across the deck.

"Where are we going? We need to help help!"

"I need your help with something else. It's time to end this battle."

Together, they ran to Artemis' cabin. The door had been left unopened and unguarded. She pushed through the false wardrobe door, revealing the secret landing deck to a very confused Nicolo. "This is how Artemis does his secret business," she explained. She didn't have time to tell him how she knew about it. She hoped someday she'd have a chance to. "But look."

From the deck, every ship in the Bianco fleet was easily visible. Avira pulled the map out of her pocket and turned it over. "Go grab me a quill and ink from Artemis' desk. I have a plan."

He did as he was told, bringing the ink quickly. Avira began charting the ships that dotted the sky on the back of her map. She knew the ink would bleed through and sully her perfect sky map, but she didn't care much. If she made it through tonight, she'd find a new map.

"Look," she showed Nicolo the dots. "The Bianco ships fly in a formation. I remember my father and Gavriel talking about it. They fly close together which means that if we take one out, they'll all knock into each other. But first, we have to get The Apollo away from their formation, or they'll take us down with it."

Nicolo's eyes looked a bit glazed over.

"We have to get Artemis to move the ship. Then, if we fire enough pepper at just one of the Bianco fleet's ships, they'll all go down."

Looking out at the little dots in front of her, Avira tried to focus. One of these ships had to be the weak link. But which one?

Everything fell away. It was only her and the sky and the map. She took a big breath in, squinting her eyes deeper, trying to imagine every scenario and how it would play out from beginning to end. It was hard to sink a skyship but it wasn't nearly as hard to drop fifteen of them. Bigger targets are far easier to take out, after all.

She pointed to a dot just little ways inward from the far left end of the fleet.

"That one. Nicolo, we have to get The Apollo close enough to take out that ship."

"But won't they know we're defecting then if we do?"
"I think they already know." Avira made a significant gesture to the chaos all around them. "Their commander's dead. Now's the time to strike. I am begging you to trust me."

Nicolo pinched his lips together. "Avi, I have always trusted you."

"Then let's go win this war."

Avira rose to her feet, and with her, something else rose, confidence maybe. Some kind of fearlessness that she'd never felt before. When she'd fought Gavriel, it had been a panic that drove her. This was different. She felt like herself. She felt powerful. For the first time in her life, she wasn't a chess piece, she was playing the game.

Chapter Thirty-Seven

Watching the night sky, trying to make sense of the fireballs, cannons, and gliders that swarmed like angry bees, was like watching a bowl of ink. It was nearly impossible to see anything. Every so often, a green flame would streak across the sky, or a falcon would arrive with an update from a Shaheeni general, but Mirjana, Rihane, and Matteo were quite literally in the dark.

"How will we know when the battle is over?" Mirjana asked.

"White flags will fly."

"But how will anyone see the white flags? It's so dark out there."

Rihane shook her head. She didn't know. They'd all expected the battle to wait until morning. But with cannon fire ringing across the sky, it was evident they were wrong. Adipe sent word once, but the letter was handwritten and almost incomprehensible.

Mirjana crumpled it up and spat something about how it was a useless update. As the night grew darker and darker, the princess grew all the more agitated. She paced in circles, tossed plums from the garden against to wall to see if they'd bounce, ran her fingers across the map at the center of the throne room.

Matteo tried to think what Adipe would want him to say to her daughter to comfort her.

"Mirjana, can I tell you a story?" he said.

"I'm a little old for stories," she scoffed.

Matteo began telling it anyway, "When I was a boy, in Veronii, we had an orchard. But orchards in Veronii aren't like orchards here. It's far colder there, so we have to grow apples and figs instead of oranges and lemons. Plums grow there, too, but sometimes it freezes over late in the spring, and all of their blossoms die.

It was a particularly cold year once, and I was worried that even our apples wouldn't make fruit. I must have been seven years old. I was still young. I still thought the snow and the Winter Lights Festival were magical and holy. Have you ever seen snow?"

Mirjana shook her head.

"Well, high in the mountains and in the Far North, they

have blizzards. Tiny white flakes fall from the sky. The most amazing thing about snow is how quiet it makes the whole world. It's like a blanket has been laid over the universe; instead of ringing out, every sound is softer. The world feels like a gentle, peaceful place when it snows."

"Can you touch it?" Rihane asked. Matteo hadn't even realized she'd been listening.

"You can, but it's very cold. Like ice.

Both women gasped.

"I hope you both get to hear how silent the world becomes after a snowstorm someday." Something in the room relaxed. All three of them were breathing again, which felt good. Like somehow talking about snow had helped them reclaim some inkling of humanity.

Dawn was breaking, the sky turning light blue and streak with orange and pink. In the light, they could make out a handful of Shaheeni ships, including the outline of The Mirage.

Matteo pointed it out to Mirjana just in time to see at least thirty cannons hit the ship directly. The ship, usually perfectly obscured by the light, erupted into flames. Everything from its balloon to its wings caught fire.

Nobody spoke.

It all happened so fast: The Mirage sinking into the sea and disappearing. As the waves engulfed it, Matteo inhaled, preparing to speak, to say something optimistic. But he didn't have a chance to. All he heard was Mirjana's scream.

She collapsed into his arms. "My mother was on that ship." Matteo ran his hand over her head, searching for words. "My mother was on that ship!" Mirjana kept repeating it, choking on her own saliva as she sobbed into Matteo. "She's dead. Did you see the flames? She has to be dead."

Matteo tried to mumble something, tried to claim that maybe Adipe could have survived. But he saw Rihane shaking her head. In the distance, hundreds of silver flags were visible. They'd risen from every mast of every Shaheeni boat and sky-ship. He could see the boats retreating.

"Silver flags? Why? What's silver mean? Are they surrendering?"

Mirjana cried harder and harder until Matteo worried she was going to faint from lack of air.

"Silver is the Shaheeni color of mourning, Matteo," Rihane whispered in his ear, her voice the sad coo of a morning dove. "Silver means our queen is dead."

Chapter Thirty-Eight

The sky was just starting to turn from deep black to the blue of early morning when Avira and Nicolo found Artemis. He and Diego were in the kitchen. Diego was binding a deep gash that ran across Artemis' thigh.

"Just another scar," Avira heard Artemis tell Diego.

"Artemis we need to move the ship." She slammed the map down on the counter next to Artemis. "If we fire all we've got at this ship, it'll send them all into the sea. It's our best shot."

Artemis scowled. "Let the Shaheeni fight them. I've done my piece."

"What?" Avira didn't understand. "We can't just abandon them. The battle is just beginning. The sun is coming up!"

"And what happens if we're hit with too many cannons on our way to executing your madcap little plan."

"Please, Artemis. You need to trust me."

"But I don't. I don't trust you. You are a little girl who ran away from home and started an entire war. I promised Adipe I'd protect you, and I did," she said, "Matteo wouldn't go along with anything if we didn't promise to protect you but look at me now. Look at my ship!"

Artemis spit on the floor, garnering a dirty look from Diego.

Nicolo, who had wandered to the window to watch the sunrise, moaned. Avira snapped her head to look at him. "What is it?"

"Look."

He was pointing out the window. Avira walked to him to see what he was seeing.

Silver flags. Hundreds of them. While the Shaheeni sky ships were still disguised against the sky, the silver of their flags was unmistakable. Avira ran onto the deck, leaning over the side of the deck to look down at the sea. All of the boats had flown silver flags as well.

"Artemis?" she called. "Artemis, what does a silver flag mean?"

Artemis' face fell. He launched himself off the counter, Diego still trying desperately to secure his bandage.

"We need to move the ship."

"Yes, I know that. But what do the flags mean?"

"It means the Shaheeni have surrendered."

"What? No. Why would they do that?"

Artemis began running across the deck, shouting to every man who would listen to hold his fire. He made it to the wheel that controlled the ship's wings and helped steer and pulled it to the left as hard as he could with his arm as injured as it was.

"Artemis, answer me. Why would they surrender?"

"Because their queen has died."

Avira fell silent. Nicolo too. Every man within earshot stopped moving and turned to listen to their captain. Avira could see the smoke cloud surrounding almost everything in the dawn light. Artemis furrowed his brow and pulled at the wheel again. The ship began to rock sideways.

"Adipe is dead?" Avira broke the silence.

"Shaheeni fly white when they surrender."

"But those flags are silver." Nicolo tried to sound optimistic as he spoke.

"I've only seen silver flags flown once before, when the king of the Shahenei died. It's how they signal to their warriors in the sky that they've lost their leader."

"So that's it? They're just done fighting? They can't just let my father win like that. They can't run away!"

"What would you do?" Artemis snapped. "Now somebody please help me with this wheel. We have to get out of here before the rest of your father's men attack."

Avira looked out over the crew of The Apollo. They'd set down their slingshots and swords. A few men were gathering the bodies of Bianco soldiers and pushing them overboard. She caught a glimpse Gavriel's bandaged head just before Malvolio tossed the rest of his body over the side of the ship.

"No," she said quietly. Artemis raised an eyebrow. "No," she said again. "We're not running. The Shaheeni can run, but we can't. Not us. Not The Apollo."

The crew, most of whom were battered, burned, and bloody, looked at her like she was crazy. Avira held her map high above her head.

"What if I told you we could end this once and for all? What then?"

She'd piqued a few men's interest.

"If the Shaheeni are defeated by my father, then who's next? He won't stop until he controls everything. Every kingdom will fall to him. You, the crew of The Apollo, will be stuck on the run for the rest of your lives. You will be remembered as cowards, not as heroes, cowards who didn't have the weapons or the wit to defend the Shaheeni against Grigori Bianco. But we can still win this. We can turn The Apollo into our weapon. If we steer ourselves right into that ship there, I promise you it will end this battle."

Avira didn't know what would happen if The Apollo collided with another ship, but she couldn't imagine it would be good. If they could take down the weak link in The Bianco fleet, perhaps it would be worth it.

"If we crash The Apollo, we all might die," one man called.

"I believe in the Goddess Aurora, protector of the skies. I believe in her love for Salicia and for the Shaheeni. I believe she will save us. Don't you?"

Blank faces blinked back at her.

"Who's with me?"

After a long pause, Nicolo raised his hand. Malvolio too. And Diego. Soon, all the men knew what they had to do. Artemis looked horrified.

"If you're frightened, I'm sure we can flag down a Shaheeni glider for you to take to land," Avira suggested.

Artemis raised his hand, too.

And the crew, once again, sprang into action. Avira cranked the wheel in the opposite direction Artemis had been turning it, causing the ship to buck wildly on the wind and flip itself around too quickly. Avira barely kept her footing and saw a few barrels of popping pepper fly off the side of the ship. She set the course steady towards the small ship she'd charted out on her map.

"Please let this work," she prayed to herself. "Please, Aurora, Salicia, protect these men."

Holding the wheel steady, Avira focused all her attention on the ship in front of her. She could see the ropes, the balloon, the golden falcon crest. Artemis, next to her, clung to the deck. The jewels in his hair shimmered in the firelight. Avira had never noticed them in such profound detail before. Nicolo, Diego, and the other men had gone to work stoking the furnace and pulling ropes so the sales were full and the ship could move faster.

"This better work," was the last thing Avira heard Artemis say before a massive *crack* rang out in her ears, and she lurched forward over the steering wheel. She could feel that The Apollo had collided with the other ship, and now they were tipping.

"Everyone, hold on tight!" she shouted futilely as the ship rocked completely sideways, its front mast stuck in the center of the other ship. She could hear men shouting from both ships as they tipped and tipped and then collided with the ship directly beside them, which tipped and collided with the ship next to it.

She closed her eyes. The plan was working. Wind whipped against her face so hard she couldn't breathe. Tiny bits of seafoam pelted her. They stung. She felt as she lifted off of her feet and tilted sideways, holding as tight as she could to the wheel. She thought of Nicolo and prayed that he would survive the collision. Even if she died, she wanted Nicolo to be with Benjamin. She wanted him to have that big Veronan wedding he'd talked to her so excitedly about. She sent out a hopeful prayer to Aurora to spare Nicolo. To spare all the men of The Apollo if she could. This wasn't their war. They didn't deserve to die for it.

If I die, I'll be with Matteo. She felt herself smile at that thought. Shouts and cracks and screams and explosions made a symphony all around her.

When Avira was young, maybe six or seven years old, her mother had been pregant all the way to term with a baby that would never survive in the outside world. The baby was a boy. Avira remembered the day he was born, the way all of the maids had been alight with energy and joy, so ready to meet the baby boy. When Avira's maid had tucked her into bed at night instead of her mother, little Avira had asked if the baby had been born yet. The maid had simply shook her head and changed the subject. That is when Avira first learned the way people are afraid to talk about death. Even as a small child, she didn't understand. Death was frightening, of course, but fearing death only wastes the energy of the living. Avira had tried to ask her maid more questions. She was worried about her mother. But she'd gotten nowhere.

The boy had been a beautiful baby, the spitting image of his father, but he'd never opened his eyes or gasped a first breath. He had been completely still, like a sculpture. It had broken his mother's heart. After so many failed attempts at giving Grigori Bianco a male heir, the loss of this perfect, beautiful infant was devastating.

Avira had risen from bed, determined to find her mother. Nobody would give her a straight answer as to if Cristina was okay. Avira was a child, yes, but she was wise enough to know something was wrong. She used a candle to light her way as she walked through the villa, past the scowling portraits of her family and ancestors, and found her mother's chamber. Avira could hear voices coming from under the door along with the amber glow of light. She heard her mother's voice first, quavering and weak.

"I'm sorry, Grigori, I don't know why the babies won't stay. It's not my fault."

"Of course, it's your fault!" Avira had wanted to go in and comfort her motherbut she was too frightened of her father to open the door. "If you weren't so miserable all the time, perhaps the babies would be more viable. Perhaps they would stay."

"I can't help my misery. I can't help it. I've given you a child, she is smart and bold and would run the company well. Why can't you just leave it to her."

A slap rang out from inside the room and little Avira drew back away from the door, her heart pounding in her throat. She hid in the shadows, hanging on every word. "You know damn well why I can't leave the company to her."

"I hate you." Her mother's words sunk deep under Avira's skin. Her mother hated her father. Her father hated *her*. Little Avira hadn't understood at the time how a father could hate his own child so much. Surely, there was some shred of paternal love left in his heart for her. But she never saw it. And slowly, surely, she began to reciprocate his feelings for her.

There were many more attempts at a son after the stillbirth of her brother, but none were viable. Avira had watched as her father's hatred for her ate away at her mother's life day by day. When she was old enough to understand the inner workings of her father's company, she'd vowed to destroy it. If nothing else, as revenge for her mother, who was barely more than a corpse among the living.

"If you don't leave me the company in your will, I'll start my own. I will!" A teenaged Avira had said to her father one night in a fit of rage. He had slapped her across the face so hard it made her nose bleed and then laughed at how stupid the idea of a woman running a company as large as his was. But Avira did not think the idea was stupid or laughable. She'd wiped the blood from her face, stood tall and strong, and spit onto her father's foot. For two weeks after that she was not allowed to go beyond her bedroom. Those were the two weeks she used to sketch out the massive trade map from memory across her bedroom floor.

Little did Avira know that the rest of the world saw her father exactly the same way she did. Her father was a liar, a hateful, angry man who would not stop until he could suffocate the world in his fists.

The night before Avira had fled, she'd had her mother up to her room. It had been a tradition of theirs since Avira was small to share a glass of tea and a discussion of politics before bed.

"I know what you're planning," Cristina had said in her same soft voice as they sipped cups of clove and orange peel tea.

"And what might that be?" Avira had tried to play dumb. It had not worked. Her mother was no fool.

"You'd rather run away and start a new life than marry Gavriel. I am your mother, don't insult me by insinuating that I don't know my own child well enough to see that."

Avira had sniffed stubbornly. "And if you're right about this plan of mine - which I'm not saying you are - how do you feel about it?"

Cristina had given a smile, a sad smile but a smile, nonetheless. "You could start a trading business. You could become a pirate queen. You could do anything you set your mind to. But, selfishly, I pray every night that you won't leave me. I will die without you here, I know it. Since you were born, the only thing that's kept me going was you. If I were to lose you. You know what? Nevermind."

Cristina had silenced herself and soon after, she'd gone back to her rooms. Avira had packed her bags and left the very next day, praying that her mother would forgive her. She had seen what marriage looks like, what it means for a young woman to become a wife. And she could never let herself endure that.

I'm so sorry, Mother, she thought as she walked away from the villa, her hair cut short. *I am not a person who stays. I don't know that I ever will be.*

Avira's body contracted like a rag doll as soon as it hit the cold water. She felt it embrace her, soaking her clothes and sending chills like lightning through her body. She began to sink below the waves, paddling with all her might to stay afloat, but her arms were floppy and hard to move. She couldn't see or hear anything. All she could taste was the burning salt of the seawater and the iron of her own blood.

She began to sink, inhaling a bit of water and choking it out as she fought to get above the surface of the water only to be engulfed by another wave. When she finally forced her eyes open, everything was blurry. Pieces of various ships, fire, even people were falling all around her into the water. She looked up just in time to see a gigantic mast with the sail still attached plummeting towards her, a beacon of flame. She didn't know what else to do so she swam down, forcing herself to keep her eyes open under the water. When she thought she couldn't hold her breath any longer, she swam deeper. Her head hurt from the pressure. She flipped onto her back, watching as the sail sank towards her through the water. Everything moved in slow motion beneath the water. She'd never been a good swimmer but with the only other option being death, she did her best.

Fighting her way towards the surface, she gasped, and air flooded her lungs. No matter how many screams for air her lungs let out, she couldn't get enough. Out of the corner of her eye, a shock of red hair glinted. She turned her body and saw an unconscious Nicolo hanging for dear life on what looked like a piece of The Apollo, a door or something.

"Nicolo?" She swam towards him as quickly as her aching body would allow her. She was close enough to touch his cold skin when another wave caught her and pulled her so far back that all her progress was lost

"Nicolo!" The desperation in her voice scared her. Still, he didn't respond. She pushed her body harder and reached him just in time for another wave to crash over them. Avira grabbed onto the piece of wood he was using to stay afloat. She ran her hand along his cheek, panicking. He couldn't be dead. He wasn't allowed to be dead. She was supposed to die. Not him. If Nicolo died, if he never got to return home to his family and his love, then she would have truly lost everything today. Matteo and Nicolo were, as much as admitting it scared her, the only people in the world who really cared about her.

"Nicolo please wake up. You have to wake up. You need to go back to Veronii and throw that big wedding for Benjamin. Remember? Remember the wedding?" Avira shook him again. She pressed her fingers to the skin below his nose and was thankful to feel the smallest bit of air coming from his nostrils.

He was breathing. *Thank you, Aurora.* She thought.

Nicolo's eyes fluttered open. "Avi?" Avira pulled him in, hugging him tight. "Why are we wet?"

"We crashed the ship, remember?" She couldn't help but let out a breathy, exasperated laugh.

"The Apollo?"

"The Apollo!"

Avira looked up, her neck burning with pain, she must have bruised something. Maybe she'd bruised everything. It sure felt like she had. Fire and debris rained down. If she squinted her eyes, she could almost pretend they were shooting stars.

"What do we do now?" Nicolo said, his usual optimism a bit dull.

"I don't know." Exhausted, Avira rested her head on the piece of wood that was so expertly holding her and Nicolo afloat. In the distance, she thought she could see the rocky cliffs of the Shaheeni coastline but she knew trying to swim to them would be futile. "I wish I knew."

Against her will, her eyes shut. She couldn't tell if she was passing out from pain or cold or shock. She couldn't stop herself. The world caved in around her.

"Woah woah woah," she heard Nicolo say. "Stay with me, Avi. I need you to stay with me." But she couldn't control it.

In an instant, everything went black.

CHAPTER THIRTY-NINE

The spray of the sea crashed against Matteo's face as he ran along the beach. He'd been searching like this for hours but to no avail. Every wave that crashed against the rocky Shaheeni shore brought with it more bodies, more rubble, more bits and pieces of what once had been the opulent Bianco fleet. The carnage was so horrific that all Matteo wanted to do was look away, but he couldn't bring himself to do that.

Matteo wasn't searching for surviving Bianco soldiers or for washed-up treasure. He was looking for Avira. He dug through the wreckage, his pants tearing along the rocks and his hands bleeding and filled with splinters. He called her name over and over but it was pointless for him to keep shouting over the raw power of the waves.

Rihane came to find him eventually. She was clothed head to toe in silver, the color of death, her eyes were sunken. She, like Matteo, hadn't slept for days.

"Matteo, come back to the palace. The child needs you," Rihane pleaded with him.

"What could she possibly need me for? I have no way of helping her I have no way of -"

He didn't finish his sentence. He broke down in tears, letting his body go limp. Rihane walked him back to the throne room and that is where he stayed.

At first, nobody knew what had happened. One moment the Shaheeni were surrendering to their enemies and the next moment their enemies were falling into the sea.

Nobody had ever seen a collision like this among sky ships. They were massive, dangerous pieces of technology but they rarely just crashed into one another. Nobody knew how to respond to it. Matteo, Rihane and Mirjana had clung to eachother and watched as the ships hooked together and pulled each other towards the turbulent waves of the sea. It was as though Aurora had snapped her fingers and struck them from the sky. Not one ship besides Adipe's shank that day. Many Shaheeni men were lost but the casualties were disturbingly low when compared to those of their enemy. It was surreal, watching an entire military sink into the ocean like that. Nobody knew what to say or do about it. There was no precedent. What's more, nobody knew why they'd all gone down at once.

For days after the battle rubble refugees and bodies washed up on the shore. None of the soldiers who survived understood what happened either.

Matteo had watched The Apollo sink alongside her sister ships, knowing Avira was on board. He'd tried hard to focus on the task at hand, Mirjana needed an advisor and though he was the least qualified person in all of Shaheen for the job, it was Adipe's final wish. Besides, Mirjana was all the family he had.

He was gutted. Every time he closed his eyes he saw Avira staring back at him. He could picture her freckles and the stubborn way she bit her lip and the little glow in her cheeks even on the darkest of days. He could see it all like she was right there in front of him but every time he opened his eyes he was reminded that she was gone, as was the rest of The Apollo's crew. The only thing anyone could guess was that The Apollo's crew had sacrificed themselves on purpose to save Shaheen. That would mean they were all heroes, Diego and Artemis and the red-haired boy Avira had shared a room with. They'd saved all of Shaheen. But they were gone now like the mist above the sea and Matteo had no means of grappling with the pain that it caused him. Why couldn't he have gone down with the ships too? Avira was the only thing in his life that had ever made sense. And now she was gone.

The battle ended and that very evening Mirjana was crowned queen. Her ceremony was splendid but there was no joy to be seen. Both she and Matteo walked through it like ghosts, going through the motions as their minds whirred with thoughts of the dead.

Matteo took an oath to be her regent and advisor. He was given a massive room in the palace complete with its own garden and a door that led directly to Mirjana's chamber. He discovered a nest filled with peacock eggs in his garden and, for a moment, felt excited to see them hatch and see the babies running through his flowers day and night. He wanted to tell Avira about it.

Mirjana had been given the option to move into her mother's old chamber but chose to leave it as it was, a sort of shrine to Adipe's last moments as queen. Matteo and Rihane had been tasked with going through every shelf and drawer in Adipe's chambers, looking for anything that would help Mirjana adjust to her role as queen. They found very little.

Rihane and a team of other soldiers went out on boats searching for survivors. Matteo couldn't bring himself to ask what they had found. There had been no sign of The Apollo in any of the rubble.

In the bottom of a box, Matteo discovered a crumpled-up pencil sketch of Adipe with another woman. The woman's eyes looked familiar. After staring at her for a while, he realized those familiar eyes were *his* eyes. It must have been a drawing of his mother - or at least the woman Adipe thought was his mother: Hamida Al Amir.

With this sketch in front of him, he could see the resemblance. But when he thought of his mother he was reminded of Avira, so he pushed the thoughts down.

The days after the battle were too slow. The time he'd spent on The Apollo with Avira had passed in the blink of an eye but the days since she'd been gone felt like years, decades even. Mirjana had been too scared to sleep on her own so Matteo laid on the floor next to her bed each night. He told her everything, how Adipe had recognized him by his eyes alone, how he'd squandered any chances with Avira the moment he lied to her about his identity, how he'd tried to get her to run away with him just a few nights earlier. Mirjana listened with wisdom and compassion beyond her years.

Matteo didn't sleep at all until the third night when his body was so exhausted that he couldn't stay awake. He'd dreamed of Avira and woken up in tears.

"We can build a statue of her in the garden for you to talk

to." Mirjana had spoken through the darkness. If he strained his eyes, Matteo could just barely make out her face.

"How did you know I was dreaming of her?"

"You said her name."

Matteo didn't go back to sleep at all that night. Instead, he walked laps around the gardens. He found Rihane, who'd been promoted to Mirjana's head guard, feeding the birds in the wake of everything. She didn't say anything to him, just let him sit by her in silence. He didn't want her to see him cry but apparently, he had no choice. When the tears stopped, she handed him a fist of birdseed to throw to the doves.

That morning, Mirjana and Matteo were sitting in the throne room reviewing funeral plans when Rihane came sprinting into the room.

Out of breath, she gasped, "Come to the beach. You need to see this."

The beach was a mosaic of rubble, and at first glance, it looked like all the rest of it had, golden and riddled with images of falcons. He thought the light was getting the better of him when the first sun caught his eye. But then he saw more and more of them. A hundred of them at least, some of them were fragments of images, but all of them were familiar.

"The Apollo," he sobbed, realizing the ship had been destroyed on the coastline's rocks just as all the others had.

"And its crew," Rihane said, pointing to a large group of men wandering towards them. He couldn't imagine why he hadn't noticed it before.

"They're alive?"

"They didn't lose a single man. Their captain said it was like Salicia herself saved them."

"Their captain?"

Hope was welled in Matteo's chest. It felt tight, like it didn't quite fit inside of him anymore and it was bursting from his body.

Before he knew it, Matteo ran across the beach, nearly tripping over his unfamiliar Shaheeni kaftan. He didn't mind any of the pain though. For a moment, a glimmering moment, he allowed himself to hope that the woman he loved was standing on the very same beach as him.

"Avira?" he shouted as loud as he could. "Avira!"

He pushed through the men, ignoring their murmurings about whether or not he looked familiar. Some of them were battered and bruised, and all had soggy and torn clothing, but they were all very much alive. That meant Avira had to be too. She had to be alive.

He heard her before he saw her.

"Matteo?" The sea of men parted and there she was, scream-ing out, "Matteo!"

She was running too, towards him. They collided in an ex-plosion of limbs and light and then she was there, her body wrapped around his.

She pulled away from him, looking hard at his face, resting her hands on his cheeks just to make sure he was real. He did the same, running his fingers along her perfect constellation of freckles, the one he thought he'd never see again.

Her eyes were black, and one of her lips was split open and scabbed over. But it was her. He kissed her hard on the forehead, not wanting to irritate any of her many injuries. She didn't appear to care, though, because she kissed him back right on the lips.

"You're here."

"I'm here."

"You're alive! I thought you died." Matteo could hear in his voice that he was sobbing but couldn't feel the tears on his cheeks.

"I thought the same about you. I thought Gavriel had killed you."

Matteo wrapped himself around Avira and lifted her up off the ground. She gave a little squeak and said something about having broken a few ribs, so he set her down gently.

"How did you all survive?" he asked.

"The impact should have killed us. As we were falling, I prayed to Salicia that I would be with you in whatever journey came next," Avira pulled Matteo in closer, "I guess you could say she answered my prayer."

The crew of The Apollo, all one hundred and eleven of them, were lauded as heroes for their bravery. They'd sunk the entire Bianco fleet by themselves. Their bravery and willingness to die saved countless lives. The celebration was heard throughout Shaheen that night. Suns were painted on every street corner and on flags flown high in the sky in their honor.

Artemis, who had sustained, perhaps, more injuries than anyone else in his crew, was bound to a chair for most of the party. But Matteo made sure he was set up with plenty of sweet wine. Matteo didn't quite know what to say to Artemis. He hadn't left the sky for a decade and a half and now his ship, and everything he owned in the world, was at the bottom of the sea.

Diego helped in the kitchen to make a great banquet and all the men, even the most bruised of them, partook in some dancing that night. Matteo even thought he'd seen Rihane dancing a little bit.

At one point in the party, Matteo realized he'd lost Mirjana. Panic rose up inside him, he looked around frantically, not wanting to leave Avira's side.

Avira grabbed his hand like she'd read his mind, "Go. Go find the girl. She needs you."

He found her in the garden, laying on the grass and watching flowers on the tree sway in the wind. He lay down beside her, not speaking, hoping she'd cave eventually and tell him what was wrong.

"A week ago, I didn't know you or Avira," she said finally. "I had a mother. I was a princess. We'd put in place a blockade against Grigori Bianco, and we hoped it would work." She rolled over and looked Matteo in the eyes. "Why does life happen so fast, Matteo?

Matteo grabbed her hand. "You're going to be a great queen."

She shook her head as though he hadn't made her feel even slightly better. "Maybe if I'd never known my mother, I wouldn't miss her so terribly now."

Matteo remembered the pencil sketch of his own mother that he'd found in Adipe's drawers. "Maybe," he said. "But maybe it would hurt more, knowing you'd never have the chance to know her."

They watched the flowers on the tree a little longer before Matteo stood up and offered Mirjana his hand. "They're still dancing in there. Will you join me?"

He led her to the floor just as the band struck up a song, unlike anything Matteo had heard. What's worse, everyone else seemed to know the steps. Even Rihane knew precisely how to move her arms to the beat of the drum in synchronization with everyone else at the party. Some of The Apollo's men were dancing along too. Artemis was doing the arm movements from his chair.

From across the floor, Avira caught his eye, clearly equally confused. She smiled at him and beckoned him over with her hand. Wrapping her arms around his neck, they swayed slowly, despite the upbeat jilting of the song. Her eyes were still bruised so dark they looked like ripe plums.

For the party, Avira had changed into a clean set of clothes, a long-sleeved kaftan with matching puffy blue pants. Matteo knew the long sleeves of her shirt were meant to cover the bruises and scrapes that ran up and down her arms. She wore a pair of glittering golden earrings in the shapes of suns that complimented her eyes.

"You look beautiful."

"I look like a toad." She laughed.

Matteo shook his head vigorously. "A beautiful toad!"

"Some days beautiful people look like toads, Matteo," she said, "and that's okay."

Out of the corner of his eye, Matteo saw Mirjana laughing and swinging herself around Rihane's arm. It felt good to see some joy in the little girl's eyes.

"Are you staying for the funeral?" Matteo asked Avira awkwardly.

"It's not like I have anywhere to go, seeing as how I just sank my father's entire fleet. I don't imagine I'll be welcome back there again."

"Oh...er... no. I just meant... you have so many adventures in front of you. I thought perhaps you'd be heading out soon."

"Matteo," she silenced him, placing a gentle hand on his shoulder and letting it slide absentmindedly down his chest. "Of course, I'm staying for the funeral."

"And how long after that?" He knew he shouldn't press. He couldn't help himself.

"I don't know." She shrunk away from him.

"Avira, I care for you," Matteo could feel himself choking on his words, "I want you to stay here with me."

"I can stay for a little while," she said. She could see the hurt on his face as clearly as if she'd slapped him.

"How long is a little while?"

Avira stepped away from Matteo, folding her arms against her chest.

"I've been made Mirjana's advisor. I'm to help her rule Shaheen until she's old enough to be queen."

"Congratulations, Matteo."

She kissed him on the cheek and then awkwardly left him on the dance floor, muttering something about wanting to find a glass of whatever wine Artemis had been drinking all evening. The rest of that night, Matteo cycled back and forth between feeling elated and terrified that this new normal would fall apart at any moment. It felt so fragile.

Two days later was Adipe's funeral. The sinking of The Mirage had left no bodies to be buried, so the Shaheeni people filled an empty casket with flowers from the palace garden and set it ablaze on a cliff overlooking the sea. The smoke rising to the heavens symbolized half of Adipe's soul going with Aurora. They spread the remaining ashes in the sea to represent the other half going with Salicia.

Avira and Matteo didn't speak a word to each other that entire day. He was too busy tending to Mirjana, who had to preside over the ceremony in royal regalia. The crown hadn't been fitted to the girl's head, yet, so it flopped down over her eyes if she didn't sit absolutely still. She was like a statue presiding over her people.

As was customary for Shaheeni funerals, all the women covered their bodies from head to toe save for their eyes. Still, Matteo could pick Avira out of the crowd, not just because of her two bruised eyes but because of the way she swayed in the wind like her feet weren't fully rooted to the ground.

The crew of The Apollo were Adipe's pallbearers, Artemis on crutches at the lead. Hundreds, maybe thousands, of Shaheeni people gathered on the cliffs in mourning attire to pray alongside Mirjana.

Still, Mirjana looked so alone standing there on the cliffs mourning an empty casket.

"At least the flowers smell sweet when they burn," Rihane whispered to Matteo halfway through the ceremony.

Three days after the funeral, an official surrender arrived at the palace from Grigori Bianco. But Mirjana didn't celebrate.

"He is a liar," she said, "and a warmonger. He may be claiming peace now, but we can't trust him. I *won't* trust him."

And who could blame her, after all.

That night Mirjana told Matteo to go sleep in his own chambers for once.

When he got to his room, Avira was there. She wore a set

of silver robes, long sleeved but sheer and billowy like a cloud. He could see through the fabric that her wounds were healing. Her hair now reached her ears and fell in little wisps all around her face. She looked angelic, sitting there on his bed.

"You're here." He couldn't hide the surprise in his voice.

Her eyes grew wide. "I can go. You must be tired."

Matteo could see her blushing, even in the dim evening light.

"No." He sat down next to her. "Stay."

Matteo had so many things to tell Avira, starting with *I love you*, and ending with, *The three days I thought you were dead were the worst three days of my whole life.*

He had so much to say, he just didn't feel ready to say a word of it yet. Mirjana must have grown impatient with waiting.

Matteo took a seat on the bed next to Avira. He sunk down into the sink blankets and feather mattress and soon they were face to face, nose to nose.

"I thought you were dead," Avira said, her voice soft and unfeeling like she'd been too afraid to say the words.

"I thought that too," he said in response.

"You almost died." The urgency in her tone was unmistakable.

"So did you."

"No. I didn't. Artemis saved me. I was fine. I was fine the

whole time."

"And what about when the ships collided? Artemis couldn't have saved you then. The whole crew of The Apollo should have gone down with the ship. You should have died."

Avira's furrowed brow knit together even more closely. Matteo noticed she was wringing her hands together like a nervous child. Most of the time, Matteo could see so much strength in Avira. It oozed out of every pore of her being. She was powerful and brave and unstoppable. But at this moment he couldn't see any of that. He saw a girl who had abandoned everything she knew, everything she was comfortable with. He saw a girl hundreds of miles away from home. He saw a child in her. He wondered if she could see the child in him too.

"I need to show you something, Matteo."

Avira pulled something large and long out from beside her. He hadn't seen it at first, she must have kept it hidden under her leg on the bed.

It was a roll of parchment. It looked like it had been through a war. Then again, it had been through a war.

"This is a map of my father's trade routes. It has every mine, port town, trade route, sand dune and canal from Polislav to Irajmi on it. It's the most comprehensive one I've ever seen."

She unrolled the map on the bed for him to see. It was indeed comprehensive. Even more detailed than the one she'd made on her bedroom floor back in Alvanii. Avira placed a finger on a red circle that sat along the coastline south of Shaheen.

"The red circles are military forts. I've never seen another map with them labeled like this. That's why I stole this one in particular."

"Military forts? Like for armies."

Avira nodded. "I think the battle with the Shaheeni was only the beginning. War is coming. My father wants the world in a teacup and I don't think I'm strong enough to stop him. I'm just one girl."

"I'm sorry Avira." Matteo placed his hand on her knee, and, instead of pulling away, she placed her hand on top of his, holding on tight.

"But, if I share this map with the world, I can warn people he's coming. I can stop him before he even gets a foothold. People who know about the world around them are far harder to control, just look at the Shaheeni. That's my mission, Matteo. Now that I'm free of Gavriel, I can finally begin." She let out a little laugh, so faint Matteo nearly missed it. "I used to think the biggest obstacle in my life was the fact that I am a girl, that I could not inherit my father's fortune, that no matter how hard I worked I would never matter as much as a boy. But now I see that harder by far is proving to myself that I deserve this life I dream of. It's in my heart for a reason, Matteo. I can't pretend it's not there. It will kill me."

Avira's dark eyes sparkled with hope as bright as the stars. But her words terrified Matteo. She wasn't saying it directly, but he knew what was coming next.

"You're leaving."

Avira took his hands frantically. "Come with me."

"I have duties here. I belong here. Mirjana needs me." Even as he said the words, he wasn't sure if they were true. He knew Mirjana was powerful on her own, and wasn't delusional enough to believe he'd be all that much help. But he'd made a promise to Adipe, a promise he wasn't keen on breaking, even if his heart yearned for Avira every step of the way.

"Why won't you come with me?" There was a girlishness to the way Avira begged.

"Why won't you stay?"

With this Avira stood and paced about the room. She was angry, he could tell from the way her slender shoulders pushed together, and she chewed on her lips. Her freckles danced under the furrow of her brow like fireworks. She didn't know what to say, but still she spoke.

"Because you know who I am, Matteo. You knew who I was

when you kissed me in the crows nest of The Apollo. You knew who I was when we made that lemonade together. You knew who I was the moment we met. Stop asking me to stay when you know I am not a person who stays." Avira held the map up and shook it at him. "I am a person who goes. Please. Either come with me or let me go."

Her words hurt. But despite the pain of what she was saying to him, despite the way her words pierced into his stomach and twisted around like a hot blade, despite it all, Matteo stood and slowly walked towards her. He took her hips in his hands and pulled her into him. And he kissed her. He kissed her hard. And she kissed back.

Her lips tasted like lemons and vanilla and the incense. Her face was hot and wet with tears. Matteo felt the tears before he realized what was happening. And then it was all happening too quickly. Avira was crying. She was sobbing into his shoulder. He wrapped his arms around her as gently as he could, placing his palms flat on her back and willing all of the light in the world into her body through his outstretched fingers.

"Nobody's ever held me like this before," she said as she wiped snot from her face.

"They should have," was all Matteo could say in response. He held her for a long time, never once letting go, never once closing his eyes. He kept them fixed on a vine of jasmine flowers blossoming in the garden. Their white blooms practically shimmered in the starlight.

"You love me, don't you?" Avira croaked.

"Of course, I do."

"Well, please, please stop. Please choose someone different."

Matteo shook his head. "We don't get to choose, Avira."

She sobbed some more, and he walked with her to his bed where they sat for a long time. They sat together until the moon rose high in the sky. Not far away, a peacock crowed in the garden. The sound startled Avira and she held Matteo even closer to her chest.

There was no world in which Avira would stay. Matteo had known that all along, but it had only just become so clear. Even if she did love him back, there were things out there in the world that she would always love more than him. He would have to live with that fact. Avira was destined to be a woman who saw the whole world, maybe even saved it. But he didn't yet know what he was supposed to be. For so long, she had been his only goal. Who was he before Avira? He could barely remember anymore.

"You have to go, Avira," he heard himself say.

She looked up at him, eyes wide.

"Where's that boy from the garden? The boy who would tear down the stars for me. He's gone, isn't he?" Her voice was soft and gentle, but her eyes glistened with pain.

He had to stay. For once, he had to do something for himself. Avira sat straight up and cupped his face in her palms. "If you change your mind, come find me. I'll be in the skies, waiting for you."

And then she kissed him again, running her hands over the braids that sat tight against his head. "I miss your curls." They spent the rest of that night together, holding one another close.

When you know a goodbye is coming with the dawn, sunrise becomes far less beautiful. But sure enough, Aurora delivered a gorgeous sunrise that morning. And sure enough, when Matteo woke, Avira was gone.

Chapter Forty

When Avira closed her eyes and tried to picture herself ten years in the future, she wasn't picturing herself as Matteo's wife, living in a palace, reading books, and tending to the gardens. No matter how much she loved him, and she knew she loved him quite a lot, she couldn't stay. She hoped one day he'd understand.

"Come find me someday," she whispered in his ear before she left. "I'll be in the skies."

She wore a silk satchel over her back. It contained everything she owned in the world, everything she cared about at least. A few items of clothing, a brick of pu'er Mirjana had given her as a parting gift, and her father's map. Everything else she'd carried with her from her old life had gone down with The Apollo. It was almost as if Avira Bianco herself had sunk into the sea alongside it. Because the woman who crept away from her lover's bed, using only the light of the stars to guide her through the palace gardens, was not the same girl who'd fled her marriage to Gavriel Castillo all those weeks ago.

But isn't that how life works? If you live long enough you wake up one day and find yourself a completely different person than you were the night before. In that way, humans are quite a lot like caterpillars.

Dawn was breaking as Avi's new ship raised anchor. It had taken about a week for her bruises to heal enough for her to fly again. She'd used that time to ask for Mirjana's help securing a small skyship for her to use.

Nicolo and Diego had been easy to convince to come along. The ship only needed a crew of fifteen and they were the first people she asked. Diego needed work while Artemis rebuilt The Apollo and Nicolo was anxious for a new adventure. A few of her old crewmates from The Apollo had been quick to volunteer as well. She'd rounded out the crew with a handful of Shaheeni guards, women who she knew were far better pilots than most men she'd known.

Diego had made fast friends with Ines, a young kitchen girl from the palace who'd practically begged to come along. Nicolo served as first mate while a few of the furnace men from The Apollo worked to keep Avi's new ship aloft.

They set off towards the rising sun. The East was somewhere

Avi had always wanted to explore. In her cabin Avi splayed out her stolen map against the wall and secured it with pins. Touching her fingers to the edge of the map she let herself smile, really smile. She was going to chart what lay past the edges of even her father's map. Her stomach got flippy floppy with excitement just at the thought of it.

Her ship was a reject of Adipe's fleet due to its insufficient camouflage but it was still far better hidden than any Alvanian ship. Standing at the helm with Nicolo, Avi let herself breathe in the cool morning air. Shaheen grew small in the distance behind them.

"Where are we headed, Captain?" a woman named Aya shouted down to her from high up in the ropes. Aya was great with knots, so Avi had put her in charge of a one-woman ropes crew, keeping the skyship running.

"How far south can you imagine, Aya?" Avi called back.

"Pretty far south."

"Well, we're going farther than that."

"Why?" Ines called. Avira had captured the entire crew's attention.

"Don't you ever wonder who makes the maps?" Avi asked. "It's us. We are building the maps of the world that people will follow someday to forge great alliances, make peace, have adventures, and tell stories. We make the maps now."

The crew seemed to like this goal, how peaceful, simple, and mysterious it was. They were hard workers and good souls. Avi felt lucky to be their captain. She knew she could sleep well at night, knowing they were keeping her ship in the air because they believed in her mission. Secretly, she also wondered if her father used to be like this too before his greed corrupted him. She didn't take long with those thoughts. They exhausted her.

Later that night Avi and Nicolo shared a pot of pu'er Mirjana had sent along as a parting gift. The sky was peaceful and gentle in the way it always is after a great battle.

Nicolo poured his second cup and swirled it around in the little ceramic cup, he was more quiet than she'd ever seen him.

"Is something wrong, Nicolo?" Avi always felt like she sounded too stern when talking to Nicolo. He was so warm and soft but she was all hard edges and ambition.

"In a week and a half, Benjamin will be expecting me back at the port in Alvanii. I wonder what he'll think when The Apollo never arrives."

Avi thought about this for a moment, sipping her tea. "Surely, he'll hear the word of the ship sinking. I do not doubt that news is all across Alvanii at this point. The entire Bianco fleet sank to the bottom of the sea."

"That's what I'm worried about." Nicolo didn't look up, he stared intensely into his teacup, lips almost white from being pursed together.

"You're afraid he'll think you died with the ship."

"I don't know why he'd think anything else."

Avi's heart felt heavy. She wanted to help her friend but had no idea how. They weren't heading anywhere near Veronii and, with her reputation, Alvanii was far from out of the question. Then an idea hit her.

"What if you could send him a letter? We have some Shaheeni falcons on board. Maybe we could send one to Veronii."

"Can they fly that far?"

"Mirjana told me they can travel the whole world if needed. They're powerful animals."

Avi got up and dashed to her cabin, grabbing a piece of parchment she'd planned on using for maps. This was more important. She handed Nicolo the quill eagerly.

"Write to him. Say you've taken up business with the Great Pirate Avi and you are going on an expedition to the South. Tell him you'll send letters as often as possible and promise you'll come home to him."

"Am I supposed to know who the Great Pirate Avi is? I've never heard of him."

"It's me you oaf. I'm the Great Pirate Avi — Maker of maps! Conqueror of the stars!"

Nicolo laughed. "It's a little on the nose, isn't it."

"Well, just don't use my full name, okay?" Avi had thought that Great Pirate Avi was an acceptable, even formidable, alias but perhaps she needed to rethink that. She had plenty of time to come up with something better. Avira Bianco didn't fit anymore, and neither did Cesario. She'd have to make up something new. She liked how many opportunities there were to choose a brand-new name. A fresh start is precisely what she needed.

Nicolo's eyes were wild with hope. "Do you think he will write back?"

"Why wouldn't he?"

"And you promise I will get to go home to him someday?"

Avi took his hands in hers and looked at him with all her softness. Nicolo had done so much for her. This was the least she could do for him. "I promise," she said.

Nicolo scrawled out the note and tucked it away to give to Diego later. He'd know how to get a falcon in the air and on its way. Avi looked out at the horizon as he wrote and thought of Matteo.

Avi smiled at the thought of Matteo teaching Mirjana anything. The child wasn't exactly the type to sit and be taught. And Matteo didn't know anything about ruling a country. He didn't even speak Shaheeni.

Nicolo caught her giggling at the thought and asked what about. She quickly changed the subject. Eventually, the conversation turned to their next big adventure.

"Have you picked out a name yet? For the ship?" he asked.

"I've had a name picked out since I was a little girl, Nicolo."

"And what's that?"

And with a signature smirk, one she'd learned from Artemis Cascella himself, she named her ship *The Falconer*.

THE FALCONER

Coming Spring 2025

The second installment in Avira and Matteo's story follows the crew of The Falconer North to Polislav where Avira reconnects with an old friend and works to undermine her father's tyranny in the Polislavic ice mines. Meanwhile, Matteo and Rihane set out together, with a reluctant Artemis in tow, following the clues Matteo's dead mother left behind. Will our hero's paths converge again? If they do, will Matteo forgive Avira for her abandonment? All your favorite characters are back, this time with even more cutthroat adventure, swashbuckling, and romance.

I started writing this book in the midst of a very dark time in my life. I was stuck in a job that had killed my creative drive and I was battling multiple chronic illnesses and great uncertainty about my health. In the darkest moments of illness and burnout, I realized that I desperately wanted to share my writing with the world. I didn't want to sit around to be the most healthy or the most inspired to tell this story. So, I started writing every day. I took ten minute breaks from my desk job, typed away in the parking lot of doctor's offices, and kept pushing. One paragraph at a time, this book appeared before me.

My love for fantasy and adventure stories comes first and foremost from my dad. My dad took the time every single night of my childhood to read us books. We read *The Hobbit, His Dark Materials, Harry Potter* and so much more as a family all curled up in my parents bed. My dad also showed me all of my favorite childhood movies. From Ghibli to Spielburg, my dad made sure my brothers and I had seen it all. On nights when my dad couldn't do it, my mom stepped in. For this reason, I have my parents to thank more than anyone for the book you hold in your hands today. As I edited, I stumbled upon dozens of callbacks to stories I first read with my parents. I was one lucky kid.

I also have to thank my incredible partner Brandon, for cheering me on as I pulled this book out of my brain. He took the time to read every page and then read them all again. Thanks for being the best adventure buddy a girl could ask for. Let's go have a new adventure now that this book is done! Yahoo!

My book design team is the best there is. Hayden Pedersen, an exceptional artist and dear friend, took the time to truly love my story as much as I do and design a cover that meshes so perfectly into the world of The Apollo. Rachael Ward, who is *not* related to me but does share my last name, designed the gorgeous map for this book. Ruben Ward, who *is* related to me, did endless concept art to support my process and my launch! I am not a visual artist in the slightest and I feel so blessed to have such an exceptional team of visual art masters who worked to make this book look and feel as dazzling as I hoped.

Thank you to my friends Calvin Pineda, Zach Pinkley and Hannah Thomas for being The Apollo's cheerleaders from day one. I can't tell you how much your support meant to me as I pushed this work out into the world. And one more thank you to ALL of my beta readers. Corban Cvitanich-Bishop, Chad Gorn, Brandon Goranson, Lauren Axness, Hannah Thomas, Debi Farber, Ashley King, Mateusz Czopek, Emily Stacey, Calvin Pineda, Ruben Ward & Trixie Zwolfer.

Finally, a thank you to my community. When I decided to indie publish this book, I felt so many feelings all at once. I was excited to share this story with more people but felt like a failure for not securing a traditional book deal. Every step of the way there have been people cheering me on with kindness and constant encouragement. I am forever blessed. Thank you all.

Grace Ward is a YA author from Boise, Idaho. She is a graduate of The National Theatre Institute, Boise State University and a current MFA candidate at Antioch University - LA. As a playwright her work has been produced with Connective Theatre Co., Surel's Place, Brick by Brick Players, The Minnesota Fringe Festival, Storyfort and more. When she's not writing, Grace loves to ski, mountain bike and read at Dawson Taylor with her awesome partner. THE APOLLO is Grace's first novel. DM her on Instagram @g.wardyy! She promises she'll reply!